OUT OF
THE RAIN

V.C. Andrews® Books

The Dollanganger Family
Flowers in the Attic
Petals on the Wind
If There Be Thorns
Seeds of Yesterday
Garden of Shadows
Christopher's Diary:
    Secrets of Foxworth
Christopher's Diary:
    Echoes of Dollanganger
Secret Brother
Beneath the Attic
Out of the Attic
Shadows of Foxworth

The Audrina Series
My Sweet Audrina
Whitefern

The Casteel Family
Heaven
Dark Angel
Fallen Hearts
Gates of Paradise
Web of Dreams

The Cutler Family
Dawn
Secrets of the Morning
Twilight's Child
Midnight Whispers
Darkest Hour

The Landry Family
Ruby
Pearl in the Mist
All That Glitters
Hidden Jewel
Tarnished Gold

The Logan Family
Melody
Heart Song
Unfinished Symphony
Music in the Night
Olivia

The Orphans Series
Butterfly
Crystal
Brooke
Raven
Runaways

The Wildflowers Series
Misty
Star
Jade
Cat
Into the Garden

The Hudson Family
Rain
Lightning Strikes
Eye of the Storm
The End of the
    Rainbow

The Shooting Stars
Cinnamon
Ice
Rose
Honey
Falling Stars

The De Beers Family
"Dark Seed"
Willow
Wicked Forest
Twisted Roots
Into the Woods
Hidden Leaves

The Broken Wings Series
Broken Wings
Midnight Flight

The Gemini Series
Celeste
Black Cat
Child of Darkness

The Shadows Series
April Shadows
Girl in the Shadows

The Early Spring Series
Broken Flower
Scattered Leaves

The Secrets Series
Secrets in the Attic
Secrets in the Shadows

The Delia Series
Delia's Crossing
Delia's Heart
Delia's Gift

The Heavenstone Series
The Heavenstone Secrets
Secret Whispers

The March Family
Family Storms
Cloudburst

The Kindred Series
Daughter of Darkness
Daughter of Light

The Forbidden Series
The Forbidden Sister
"The Forbidden Heart"
Roxy's Story

The Mirror Sisters
The Mirror Sisters
Broken Glass
Shattered Memories

The House of Secrets Series
House of Secrets
Echoes in the Walls

The Umbrella Series
The Umbrella Lady

The Girls of Spindrift
Bittersweet Dreams
"Corliss"
"Donna"
"Mayfair"
"Spindrift"

Stand-alone Novels
Gods of Green
    Mountain
Into the Darkness
Capturing Angels
The Unwelcomed Child
Sage's Eyes
The Silhouette Girl
Whispering Hearts

V.C. ANDREWS®

OUT OF THE RAIN

G

Gallery Books

New York   London   Toronto   Sydney   New Delhi

G⌐

Gallery Books
An Imprint of Simon & Schuster, Inc.
1230 Avenue of the Americas
New York, NY 10020

Following the death of Virginia Andrews, the Andrews family worked with a carefully selected writer to organize and complete Virginia Andrews's stories and to create additional novels, of which this is one, inspired by her storytelling genius.

This book is a work of fiction. Any references to historical events, real people, or real places are used fictitiously. Other names, characters, places, and events are products of the author's imagination, and any resemblance to actual events or places or persons, living or dead, is entirely coincidental.

First Gallery Books trade paperback edition November 2021

V.C. ANDREWS® and VIRGINIA ANDREWS® are registered trademarks of Vanda Productions, LLC

GALLERY BOOKS and colophon are registered trademarks of Simon & Schuster, Inc.

For information about special discounts for bulk purchases, please contact Simon & Schuster Special Sales at 1-866-506-1949 or business@simonandschuster.com.

Interior design by Erika R. Genova

Manufactured in the United States of America

10 9 8 7 6 5 4 3 2 1

Library of Congress Cataloging-in-Publication Data

Names: Andrews, V. C. (Virginia C.), author.
Title: Out of the rain / V.C. Andrews.
Description: First Gallery Books trade paperback edition. | New York : Gallery Books, 2021. | Series: The umbrella lady ; 2
Identifiers: LCCN 2020049508 (print) | LCCN 2020049509 (ebook) | ISBN 9781982156251 (paperback) | ISBN 9781982156268 (hardcover) | ISBN 9781982156282 (ebook)
Subjects: GSAFD: Suspense fiction.
Classification: LCC PS3551.N454 O93 2021 (print) | LCC PS3551.N454 (ebook) | DDC 813/.54—dc23
LC record available at https://lccn.loc.gov/2020049508
LC ebook record available at https://lccn.loc.gov/2020049509

ISBN 978-1-9821-5626-8
ISBN 978-1-9821-5625-1 (pbk)
ISBN 978-1-9821-5628-2 (ebook)

OUT OF
THE RAIN

PROLOGUE

In a dream I had many times, I was walking up the stairway. Flames were licking at my face and hair, but I didn't feel the heat. Somewhere below, my father was calling to me, demanding I come back.

I didn't stop.

At the top, the flames looked more like they were beckoning to me, inviting me into them. There was a clear but narrow strip of floor that I followed until I was in Mama's room. She was still sleeping.

I yelled for her, and she opened her eyes and then sat up.

I think she saw me, but instantly she turned into smoke and was gone.

And like always, I woke up with a scream.

CHAPTER ONE

There were a little more than a dozen or so people on the last train leaving Hurley the night my grandmother Mazy died. Only two other people had gotten on with me, both strangers. We had but two stops before I would reach the town in which my father now lived a new life with a new family. By the time I stepped off the train, there was only one other passenger left, a young woman with light-brown hair. She resembled my mother, and so my imagination played its tricks on me. I imagined her turning and smiling at me, telling me I was doing the right thing.

Although I had never revealed it to Mazy, I had memorized the entire train schedule—where I could make connections to continue north, south, or west—because I didn't know what my exact destination eventually would be until I found the secret letters my father had sent to her. However, the trip itself had always been out there, like a promise dangling. Maybe it was a fantasy most of the time, but I had believed that someday I would continue the journey to a new home and a new life, just as my father had done.

After I boarded and sat, no one gave me more than a passing glance before returning to his or her reading, texting, or sleeping. To everyone else, there was probably nothing unusual about my appearance, even though I felt like I was exploding with anticipation. My face felt on fire. I imagined that the excitement in my eyes had turned them into hot coals brightening and fading, brightening and fading with every breath and every heartbeat.

Why didn't anyone else seem to see it?

Or did the sight of me upset them so much that they had to look away?

Although there was central lighting and anyone who wanted it had a light above his or her seat, darkness soon seemed to be seeping in like water into a sinking ship as the train continued on its route, every bolt, screw, and wheel locked in its predestined journey, just like me. It could never leave the tracks, it could never turn around before its final station, and it could never simply stop short of a set location. I had to go where it would lead me, and do what I had to do. Mazy had died.

The train whistle sounded. The future was out there, hovering like a hawk, waiting to pounce on me and take me to my fate. As the car rocked gently, soothingly, I could feel myself drifting back through time.

The moment I closed my eyes, it was as if everything that had happened between my original train ride with my father and the current ride was truly imaginary. As long as I kept my eyes tightly shut,

I could feel him sitting beside me, even smell the fragrance of his aftershave, despite how long ago that was. There are scents that are embedded forever in your memory. For me, his aftershave was one of them, though no odor was stronger than the painful, bitter smell of smoke coming from our house fire.

Despite all the years I had taken care of Mazy's fireplace and sat with her in front of those dancing flames, they really never became comfortable, nor did the sharp pain in my lungs and heart diminish. Flames, no matter where I saw them, would always be frolicking in glee, even a tiny one on a birthday candle.

Daddy and I had said so little to each other on the train that day.

He had fallen asleep first. I could hear his soft inhales and exhales. Their rhythm was enough to help me fall asleep, too. I felt safe again. I had lived below bruised, angry clouds that rumbled long after the night of our tragedy. However, no one else, not even Daddy, seemed to hear them. The rumbling was there only for me, even if there wasn't a cloud in the sky. I was trapped in the surrounding flames and deafened by the high-pitched scream constantly ringing in my ears. The moment I began to stand still, no matter where we were, I started to tremble. My lips felt like they were bubbling. I was living in a shell with spidery thin cracks that was threatening to shatter and fall at my feet, leaving me as naked and alone as a newborn abandoned in the cold, dark night.

Despite how calm I might have appeared to a stranger back then, inside, the real me was crying hysterically for my mother. When I looked at other people, I was surprised they didn't hear it. They smiled at me, held my hand, and couched their words carefully in expressions of compassion and hope. Their assurances fell into distant echoes. How could everything ever again be all right? After a while, I didn't hear them at all, just as they didn't hear me. The whole world might as well have been deaf.

When Daddy had told me we were leaving to start a new life, I unashamedly felt joy. We were escaping from the darkness, maybe from those flames in my memory, too. Because I was so young, I had believed we would just go a little ways and every terrible thing that had occurred would disappear. I recall even thinking that maybe Mama would be waiting for us at our new place. That her survival of the house fire had been kept secret. That after we had stepped off the train, no matter where we were, she would be standing there waiting. The smile I remembered would be back where it belonged, nestled on her face, brightening her eyes and filling her lips. I'd rush into her arms, and the three of us would walk off into a scene as happy as the last scene of *Alice in Wonderland*. We'd be holding hands and laughing that everything horrible that had occurred was now only a bad dream. None of us had followed a rabbit down a hole. Everyone has bad dreams.

Why couldn't that be true for me?

Couldn't someone say, "You're safely back in Kansas, Saffron?"

And so, when Daddy had left me at the Hurley train station, filling out figures in my new coloring book with new crayons, I had never doubted that he would come back for me after he had bought some of our necessities, and then we would take the next train to our new home. The speed with which he walked off, practically ran off, convinced me that he didn't want to leave me alone for too long. I actually was proud at the start, delighted that he would consider me old enough to wait by myself in a strange place, even though I knew in my heart that my mother would be furious at him for doing so.

Thinking back to it now, I suspect that Mazy, the elderly lady who had appeared suddenly and would turn out to be my real grandmother, had deliberately waited until the train station was deserted and I was alone. If she had appeared earlier, while trains and people were still going to and fro, I would never have taken her hand and permitted her, a total stranger at the time, to lead me away to her home and her lonely life. Time, the realization that Daddy wasn't returning for me, and the chill of darkness had to embrace me first.

After Mazy had taken me in and after days and then weeks had passed, I grew more skeptical of her true intentions, but she was very methodical, cleverly answering every one of my questions and seemingly honest about her efforts to reunite me with my father. She drove back my doubts almost as soon as they occurred.

Now, when I recall those early days, I realize that her experience and training as a grade-school teacher had enabled her to ease me into a new reality, with the main realization being that my father really had deserted me. She'd had to lower me into the truth the way a parent would lower her child into a very warm bath. Even so, what child could live with that revelation? Where could he or she ever find self-respect after having been discarded with maybe little more than an afterthought?

Daddy's one saving grace was that everything had been pre-arranged, as heartbreaking as that was to realize. At least, I eventually learned that he didn't out-and-out desert me and just leave me dangling in the unwelcoming night. Mazy had lost her daughter, my mother, when she had given her up for adoption practically the same moment she had been born, but she could and would enjoy her granddaughter. My father had kept in touch with her while his parents brought him and my mother up in the same home. They were supposed to be more like brother and sister, but they weren't.

As the train carried me farther and farther away from Mazy and the life she had tried to make for me, I felt deep sadness for her and the pain she had kept hidden in her heart most of her life. Despite the way she had encouraged me to keep hoping my father would return for me, especially in the very beginning, I bore her no resentment and, in the end, blamed her for nothing. In a way, everything she had done to keep me isolated and protected was born out of her own guilt over giving up her daughter, despite how difficult it would have been for an unmarried woman to raise a child with no visible means of supporting herself at the time. That night when she led me to her house from the train station, she finally was doing what she wished she had done the first time around. I was to be her redeeming light. How could I fault her for that?

Mazy was possessive and domineering, for sure, but her intense need to weave her love and her worldly knowledge into me drove her to hover over me, spreading her wings like an angel, to be sure no one would harm me. She wanted to be certain that I'd be well prepared to do battle in this world, for that was how she saw it . . . filled with a constant series of challenges and conflicts. It had made her quite bitter. Countless times she told me that if I listened to her, I would be strong enough to survive and happily so. It got so I feared stepping out of the door on my own, even if simply to play in the backyard.

The proof that she had prepared me well lay just ahead in a whirlwind of what I expected would be major challenges even if I were older. Both mentally and physically exhausted from my stream of memories and all I had just done to effectuate a good and safe escape after Mazy had died, I welcomed the deep sleep that overtook me during the trip. Just as on that first train ride years ago, this train's slowing and coming to a stop at the station I wanted was what woke me. When I sat up and looked out the window, I felt like an astronaut gazing out at a new planet.

The young woman I had imagined resembled my mother did not disembark, and when I walked by her and she looked at me, I saw she was nowhere near as pretty as my mother had been. Outside, there were no passengers waiting to board. The train lingered like a great beast catching its breath. Being alone on the train platform when I stepped off made it all seem more like a recurring dream. Was I really here?

This train station was cleaner and more up-to-date than the one I had left. I was both happy and angry that I didn't have to travel too far, just a little over two and a half hours. I wondered whether my father had taken this exact trip in the opposite direction from time to time to catch sight of me. Was he ever on our street waiting for a glimpse of the little girl he had left behind? Did Mazy alert him ahead of time when we would be in the village so he could stand in some storefront and look at us passing by? I wanted to believe that. I wanted to imagine that he still harbored some love, some curiosity, and still possessed something of any father's need to know his own child.

But I wasn't completely convinced he would welcome me now with open arms. Before I had left, I had read all his secret letters to Mazy and looked at the pictures of my mother as a child and then as a woman, a mother herself, pictures he had sent to my grandmother. Even as a very young girl, I had spent hours and hours trying to understand why he would have deserted me in the first place. The letters explained so much, but most of what he had written had stunned me and left me cold. Now I suspected that he had been planning to transfer me into Mazy's care for a long time, perhaps even before the fire. He had kept his intentions hidden that well. But even if there were clues, why would I have noticed and read into them back then?

Whom can you trust more than your own father and mother? Who did you least expect would betray you? There wasn't a hint in his eyes or in his voice to warn me he was going to do just that on that fateful day. For so long, I had wondered why he didn't want me with him. Buried deeply in my heart and mind was the realization that leaving me behind couldn't only have been for the reason he had given to Mazy in his letters, his desire to repair her loss. But why would he make such a sacrifice for someone he barely had known? He had to have had other reasons. And besides, why ignore my losses and what the desertion would do to me? I read no lines of regret about that in those letters. There were no apologies to be given to me and no expressions of worry for my emotional well-being.

That only reinforced the dark places in my heart and the ugly answers hanging like bats in a cave, answers to questions that I had always fought against exploring. Wasn't it Mazy who told me, "You never ask a question for which you don't want an answer. There is much truth to the adage 'Ignorance is bliss' "?

None of this denied that my early life had its moments of sunshine, but mainly before my father and mother had become more like strangers to each other and my mother had fallen into a deep depression. Images and parts of sentences between them lingered in the air filled with static, all of it threatening to connect and then eventually force me to realize the truth, a truth a little girl my age was unable to face at the time. It meant that the bond between my mother and father, the bond that keeps a child feeling safe, was already shattered. Much of who and what they had become to each other had really gone up in smoke with that fire.

What was left of love and tenderness before the first spark leaped out? Where did the wind carry the ashes of all the anger and unhappiness? What greater horror lay in wait out there? What monster, uglier than any I could imagine, sneered and clawed the ground, anticipating its opportunity to seize me and destroy what little remained of faith and love? I would soon know.

Nightmares had become more like movie trailers, snippets of the terrifying reality that had my name across its forehead. But I had little choice. I had to head toward it like someone driving on a road that she knew would end at a cliff. How long would the fall take? Would there be anything left, any reason to continue? Perhaps that was the biggest, most pressing question of all. Even if I found a hint of love, it would pale in the presence of what had happened, what had been real and not imagined. Could I live with it? The simple questions that followed me off the train were: Did any of what I was hoping to find matter? Did family matter? Did everything Mazy had done for me matter under the shadow of all that?

Did knowing who you really were matter?

Was I in a different shell, and should I bother to emerge?

I almost turned around and crossed the platform to take a train going in the opposite direction. If I didn't continue to go forward, would I never have to confront those answers? "Ignorance is bliss," Mazy had told me, but could I really live on without knowing these answers? I feared how they would haunt me forever.

I stood there, indecisive. The train that had brought me started away. There was another choice. I was tempted to rush back on and continue into the unknown, go on and on. I felt like a deep-sea diver who, after she had jumped from the edge of a cliff, wondered in mid-air if she should have. But I didn't return to the train.

No, I told myself, *it's far too late to change your mind, Saffron. Let yourself keep falling.*

In the end, what kept me going wasn't a young girl's need for love or truth or justice. My motives weren't that noble. Truthfully, where else could I go now? There were no family friends, no living relatives. I had a fake birth certificate, but what kind of a life could I have alone?

What had brought me here was just a brutal need to survive first and a hope for restoration of any family, any love, second. In no sense was I coming home, no matter how I wished and pretended I was. Living with Mazy had made it more difficult to lie to myself. Because she wouldn't tolerate deception in any form, I found it distasteful, too.

I walked slowly off the train platform to a taxi parked nearby. The driver had his bushy, gray-haired head back and his mouth wide open, looking more like someone who had just died. He did resemble who I imagined to be someone's grandpa driving a cab. Mazy once told me that older people show their age the most when they sleep. I thought about Shakespeare's line in his sonnet about getting older, "Death's second self." Mazy had been amazed when I ruminated about it and I asked, "Isn't every sleep a taste of what's to come?"

That day, she had stared at me hard before she said the strangest thing.

"I'm sorry you're so intelligent, Saffron. You'll suffer more."

"Should I stop reading?" I asked, terrified.

She laughed. "Not for an instant," she said, smiling.

I tapped on the window, and the driver stirred, realized where he was and what was happening, and jumped up instantly.

He rolled his window down and said, "Hey. Sorry, missy."

I gave him the address and got into the back of the taxi. The moment I did, he started to talk, beginning with why he had fallen asleep. I smiled to myself listening to how guilty he felt. If he had only known the forest of guilt through which I had come, he would laugh at his meager shame.

"This is the last train stoppin' at Sandburg Creek," he said. "Most of the time, no one gets off, or if they do, someone is waitin' for 'em, but I can't afford to miss a possible fare. Still, ya'd think a girl as young as you would have someone waitin' for her. I tell ya, the risks parents take with their children in this day and age are astoundin'."

I'm really not that young, I wanted to tell him. *Your real age is inside you because of what life has done to you.* But I didn't want to get into any deep discussions. I was trembling.

"I have the last shift, so I see what goes on. Kids no older than you, and girls especially, are wanderin' the streets in the early mornin' hours. Who knows where they came from or where they're goin'? Who's checkin' ta see if they ever came home? For a lot of 'em, I bet no one.

"I'm not married and don't have no children, but it doesn't take much ta realize that's bad. So where ya been, missy?"

"Away," I said, looking anxiously at the houses we were passing. They were bigger than the ones in Hurley, with more elaborate landscaping. The streets were wider, too. There were pruned medians and modernized, stronger lights, making the macadam glitter as if there was a thin layer of ice over them. Here and there were wooden benches.

It was still early enough in the evening for windows in all the homes to be well lit. Traffic was light in both directions. I saw people walking dogs and talking in the early evening. The taxi driver was right. Girls as young as I, if not younger, walked with older kids who poked and teased each other playfully. Others about my age were walking with their parents. It looked like a dream world, the idyllic community Mazy would describe as a painting by Norman Rockwell, her favorite artist. People were laughing and looked friendly in many of his pictures capturing rural scenes. Was this that world? Could there really be one? Was I too desperate to believe a place like this existed? I was afraid of hope. I knew too much disappointment.

"Ya live here in Sandburg Creek, right?" the driver asked. "Or are ya visitin' someone?"

"I'm coming home," I said. It was noncommittal enough for him to look at me in his rearview mirror.

"How long have ya been away?"

Was he writing a book? This was my first taxi ride. Were all taxi drivers this talkative and nosy? The silence in my hesitation was uncomfortable, even for me.

"A while," I said. "I am in a private school," I added, to hopefully shut him up. In a true sense, I had been in a private school with Mazy, not that it mattered too much to me that I might lie to a taxi driver.

"Oh. Well, welcome home," he said, turning onto a new block.

I caught the house numbers. This was my father's neighborhood. All the homes had good-size plots of land, so they weren't on top of each other. They weren't modern in style. Most of them were Queen Anne, more reason to believe I was in a Norman Rockwell painting. It felt as if I had dropped through time to a place where people might still leave their houses and cars unlocked. Strangers were people to be curious about and not to be suspected of some evil intention. Lights that looked like candles flickered in windows. Maybe mothers and fathers were with their children watching television, the way Mazy and I had done. Perhaps that was what my father was doing right at this moment, never dreaming he would be seeing me in his doorway.

Now that I was really going to ring his doorbell, what really made me tremble inside was the idea not only of confronting him but of meeting his new wife and his new children. I finally faced the thought, the frightening thought, that I had a new family. What would they see when they looked at me? How much did they know? I wasn't just carrying some of my clothes in a small bag; I was bringing along a horrific past. The flames would be snapping and crackling right beside me. Maybe he had told them that I had died in the fire, too. When he and his family saw me, they might all chant it together: "You can't come here; you don't belong here. You're dead; you're gone, forgotten."

They would probably be more frightened of me than I of them.

If so, where did I belong now? Would I join the homeless whom Mazy and I had seen on television news? Would I live in shadows, covered in the filth of the street? Would I die in some alley like a scrawny cat, scratching at the approaching image of death with its smile full of sharp, yellow teeth and its eyes swimming with cold glee? In a few more minutes, my whole life would be decided.

Dare I breathe?

As the taxi began slowing down, I wondered if I ever could be more terrified and my body ever be more frozen in fear than it was at this moment.

We stopped in front of one of the larger houses. It was a brick three-story with a veranda and an octagonal extension on the right and a three-story octagonal tower on the left. A half dozen matching brick steps led up to the front entrance at the center of the house's wide veranda. My father's home was easily almost three times the size of Mazy's house. Even though there was no one on the veranda, it was well lit. The lawn looked more like a rich, dark pool of green soaking in the light. Well-pruned roses grew close to the veranda, hugging its shadows. On the right was a dark-pewter fountain with a sculptured little boy and girl under an umbrella off which the water flowed back into the bowl.

An umbrella, I thought, remembering the first time I had seen Mazy with hers and how she wouldn't walk out of the house without it, rain or shine. I would never look at one, even in a picture, without thinking of her immediately.

"Wow. Nice house," the driver said. "Yer family live here long? What's yer father do? Is he a doctor or somethin'?"

"How much?" I replied, as if I hadn't heard a word.

"Nine fifty will do it."

I gave him a ten and opened the door slowly.

"Say," he said. "Really. How come nobody met ya at the station?"

"I'm not supposed to be here yet," I said, smiling. *Lies as tools*, I thought, remembering how Daddy once had explained why sometimes a lie was okay. "It's a surprise."

"Oh. Gotcha."

I closed the door before he could ask anything else. He watched me in his rearview mirror until I walked around and started down the cobblestone walkway to the stairs. He didn't drive off until I was nearly there. I could hear the television in the house, some comedy show with its usual canned laughter. Visions of Mazy smiling when she and I had sat together to watch television gave me some courage.

You're his daughter, I thought. *You're his daughter*, I chanted to myself. *He can't turn you away.*

But what would he do? a little voice inside whispered. *He turned you away once, didn't he?*

As soon as I stepped onto the stairway, another light came on above it, a motion detector. I felt like I had stepped into a spotlight. For a moment it blinded me, and I seriously considered turning around and rushing away. My heart was pounding. I tightened my grip on my shoulder purse and simply stood there, unable to take another step.

But before I could change my mind, I realized that the burst of light had alerted someone inside. There was a rush of footsteps, and then the front door opened.

For a few moments the expression on my father's face said he didn't recognize me, but that quickly fell away to be replaced by his shock and even fear the moment he did. He looked unable to move, unable to swallow, and even unable to blink. He had gotten older, his face rounder, softer. He was no longer his svelte, athletic self. He had a bit of a potbelly. Maybe it was just the veranda light, but it appeared that he had some gray at his temples. The hair he had mourned losing years ago had only receded more. Perhaps to deny what was happening, he had let his sides grow thicker and the back grow longer. His white shirt was gathered at his waist, some of it sticking out. My father had never looked this disheveled. Actually, he looked like he had just been wakened.

"Who is it, Derick?" we heard a woman cry from inside.

He stepped closer, his eyelids narrowing.

"Saffron?" he said. Just hearing him say my name began to defrost the icy fear in my body.

"Yes, Daddy," I said.

"Derick?" we heard.

"Just a minute, Ava," he shouted back, and closed the door behind him.

I almost retreated in fear when he moved us to the edge of the veranda so quickly.

"What are you doing here?" he asked. Fortunately, he sounded more curious than angry.

"Mazy died," I said. Even in the yellow-tinted light, I saw his face whiten.

"Died?"

"I found your letters to her. I know everything about you and Mama and why Mazy is my real grandmother. I have money she left me. I called someone, a nurse friend, to go to her house and take care of her body and her cat. Then I got on the train. No one knows I've come here. No one back there knows anything. I threw the letters in the garbage before I left."

I rattled it all off in one breath, hoping it would be enough to convince him it was safe to love me again.

His eyes seemed to roll in his head as he digested what I was saying and sifted through his mind to find some way to deal with what confronted him.

"Listen, listen," he said, coming down the steps and reaching into his pocket as he did so. He took out a wad of money. "Go down the block and turn right. Go two blocks and turn left. Two blocks later, you're in the downtown area, and there's a hotel on the right called the Dew Drop Inn. It's more of a motel, but the rooms are okay. I'll call ahead so they'll be expecting you. We're part owners of it."

"Part owners?"

"I'll explain it all tomorrow. Check in, get something to eat, and go to sleep. I'll meet you first thing in the morning."

He shoved the money into my hand.

"I have money."

I wanted to add that wasn't why I'd come, but he did look frantic.

"Don't worry. We'll talk about how to do this," he said.

"Do what?"

"Just go. Do what I say. We'll work out everything. Check in to the hotel. I'll make a call so you'll be expected. There won't be any problem."

He glanced nervously back at the front door.

"Go ahead."

"If I check in, I'll be using my new name. Mazy had a birth certificate created for me," I warned. I was hoping that would upset him, but he nodded, close to smiling.

"Saffron Dazy. I know. It'll be all right. That's perfect. Just go." He looked poised to shoo me off like a fly.

I hesitated. *That's perfect?* His name and mine had been sliced apart. Wasn't he even going to hug me? I glanced past him at the front door, and then, when he didn't move toward me, I turned and walked to the sidewalk. He watched me for a few moments and then hurriedly went into the house.

I thought I heard the door lock. The motion light went off. It was as if a curtain had closed.

I continued walking through what felt like a fog, not really looking at, seeing, or hearing anything. This was what I had feared, this feeling of being in limbo, floating, dangling. Suddenly, the streets were so quiet, with hardly any traffic. I felt as if everyone and everything around me were pausing to watch me walk alone. I caught glimpses of families through the warm light of their front windows. Somewhere off to the left, a dog began barking. The barking grew softer, lower, as I walked faster. When I made the turns he had described, I saw the Dew Drop Inn sign ahead in a purplish blue light. I paused.

Why not keep going? I thought. I had enough money for a while. Maybe I should find a bus station rather than return to the train station. But if I did, what could I possibly do? I couldn't get a job. I'd be that girl of the streets I had envisioned on my way here. Any other girl in my place surely would be terrified and crying by now. Her father had just sent her away a second time. I credited Mazy for my stoic attitude and strength. She had raised me to be strong.

I walked on. Practically indifferent to where I was going and what I was being forced to do, I entered the small, brightly lit lobby with pale yellow walls and black-framed windows. Posted rules and regulations and No Smoking signs were scattered about. A short, elderly man with bushy gray eyebrows and an almost childlike body, small hands, and light-brown hair, still quite thick, stood up instantly and smiled. His thin pink lips seemed stretched to the point of snapping, losing their color, too. He obviously wanted to make a good impression. What had Daddy told him about me?

"Saffron Dazy?" he said.

"Yes."

"Everything's arranged." He brought a key on a small chain with a Dew Drop Inn blue plastic tab to the counter. "Got my nicest room for you, twenty-one A. You just go out, walk to the left, go down the short walk, and it's the first door on the left."

He pumped the key at me until I took it.

"There are bottles of fresh water in your room in the minibar in the dresser. There's an extra blanket and pillow in the closet. If you want something to eat, you'll find a Birdie's menu right next to the phone." He smiled again. "My son owns Birdie's. Great pizza. They deliver," he quickly added. "Don't worry about expense. Everything's taken care of. Anything else you think you might need?"

A life, I wanted to say, but instead shook my head.

"Don't I have to sign anything?"

People always did that in movies.

"No, no. I know your uncle for a long time. He explained everything."

I stared. Did I hear him correctly? My uncle? Explained what? I was afraid to ask.

He smiled again.

"You just hit zero on the phone if you need anything," he said. My silence unnerved him, I guess. He had to keep talking. "I'm on alone all night tonight, or I'd show you to your room. We're not too busy today, but we do get busy on the weekends. Lots of hikers, and the lake still offers great fishing. Fed by a natural spring. People rent rowboats, have picnics. They come from hundreds of miles, some of them."

I was simply staring at him, or through him, really. His words flew over me.

"You okay? I guess I can walk you to your room if you'd like," he said reluctantly. He could have said, *What are you waiting for? Get going. You're making me uncomfortable.*

"No, I'm fine," I said, and started out.

"Just hit zero on the phone," he called after me. "I'm here for anything you need."

Right, I thought. *I'll hit zero and say, "I lost my father. Can you send around a new one?"*

As I walked to the room, I kept repeating the word in my head as if I had to memorize it for a play or something: *uncle.*

When I unlocked the door and turned on the light, I stood there looking at the strange bedroom the way someone might look at a prison cell. Maybe the old man would come by and put a lock on the door so I couldn't go back to my father's house.

I hadn't slept anywhere but my room in the house that had gone up in a fire and in Mazy's house, my robin's-egg blue room. Those were the only personal walls and windows, closets, and rugs I had known. People go on trips, vacations, and sleep in different places, but I imagined that sleeping in a new place without anyone you knew coming along with you had to be quite different from going somewhere with your family or friends.

Loneliness was such a cold feeling, and what could be lonelier than coming into a room like this? There was nothing warm about it. It was clean but bland, with light-brown bedding. There was a darker brown night table beside it with a phone and a pad and pencil on it. A small desk with a chair was in the left corner. The walls were papered in white with thick brown lines, and the floor was covered in a vacuumed but well-worn carpet. On the right was a dresser in dark brown with a cabinet I imagined was the minibar, just like I had seen on television. The oval mirror above was in a matching dark-brown frame. To the right of it was a television set on a metal wall shelf. The remote was on the shelf, too.

It's nobody's room, I thought, *and also everybody's.*

I stepped in and closed the door. The bathroom was straight ahead and as bland as the room. The floor was a gray tile. There was a tub and shower and a sink with a cabinet above it. I looked in at empty shelves. It wasn't until that moment that I realized I had left home without a toothbrush and toothpaste. I went out and sat on the bed, still feeling caught in a daze. The trip, although not terribly long, combined with my confrontation with my father and his hiding me away in a motel, swept me up in a wave of exhaustion. Without taking off a thing, I fell back on the bed and looked up at the bland white ceiling.

Mazy used to say that some motels and hotels are nothing more than human storage. I never understood what she meant until this moment. I had been put on a shelf until there was a decision about what to do with me.

Uncle, I thought, before falling quickly into a deep sleep.

I didn't realize that my legs were hanging off the bed until I woke up in the morning, just as the sun was rising. Almost immediately, I felt, as Mazy would say, morning grimy, so I took a shower and changed my clothes. I was hungry, too. It had been almost a full day since I had eaten anything. After I bundled my dirty clothes and put them into my bag, I picked it up and my purse and started out. Daddy was approaching just as I closed the door.

"Good. You're up," he said. "I'll take you to breakfast, and we'll talk."

He was dressed in a dark-blue suit and a light-blue tie, now looking well put together. It was how I remembered him. He started to turn, but stopped when he saw I wasn't moving.

"Saffron?"

"Why did you tell the hotel manager you were my uncle?"

"You'll see. It's a good idea. You'll see."

Good idea?

When I just stared, he looked away for a moment and then turned back to me.

"I'm not going to send you away," he said. "I want you to live with us. I'm just finding a way to make it happen."

"You're my father," I said. "You already made that happen."

He smiled at my firmness.

"I've got to remind myself," he said, "that Mazy's been bringing you up. Let's just get some hot food in you and talk, and you'll see that I'm finding the best way to be your father."

I didn't say it, but I thought it.

I hope it's better than the way you found after the fire.

He surprised me by reaching for my free hand.

And I surprised myself by taking his.

That's what being desperate really meant.

CHAPTER TWO

"My wife, Ava, never knew I had another daughter," he began, "but don't worry. I have prepared for this day."

He said that like an insurance agent would. That was what he used to be. Mazy told me often that what you do becomes a part of who you are.

We were sitting in a small restaurant in the village of Sandburg Creek. It was just off its Main Street, which in many ways, although longer and wider and with many more stores, restaurants, and supermarkets, resembled Hurley with its similar early-twentieth-century architecture and more modern structures here and there. The traffic grew quickly; people seemed to have popped up out of the sidewalks. There was an air filled with far more activity here. People were walking faster and talking louder. I thought maybe it was a couple of thousand people away from being considered a city.

Before Daddy began talking, dozens of questions about his life here, his life without me, flooded my mind, but I pushed them all aside to listen. One of my biggest questions was, what did he remember about me? It seemed to me that every parent should recall the slightest details about his or her children, but especially what made them sad and what made them happy, as well as what frightened them. The smallest things became so important, even as they grew older. How much of me remained stored in his mind, written indelibly in his thoughts and memories? He ordered our breakfast, telling the waitress to scramble my eggs well and bring cream cheese with the toast. "And a large orange juice with an ice cube," he added.

I said nothing, a part of me cringing in anticipation of what he was going to say about my unexpected arrival. Had he already arranged for me to be taken somewhere far away from his new life? Was that what the word *prepared* meant? Was that his insurance policy? And what about Mama? Did he think about her at all? Did he wonder if I still did or if Mazy and I often talked about her, even before I knew she was Mazy's daughter? What did he think or know about my life away from him all these years?

My questions were coming to my mind quickly, but I kept my lips pressed closed so tightly that I could feel the muscles straining in my jaw.

He hesitated, finally really looking at me, I thought. Up until now, he'd glanced and looked away quickly, almost as if he was afraid to convince himself I was really here. How many times had he dreamed of this moment? More than I had? Or was *dreamed* the wrong word? Should I think *feared*?

"Do you drink coffee now?"

"Sometimes," I said.

He ordered coffee for both of us. As soon as the waitress left us, he smiled. He moved to take my hand, but I put my hands in my lap. Everything he did drew my suspicion. I wasn't subtle about it. I could see how uncomfortable I was making him, and that made me angrier, probably because I was so fearful of what was coming. He forced a smile and sat back.

"Mazy was right. You do look grown-up, years beyond your age. You're about as tall as I imagined you to be, and filling out well."

That answered my question about whether he had ever come to Hurley to sneak a view of me. I could feel the chill surround my heart, my vulnerable, innocent, and still childish heart. That air of comfort I remembered when I was with him years ago could have gone up with the smoke spilling out of every window, under every door, and through the crumbling walls and ceilings of what was once the only world I really knew. I certainly didn't feel it now. My body sank with the disappointment. He hadn't been intrigued about me as a father should be. He hadn't gone to Hurley to sneak views of his daughter. Hope seemed to fold inside of itself like a balloon quickly leaking all its air. Daddy was still more like a stranger, and for now, every minute together was not changing that. It was reinforcing it.

"My new birth certificate says I'm fourteen—fifteen almost," I said. He nodded. Did he even remember how old I really was?

"Oh, I can believe that easily. So," he said, "you read some of my letters to Mazy?"

"Not some. Every one of them. She never threw out any. She kept them in a box in a closet in her room but never revealed anything that was in them or even that she had any."

He nodded. The waitress brought my juice and our coffee.

"I never expected her to show them to you."

"She didn't," I said. "She died first. I remembered the box in her closet and always wondered why she had to keep it under lock and key. Nothing else was hidden from me. It was the first thing I thought of when I realized she was gone."

"What happened to her?"

"I don't know exactly. She died. She went up to her room, lay down, and probably had a heart attack. If she was seriously ill, she never told me. I never ever heard her say she had gone to a doctor. She said doctors were mostly pill pushers. She had her own cures for anything that happened to either of us."

"Oh, I believe that. She was quite a tough lady. You needed only to meet her once to sense that."

We stared at each other. He smiled, but I didn't. I drank my juice and waited, even though my questions wanted even more to gallop off my tongue. Mama, I thought. Mama would want me to ask the first one, but it was painful to find the words.

"So when did you have this other daughter? How old is she?" I asked.

"I thought about it all on my way to pick you up and decided I would be completely honest with you," he said, pressing his palms flatly on the table. "I can see that you're old enough and smart enough to understand everything now."

Did I want complete honesty? Wouldn't I rather he made up one of his fantasies the way he used to and make it easier for me to accept where we were and how we got here?

"Your mother and I had drifted apart even before I began my affair with Ava Saddlebrook. By the way, you'll see the name Saddlebrook on a number of properties here. Her father, Amos Saddlebrook, owns a great deal of real estate, has an interest in many of the local businesses, like the Dew Drop Inn, and is on every important committee. He's still quite active at age eighty-one. Fit, too. You'll think he's in his sixties. Ava's mother died a little over fifteen years ago. Ava was an only child like you."

"I'm no longer an only child," I said dryly, and finished drinking my juice.

He smiled, but it wasn't the smile of a proud parent. This smile was tinged with some anxiety. I couldn't help but enjoy how tense and nervous he was. Why couldn't it be at least as hard for him as it was for me? That was my anger speaking, but a bigger part of me wanted there to be no anxiety at all. This should be a wonderful reunion.

"I fear that there's a lot more of Mazy in you than I know."

He sipped his coffee.

"Why shouldn't there be?" I shot back. "She was my grandmother and all the family I had for years. She nursed me when I was sick, clothed and fed me. She taught me anything and everything a parent might, probably more."

"Right, right. Okay," he said, lifting his hands like someone surrendering.

"When did you have this other daughter?" I repeated.

"It's a little complicated."

"When?" I insisted. There was no longer any tolerance in me for any of his sins. He owed me the truth, and I wanted it all here and now.

"A few months after you were born."

"Months?"

He looked down at his now-clasped hands. How does a father tell his daughter that he had betrayed her mother? I enjoyed seeing him squirm. I was enjoying it for Mama.

"I didn't think Ava would go through with it. She didn't tell me until she was nearly seven months along. She didn't show like most other women do. Sometimes I think she did it solely to torment her father. Or maybe to force me to leave your mother. When she started to show, she basically dropped out of sight until months after she had given birth."

"But everyone knew about you?"

He was silent.

"I mean here."

"No one knew that she had a child for some time," he said.

"Some time? How long?"

"Long."

"Why?"

"Her father preferred it that way, and she was waiting . . ."

"For you? Her father preferred it?"

"Yes. I told you it was complicated," he added quickly.

"So explain it, Daddy."

"After she realized she was pregnant and decided to have our child, she had a nanny, and our daughter was basically kept hidden away at the Saddlebrook estate until our accident. As I said, her father insisted on it. She was dependent upon him at the time, and as you will learn, he's a very powerful man in this community."

"Accident?" I fumbled for a meaning until it came like a slap across my cheek. "You mean the fire?"

He nodded.

This felt like I was reaching into a beehive.

"When I left with you afterward, I had decided to accept my responsibilities and move here."

"Did her father know about me?"

"No. He disliked me as it was, because Ava became pregnant and I sort of disappeared for a while. I mean, I saw her but didn't spend any time with Karen until she was nearly three. Her father wouldn't have anything to do with me until we had eloped. By then, Ava had already chosen the house we're in. After we made our relationship legal, her father reluctantly bought us the house."

"Why reluctantly?"

"He wanted us to live at his estate, Saddlebrook."

"Why didn't you?"

"Ava wanted us to have at least the semblance of independence, especially after her father had treated her like some stain on the family name."

"Didn't people ask questions about it all?"

"Behind our backs, for sure. The Saddlebrook family is powerful here. Nevertheless, the early days of our marriage were a little difficult, actually quite difficult, but in the end, money has a louder voice than conscience or religious principles . . . whatever. Who doesn't have a skeleton in a closet?"

"Your new wife waited all that time? She never had another boyfriend?"

"When you're older, you might understand. Despite having lived so long under her father's thumb, Ava . . . Ava is quite independent. She's a lot like him in that way. When she wants something, she gets it, no matter how long it may take.

"So you see, I really did have a lot to work out before I could bring you into all this. Before that, your mother found out about my affair with Ava and became very bitter. Sometimes I used to think she wanted to stay married to me just to make me suffer. I did, and I know you were suffering, too, especially when she was keeping you practically a prisoner in the house with the homeschooling. Maybe she thought that was another way to punish me. I'm sorry I let that go on so long."

"My life with Mazy wasn't much different," I said. "I didn't enter public school until just recently, and that was a disaster, because kids who had seen me already had made up crazy stories about me and Mazy. They were actually afraid of her. Some thought she was a witch and had taught me weird stuff."

"You'll have to tell me more about that when we can talk privately. Mazy and I didn't communicate as much recently, maybe because she was getting sick. I mean, I knew you had entered school, but . . ."

The waitress brought our food.

He started to eat and gestured at me to start as well. I did, but I didn't take my eyes off him. My memory felt like it was twirling back through a tunnel as I caught the gleam of his blue eyes, eyes that had once brought calm and a sense of safety to me whenever I was troubled or afraid. The strength in his firm lips was still there, and despite the weight he had put on, making his face look chubby and soft, there was that air of authority, that sense of control I not only saw when I was a little girl but craved often whenever there was tension in our home. Call himself whatever he wanted, he was still my daddy.

I fought back needing him. I was afraid I would cry.

Anyway, what I really wanted to bring him was my anger. I was disappointed in myself, in how quickly I was becoming a little girl again as soon as I was with him. How could I still love him, respect him, and want him after all that he had done, had just revealed? There is no disappointment greater than a disappointment in yourself, and I was feeling it. I ate, but I didn't taste anything, and although I was battling as hard as I could, the tears were seeping into my eyes. *No!* I shouted inside myself. *Do not cry; do not be a little girl again. That's what he's hoping you'll be.*

"So," he continued, "when I began with Ava, she knew I was still married, but as I said, she didn't know about you. I wanted to tell her, but Ava back then wasn't the sort of young woman who would willingly take on the responsibility of bringing up another child, especially someone else's child. And it might have made for more complications with her father at the time."

"So you lied to them both?"

"I didn't lie so much as I left out some of the story."

"What about your other daughter? Did she know you were her father back then? I mean, when you spent time with her?"

"Yes and no."

"What does that mean?"

"She was too young to understand what was happening and was kept quite content at the estate. And I thought I could manage it until . . ."

"Until what?"

"Eventually, I thought maybe I could divorce your mother and give her sole custody of you. I even revealed I had another child. I planned on telling Ava about you after the divorce, because even though your mother would have sole custody, I'd have visitation rights, but . . ." He paused. "Go on, finish eating before your food gets cold."

"I ate enough," I said, pushing the plate away. I could feel the food sticking in my throat.

"Yeah, okay. So what happened was it became clearer that your mother couldn't handle the responsibility, and whether I liked it or not, that plan wasn't going to work. I started to tell Ava about you a few times but lost my courage each time. I was really in love with her, and once you meet her, I think you'll understand why. She is beautiful and intelligent, elegant and—"

"Mama was all that," I said sharply.

He nodded. "She was. I would be the first to admit it. I remember often telling you about what she was like before . . . before all this happened. It broke my heart to see the changes in her."

"The changes due to your affair," I said dryly. "And knowing you had another child with another woman."

He looked like I was stabbing him with the sharp end of a scissor. Mazy surely would have said it. After all, he had broken my mother's heart.

"Well, yes. I bear a lot of guilt, but there was more to it. Your mother always showed some signs of emotional and mental issues. Our parents had her see a therapist. I don't think she ever got over being adopted once she found out, even though that meant we could fall in love. I guess I was fooling myself when I told myself I could fix all that.

"Anyway, when I discovered your mother's real history, the adoption, and how it had happened because Mazy was single and alone, I felt sorry for Mazy. Maybe I shouldn't have done it, but I contacted Mazy. I never told your mother, of course. I even secretly met Mazy a few times. My parents didn't know. I sent her pictures and told her about your mother, how she was doing in school, in college, and how wonderful she was. I'm sure you saw all of that in the letters.

"My parents did love her and tried to give her everything she wanted and needed. But every time I saw how beautiful and intelligent your mother was, I thought about Mazy, how she was missing it all and, if it wasn't for me, how she would never know. Eventually, you were kind of a solution for Mazy's sadness and regret, you see."

A solution? Maybe I smirked at how much I didn't believe he felt so sorry for Mazy; maybe he could still read my feelings and thoughts in my eyes.

"Is that what you meant when you said you were preparing? Even before I was born?"

"What? No. If you think I was doing that back then, writing to Mazy and keeping her up on your mother to get Mazy to take you in eventually . . . I mean, I wasn't even sure your mother and I would be together in those days. We were married after your mother became pregnant with you."

"Sounds like a pattern with you and your marriages."

He shook his head. And then nodded. "I understand your bitterness."

"Do you?"

"Of course. Anyway, when the time came and I thought about Mazy . . ."

"It was convenient," I said.

He looked stunned for a moment. "I don't know if I'd use that word. I really believed that everyone would be happy. That I'll admit. Maybe I was wrong, but I knew that even if I convinced or forced Ava to take you in with us, you wouldn't have been happy. Who knows how Amos Saddlebrook would have treated you? Ava . . . another woman's child . . . it wouldn't have been pleasant. However, Mazy was certainly elated."

He shrugged. "To my way of thinking, it was a nice, wonderful thing to do for someone who lived with so much guilt."

I stared at him coolly and then finally asked a question I didn't want to hear answered.

"What about me, my happiness? Didn't you care at all? I was your daughter, too."

"It hurt me to leave you, of course, but as I said, I believed that if I truly loved you, I wouldn't bring you into an unpleasant life after such a tragedy. Ava would feel I was forcing her to accept you. She'd know I had lied to her, and Ava's not someone easily lied to. She's quite intolerant of deception, as is her father. We'd probably have broken up, too. It would be like another fire," he said, and I could feel my eyes threatening to explode.

"Fire? You compare a breakup to *that*?"

"Anyway," he quickly continued, ignoring me, "I kept up with your upbringing, development. Mazy wrote detailed letters like the teacher she was. She didn't need any money, but I sent her some from time to time."

"And even after all these years, your new wife never knew I existed?"

He nodded, but he didn't look as regretful as I wanted him to look. Maybe I never really knew my father, and all the feelings I had felt for him and thought he had for me were imagined.

I pushed the plate farther away and stared out the front window of the restaurant, which advertised itself only as a breakfast and lunch place. It was simply decorated, with some pictures of the family who owned it on the dark-blue-painted walls. Two paintings of lake scenes were hung near the entrance. There were three other booths like the one we were in and then about twenty tables of two and four seats with a small counter that had a half dozen stools. Nobody was looking at us in particular. No one had smiled at him or nodded when we had entered.

"You don't come here much, do you?" I asked.

"No, why?"

"No one's said hello. No one asked you about me. That's probably why you chose for us to come here."

"Oh." He smiled. "You pick up on things quickly."

"Mazy used to call me Miss Marple. The famous woman detective," I added. I wasn't only clinging desperately to my happier memories with her. I was trying to tell him that he couldn't fool me. No more lies. I almost told him what Mazy once said about liars. *Liars have to have good memories.*

He smiled and looked at the other patrons.

"Yes, I don't know anyone here, really. I mean, I've seen some of these people. It's not that big a town. If I go out for breakfast or lunch, I usually go to the Sandburg Club. It has a pool and four tennis courts. You'll be able to go there, too. My father-in-law created it."

"You're my father, but you can't admit it, but you can admit to being my uncle? How can you make this work?"

The waitress came to take our plates, and Daddy ordered more coffee.

"I was always anticipating last night," he said. "I mean, I hoped Mazy would live long enough to see you through public school and maybe even college. The money's there, but . . ."

The waitress brought the coffee. He sipped some and looked up, as if he was trying to remember everything.

"I told sort of a half-lie to Ava. Your mother and I for the longest time were really brother and sister, as you know. I just . . . never told Ava that the woman I married was the woman brought up as my sister. She would have hated that."

"Why?"

"It sounds incestuous. Anyway, I told her I had a sister who married a man in the navy and was a bit—well, not a bit, but completely estranged from our parents because they disapproved of the marriage . . . which our parents did, by the way, disapprove of us."

"Felt it was incestuous?"

"Obviously it wasn't, but as a result of all that, she and I were estranged from our parents as well. That's what I told Ava."

"Half-truths," I said. "Lies as tools."

He raised his eyebrows. "You remember that?"

"Why not? There's so much of it in my life. And apparently, so much in yours."

He winced now like someone slapped across the cheek.

"Anyway. So I had told Ava about my sister and told her that we were never close. I kept it vague enough, claiming it was painful to discuss. That's worked."

"I always believed that people who love each other can easily tell when one is lying," I said. "I guess I was wrong."

He closed and opened his eyes. Maybe I really was Mazy's granddaughter in more ways than I had anticipated.

"It's not lying so much as being creative to protect everyone. Anyway, I told Ava that my sister had a daughter, and last night, I told her a messenger had come to our house to tell me my sister had died. I didn't know my brother-in-law had deserted her a year after you were born. Which is perfect, by the way."

"Why?"

"This way, you don't have to recall anything about your father."

"You mean for me it's like my father didn't exist?"

"Yes," he said, missing my point about him entirely.

After a moment, I asked, "What do you mean by a messenger?"

"I implied it came from the police, the chief himself. It's all carefully laid out. You'll see."

"What if she asks the chief or says something and he tells her he doesn't know what she's talking about?"

"He won't contradict what I said. He'll play along."

"Why?"

"I'm on the town board. I voted to give him the job, and my vote counts the most now.

"So," he continued, "I told them that my niece was coming today. I sat with Ava and your . . . cousin Karen and explained you were coming to live with us and that I knew little about you except that you were an excellent student, in the tenth grade although you were only fourteen, because you were in an honors program, which is true, right?"

"I thought you said Mazy didn't keep you up on all that."

"Oh. I didn't mean that part. I never heard about your having trouble at school or that stuff about witchcraft."

Where were the lies, the tools? Where was the truth? How would I ever know? Could I live, even just breathe, in a world of so much deceit? I seriously now wondered if I should have done what I had been tempted to do last night and walked on past the Dew Drop Inn and caught a bus to anywhere.

"That trouble happened pretty soon after I began school," I said. "Then she must have called you about my honors status. How else would you know?"

"Yes. A phone call from her was unusual. We only spoke when I called her."

I thought for a moment.

"Maybe she thought something was happening to her and she had to call you finally," I said.

"I don't know. She didn't say anything about herself. She was kind of proud of how you had handled your first day and your achieving honors status."

"She was," I practically whispered. She was so proud of me, I thought, and I had left her lying on her bed alone and her cat, poor Mr. Pebbles, wandering about looking for me.

"So let me tell you more," my father said, his smile returning. I could see how proud he was of how well he thought this was going.

For me, it was turning my stomach. I was sorry I had eaten anything first.

"Your cousin Karen's in the ninth grade, and your baby cousin Garson, named after his great-grandfather, is almost a year old. We weren't going to have any more children, even after we were officially married, but Ava was bored with her work at her father's company, and with Karen a real teenager now, we just let it happen before Ava was too old to get pregnant. She's thirty-nine."

I was silent. I don't know what he expected me to say. *Great, I'll have a new young mother? I'll have a cousin instead of a half sister and a cousin instead of a half brother? Does that make it easier to accept?* Did he really think this solved it all?

"My cousins," I muttered.

"You could be a great help with Garson," he added.

"What if I forget and call you Daddy?" I said. I think I said it more just to be difficult, to throw new problems in his way and maybe make him rethink his lies as tools. He was looking too confident.

However, I really could see myself doing it, calling him Daddy, especially when I was frightened or sad.

"Well, everyone will just think you had made a mistake or had come to accept me as someone in that role. I think Ava and Karen would feel sorrier for you than anything else."

"Feel sorrier? Why?"

He shrugged. "Your need to have a father."

"Don't you think I did? I do?"

"Sure. You'll claim that your fictional mother had boyfriends after her husband left you both, but none of them stuck."

"None of them stuck? What if they ask me why not?"

"You can say anything that comes to mind. They drank too much, were on drugs, worthless, trying to live off her, anything you want. Those are good reasons why none of them stuck."

"And what about describing my mother?"

"Just tell them what you remember about your real mother. I have some pictures you can use of Lindsey when she was in college. You don't have any pictures of your father because he left so quickly, even before you were born."

"Well, it's true. I don't have pictures of my father," I said. "You didn't leave any pictures with me. Just a coloring book."

"Saffron . . ."

"I have it in my bag, you know. There are pictures still left to color."

He pressed his lips together.

I looked out the window again. I could still just get up and run out.

"I really hope this will work," he said. "For all of us."

"Isn't it easier to just tell the truth?"

"I'd have to explain everything," he said.

"Everything? You mean leaving me at a train station and then pretending I don't exist for years?"

He sipped his coffee, his eyes suddenly cooling, making him look distant, lost in his thoughts. I waited until he looked like he realized I was really sitting across from him. I imagined I looked ready to explode.

"Why make it so difficult, so complicated, for everyone now? If we do what I've planned here, the result will be the same. You'll have a new home, a family. And as I told you, we're an influential family in this community, too, Saffron. There are benefits."

"So you work for Mr. Saddlebrook?"

"Yes. I'm his senior adviser. You'll like the private school, Karen's friends, everything."

"Private school?"

"Yes. Grades kindergarten to twelve, too. It's quite impressive, small class sizes, on a great property with a beautiful athletic field and running track. My father-in-law paid for the gymnasium. There's a thousand-seat theater. Community theater projects often use it. Karen's in the dramatics club. She's quite the little actress already and very popular in school. She's doing well in all her subjects, and she's very helpful around the house and with Garson. In fact, Ava depends on her. We have a part-time nanny and a maid. It's how Ava likes it. Karen's very responsible, and she's pretty because she looks more like Ava."

The pleasure in his face when he talked about his new daughter was like a bee sting. Would I ever bring that pride and joy back into his face? How could I if he wasn't even permitting me to be his daughter?

He stopped, probably because of the expression on my face.

"I know, I know. This is all making it tougher on you," he said. He reached for my hand again; this time, I let him take it. His fingers felt warm. I was thrown back for a moment to his taking my hand when the three of us went somewhere. Sometimes in the later days, Mama would forget to hold my hand.

"But it's going to be all right, Saffron. It will be. I'll take care of all the arrangements at your new school. I'll use a lot of what Mazy did. We have a great deal of influence there, obviously. Once you start, no one will question anything anyway."

He signaled for the waitress to bring the bill.

"Where am I supposed to have lived?" I asked.

He reached into his pocket to produce a notepad.

"It's all here," he said, handing it to me. "The important facts. If you look troubled when answering questions Ava and Karen ask, they'll slow down and maybe stop asking altogether. Last night I laid the groundwork. I explained how hard things have been for you and how it's better to help you forget the life you had before this. So they'll take it slowly, I hope."

Maybe, as Mazy would say, that would be the silver lining in all this: I could forget the past.

I opened the cover of the notepad while he was paying the bill. When had he done this? Last night? Years ago, anticipating my arrival? When? Then again . . . why did it matter when?

Reading the fictionalization of my life wasn't a shock. I had lived with fabrication ever since my father left me at the train station.

"Costa Mesa, California?"

"You mother moved there after your father deserted you. He was stationed in San Diego. You'll see when you read through the details. Then you can go on the computer and study up on Costa Mesa and the whole area so you'll feel more comfortable talking about it."

"What computer?"

"Oh, I'll buy you one right after we leave here. Didn't you have one at Mazy's?"

"She wasn't fond of the way young people use them, but she had promised to buy me one for my next birthday."

"Oh. What I think you should do is return to the Dew Drop Inn. I kept your room for the day. I'll bring you the computer in an hour and make sure you know how to use it. After work, I'll come get you, and we'll say you flew into the Albany airport and took a bus to Sandburg Creek. You just arrived, and I picked you up at the bus station. You made your own travel arrangements because you didn't want to be in the hands of any social service agency. You had no one else to help you. That will make Ava and Karen feel even sorrier for you."

"I did flee to be sure I wasn't in the hands of any social service agency."

"See? We're building around the truth. It'll be like the first time you and I met, too. That will help make it work. Don't be shocked or surprised at the questions I might ask in front of them. Just study those notes. Don't worry. It's all going to be just fine. You'll have everything a daughter of mine would or should have."

"Except a father," I said.

He blew frustration through his lips.

"You'll have a father in every way. I'll be involved in your education, everything you do. You'll be part of this family. There'll be birthdays and Christmas. If you want, if it's easier, call me Derick after a while. Karen fools around and calls me Derick sometimes. You guys are going to be great together." He smiled. "I'm getting excited about this."

Was he serious? Excited about being my uncle and not my father?

"Excited?"

"About making it work. Ava will be taking you for new clothes the moment she realizes you left with practically nothing. You could actually wear some of Karen's clothes for the time being. I can see you guys wearing each other's things. You're about the same size, height. I wouldn't be surprised if you were the same shoe size. Karen's a generous girl. She'll be willing to share.

"We'll work on the guest room and make it really your room. Ava will enjoy doing that. You can tell her what your favorite color is, and she'll buy more for your room."

"Fictional or real color? Is it in the notepad?"

"What? No, real, of course. There's nothing like that in there, just important basic facts. Ava will get you new bedding and maybe change curtains and get area rugs, bathroom towels, everything. Karen will love being involved, too. She'll be happy to help you make decisions, share ideas, I'm sure."

I stared at him. It seemed redundant, useless to ask, but I wanted to ask if she was generous enough to share her father.

"Look," he said, "I know in the beginning this is going to be hard for both of us, but it will work, and you'll have a real family again. And eventually, we'll all be living in Saddlebrook. It's a magnificent estate. We could live there now, but as I told you, Ava likes being independent from her father. It's going to be fantastic." He paused, then added, "Trust me."

It was as if those two words were the magic words that would unlock a chest of images. *Trust me?* If I closed my eyes, I could remember and see him taking my hand and leading me to the train. I could hear him talking about our new home, our new beginning, how now I would go to a real school, not a homeschool, and have friends and parties. He was going to buy me so many nice things to replace what went up in smoke. He'd be with me all the time and work hard at making me happy.

Didn't he fix my collar and give me a kiss on the cheek before he turned and closed his eyes as our train began to leave?

And what about Mama? What about the way we stopped talking about her?

"You want something more to eat? You hardly ate."

I blinked, returning to today.

"No," I said.

"Then let's go. I'll walk you back to the Dew Drop Inn and then go get the computer. I'll show you the basics before I leave you for work. Kids your age pick it up quickly. Karen had a computer when she was four. And I'll get you a cell phone tomorrow, too, one of those great smartphones."

"Whom am I going to call? Certainly no one back in Hurley."

"Oh, you'll have friends, lots of friends, and you'll have my number when you want to talk or need something, and I'm sure Ava will want you to have her number, and Karen will want you to have hers. Kids your age practically live and breathe those things. Give it all a chance, Saffron. You'll see. After a short while, it will be like you were always here."

Was I always in your heart? Did you ever dream about me? Did you ever cry about me? I wanted to ask so many questions, but he rose. I put the notepad in my pocket and followed him out. We walked quickly back to the hotel. I felt like I was being smuggled into it. He kept his head down, avoiding greeting anyone. Before he left to buy my computer, he handed me an envelope.

"There are fourteen pictures of your mother when she was in college and three of you around age two with her. Put them in your bag," he said, "with your new birth certificate. Okay?"

"So you'll tell people my real father's name was Dazy?"

"Nothing to worry about," he said.

I took the envelope so gently someone would think it was hot.

"I'll be right back," he said.

After he had left, I sat on the chair by the small desk, with the envelope in my hand, and just stared at the door. Despite all his assurances, I was more frightened than I had been when I stepped off the train and walked to the taxi. From the moment I had laid eyes on it, there was something about this world that had seemed unreal, a too-picture-perfect place. I was afraid that anyone who saw me would know immediately that I didn't belong here. It was as if I had walked onto a stage and everyone around me was an actor. They would take one look at me and know I wasn't one. How did I get on their stage? Why?

I took out the small notepad. My part was in here. Later, when my father picked me up to take me to his new home where his new family lived, I would be the character in this pad, in this play. It had been so long since I had thought of myself as Saffron Faith Anders anyway. Mazy was the first to write a new part for me to play, when she had my name changed and got me my new birth certificate. Last night, the train had only brought me to a new stage, not to the reunion I had imagined.

What of my real self would remain after all this began?

Before I went back to reading the information in the notepad, I opened the envelope and spread the pictures out on the top of the small desk. All those tears that had been threatening to rush out at the restaurant emerged. I felt them zigzagging down my cheeks and dripping off. The sight of my mother released so much more. Childhood memories flowed as if the dam that had held them back for years had crumbled. I could hear her voice and her laughter. I heard her singing me to sleep and going through my spelling and math lessons.

My body was trembling so hard. My screams flooded my throat. The rasping sobs kept them from emerging. My ribs ached. I embraced myself and rocked in the chair the way I had rocked on the train-station bench years ago when I realized Daddy had left me and felt the cold night, trying to claim myself forever in the darkness.

Finally, I caught my breath, sucked back my tears, and went to the bathroom to wash my face and clean away the streaks the tears had drawn across my cheeks. Then, after a few deep gasps, I returned to the desk and put the pictures back in the envelope and into my bag with my new birth certificate and my coloring book with its yellowed pages.

I returned to the pad and began reading details about myself. As he had said, he had noted that I wasn't happy with any of the men my mother had dated, and there was even a reference to one being too familiar with me. That was the reason my mother dropped that particular one. Everything was done in a general way. I could elaborate on the details of anything I wanted. It would be like he and I were coauthors of the same fictional biography, my own soap opera.

Was I going to be born again, emerging from the cocoon that had been my world with Mazy? I hated to admit it, but I could probably accept this fiction and convince anyone else that it was true. This was the ultimate lie as a tool, I thought. It didn't surprise me that my father was so good at it. He had been for so long.

And now maybe I would be.

He knocked on the door and rushed in with my new laptop computer.

"It was all set up in minutes," he said. "Take a seat."

I did, and he showed me how to connect to Wi-Fi and begin the research, pulling up my fictional hometown immediately.

"Enjoy it. You can see the world on a computer these days."

He checked his watch.

"I'll return at four thirty, and we'll take you to your new home."

I sat there looking up at him.

"Oh, just call reception. They'll order you whatever you want for lunch. Okay?"

How had such a simple word as *okay* become so hard to say? It was almost profanity. Okay to what? To no more Daddy, to no more truth?

My new life had become very expensive.

I just nodded.

He put his hand on my shoulder. Did he want me to look up at him, invite him to kiss my cheek? I stared at the computer screen.

"See you later," he said.

Yes, I thought, *see you later, Daddy, just the way I expected I would when I sat on a train-station bench and opened my new coloring book years ago.*

CHAPTER THREE

It was a long day, but all the study habits and techniques Mazy had taught me certainly made a difference when it came to learning something new quickly. Concentrating with her methods also kept me from falling into the whirlpool of emotions swirling beside me. The reality of what I was doing, what my father was making me do, continually prodded at my tears, pushing me to let them gush and simply scream at these bland nobody walls. Keeping busy was the only way to hold down the lid. I could almost hear my blood boiling.

If I wanted a father, I had to become someone else.

I took notes on the notes as if I was studying for a test, and in the process I tried to imagine this new Saffron Dazy my father had created. Truthfully, despite the fictional biography, there was so much she and I shared. Daddy had cleverly or subtly suggested what we would have in common. I certainly felt the same vulnerabilities, the same desperation the girl outlined on these notepad pages would feel. My mind was a workshop in which I weaved so many possibilities. Both of our mothers had died unexpectedly from heart attacks. Why not add that we both were the first to discover they had died? Chances were that Daddy's second daughter, Karen, my so-called cousin, had never seen a dead person. I could certainly describe how I felt. I could do it so well that she would have nightmares. Right now, that result seemed pleasing. I couldn't top the resentment taking seed in my heart.

But the story was there. Both my imaginary self and I had our fathers desert us. How clever my father was to make my imaginary self less than one year old at the time. What could I describe in the way of emotional and psychological damage? My father's voice wouldn't even be a voice I'd remember. Maybe that was what my real father had wanted when he left me at the train station. I had to swallow back those thoughts, press them down like rubbish in a garbage can and close the lid, but there it was. What are the memories for a child who had no father to recall, no father's voice singing "Happy Birthday," no laughter and smiles on Christmas morning, and no hand to hold crossing the street?

I certainly could talk about what it was like to see other girls my age with their fathers, talking about their fathers, when I was older. "My daddy this and my daddy that." Certainly, I was drowning in envy, and why not? The first hero in your life was your father. If it was a good marriage, a good family, you loved him first through your mother's eyes. You could fill a book with quotes like *Your daddy will fix it. Your daddy will make it better. Your daddy will take us. Let's wait for your daddy. He might have a surprise.*

When you realized what romantic love was or could be, you were always asking your mother to tell you how she had fallen in love with your father and how your daddy fell in love with her. What greater romance was there, then?

And so I would tell Karen how it became painfully clear to me that fathers meant more as we grew older. I didn't love or respect my mother less. In fact, she became more of a hero in this fiction. All responsibility was loaded onto her shoulders, and I felt a deep sadness for her as well as deep pride. Surely, Karen would know what I meant and feel sorrier for me. I wanted her pity. It might stop her from asking too many questions.

Taking my cue from the details in the notepad, I would describe how when I was younger in my fictional life, my mother hired someone or got someone to do her a favor and watch me while she worked. She had no higher education and worked as a waitress. We moved around Southern California a lot before we settled in Costa Mesa because my mother had gone from waitressing to a good job managing a clothing store in the Southcoast Plaza. From when I was nine, she often left me alone when she went out at night. In this world my father had created, he had laid the groundwork for Karen to feel sorry for me because of that. And with the way he had described my mother in the notepad, it was obvious that I could come up with any explanation for her heart failure that I chose: cigarettes, drugs, alcohol, or simply great stress and physical exhaustion. I could choose two or three or maybe all four. Maybe, in fact, as I had done with Mazy, I didn't hang around to find out. Why would it matter? I was alone now, and blaming something like cigarettes and/or booze didn't change that.

According to a note in the pad, both my imaginary self and I were by ourselves during so much of our early lives with no close friends because of how often we had moved. I easily could imagine what psychological and social issues my fictional self had endured, especially the loneliness and the insecurity. We surely cried similar tears and had the same daily worries. Lies as tools were being molded and woven into a steel image for me to manage. This phantom would soon slip inside me and push the real me out to become the ghost. Someday I might even question my real memories and wonder what was fiction and what was the truth.

As the picture of my imaginary self began to form in my imagination, she gradually stepped out of the shadows and stood beside me with that same dark, depressed look on her face that I wore on my way here and now. Give her any reason, simply break a glass in her presence, and she would start to cry. The world she was in, like my world, was so tender and fragile that nasty words, sarcastic remarks, anything that made us the object of ridicule, cut like shards of that broken glass. We would bleed where no one could see us, especially in the dark, and especially in dreams. I felt like turning and saying, *Hello. Welcome to me. I'm all yours now. Good luck.*

Reading about her, imagining her, actually did bring me to tears.

I ordered lunch early because I had really not eaten much at breakfast. For a while afterward, through my new computer, I continued exploring what was to be my former world. Daddy was right about my picking up quickly on how to use it, especially for research. Traveling over roads and city streets using something called Google Maps gave me the feeling I had been there. I made note of any and every site a visitor or local resident would surely know. Finally, it was my tired eyes that told me how long I had been intensely concentrating. I took a break and fell asleep for a while.

When I woke, I suddenly thought about my appearance. How odd that it had not occurred to me to think about it until some vagabond gazed back at me in the mirror. My hair looked like spiders had woven it together. Besides not taking a toothbrush, I hadn't taken a hairbrush. I should have had my father stop to get me some basic things on our way back from breakfast, but he almost had been in a panic, rushing me along to avoid contact with anyone he knew. I couldn't help but recall being left at the train station with nothing really but my coloring book. It gave me a chill I had tried to stop so many times. I ran my fingers through my hair, brushed down my clothes, and returned to the computer.

Now, a little dazed, I was simply staring at it, feeling more like someone who had just stepped off a roller coaster. Moments later, I heard him at the door. As soon as I opened it, he rushed in. His eyes were electric. I didn't know whether he was really excited or really very nervous.

"Let's get it all together and get on our way," he said, and went immediately to the desk to pack up my new computer. "Ava and Karen are eager to meet you. They've been preparing a great dinner."

He looked at his watch.

"I told them I was picking you up at four forty-five at the bus station. This is the schedule you followed, the plane you took, etcetera, in case you're asked anything about your trip here."

He held out another slip of paper with dates and times. I didn't move, didn't speak.

"What's wrong?"

"What if I make a mistake about this fake history?" I asked.

"You read through my notes, right? You probably memorized them by now."

"Yes. At least, I think I have."

"And you've been using the computer all afternoon and studied where you lived, all the important details, I'm sure. Right?"

"Yes."

"So you know enough about where you came from and what your basic facts are, Saffron. You're a clever girl. You'll fill in the blanks beautifully when the questions arise, I'm sure."

"But what if I do say something that reveals the truth and they jump all over it and then all this fizzles like some balloon?"

"Don't worry about it," he said, looking more annoyed than worried.

"But if that happened, your new wife would know you'd been lying for so long. You said your love affair would have broken up over your lies years and years ago. Would your marriage?"

"We don't want that to happen, Saffron. It wouldn't be good for either of us," he said. I wanted to convince myself that it sounded more like a fact than a threat.

"What does that mean?"

"Jesus!" He closed his eyes so hard that it made his whole face scrunch. Then he took a breath and spoke calmly. "It means be good at this, Saffron. For both our sakes. Nothing more. C'mon. The longer you think about it, the more nervous you'll make yourself. It's going to be just fine." He found a smile. "Karen's no Miss Marple, and Ava, well, Ava avoids thinking about anything that would make her unhappy. It couldn't be any easier for you."

He pumped the slip of paper at me until I took it. *Couldn't be any easier for me?* I thought. *You could make it very easy. All you'd have to do is tell them who I really am.*

He looked away quickly as if he could hear my thoughts. When I was very little, I thought he could. I especially believed my mother could. I believed it was something parents could just naturally do because you were a part of them.

Once again, I wondered, is deception easier or harder between people who love each other? I still believed that love requires so much trust. But if you knew someone so deeply in your heart, couldn't you see a false face immediately? For Daddy, that never seemed to be true. Look at all the deception. Was I learning something new about him every moment? It seemed like every day was a Columbus Day now, a day to acknowledge discoveries.

I picked up my bag and my purse. He stood there for a moment, suddenly looking indecisive and concerned, but it wasn't about the issue I had raised. When he spoke, it was more like he was arguing with himself, reciting his train of thought.

"You can't fit the computer in your bag. You left quickly and brought it all on the plane and then on the bus. You could have carried it alongside your purse, I guess. Yeah, that makes sense, but I'll carry it now."

"Are they going to be questioning every little detail like that? I've never been on a plane."

"No, no, I was just thinking aloud. It's nothing. No worries," he said. "You boarded and then fell asleep. Simple. Let's go." He smiled. "You didn't leave anything, right?" he added, gazing around.

"Not a clue to prove I was here," I said. "They should change the name of this place to Limbo."

Mazy would have enjoyed my saying that, but his smile dissolved into a smirk. He shook his head, sighed deeply, and opened the door. I half expected a gaggle of reporters with cameras shouting questions. *Is this your real daughter? What happened to your wife? How did your daughter get here? Where has she been? Why did you leave her behind?*

Maybe I was wishing they were there.

"Remember," Daddy said as we stepped out, "they expect you to be shy. It will be to your advantage to listen and not volunteer any information. When you're asked a question, ask yourself the same question before you answer. I find that to be a very helpful technique."

"Technique? To do what?" I asked. Did he spend his days telling lies?

He didn't answer. We walked to a silver car. It looked new, and when he opened the door for me and I got in, it smelled brand-new, too. He took my bag and put it with the computer on the rear seat.

"This a new car?"

"Oh, yes. It's only two days old," he said proudly. I didn't know anything about cars, but it looked very expensive.

He closed the door and hurried around. When he started the engine, he smiled. "Won't be long before you're old enough to take driving instruction and get a license. I'll get you your own car."

"My own car?"

"Sure. Why not? I can spend anything I want on my orphaned niece."

The moment we pulled onto the main street, he started to talk quickly. It was as if he wanted to stuff years into five minutes. Or maybe he was really nervous, now that we were almost there and this was all about to begin. Maybe it finally occurred to him that we had little time to prepare for such a big deception and he was relying too much on whatever Mazy had told him about my abilities.

"I can envision you driving Karen to school until she gets her license, too. Ava will love having someone else able to pick up stuff for her. I have a tendency to forget what she tells me we need. I write myself notes, but I forget the notes and even forget to put it on my phone. When she's nice about it, she calls me her absentminded professor. But she can have less pleasant ways of putting it. She might look pretty and dainty, but she's a Saddlebrook through and through. Sometimes I think she was cloned."

"What's that mean?"

"Her father is one of those businessmen who believe weakness or mistakes when it comes to business decisions, almost any decisions, are sins. If he could, he'd rewrite the Bible and say, 'God created the earth without any union members helping.'" He laughed. "Don't worry. He'll be impressed when he meets you. He likes people who have an independent streak."

"I didn't choose to have it," I said sharply.

He acted deaf for a moment, like he hadn't heard a word.

"Despite all that, we're a family, a real family. We've even been talking about getting a dog, but Ava is a little worried about having a pet while Garson is so small. I'll warn you ahead of time that she reads those rag newspapers as if they're gospel. Sometimes we argue about the nuttiest things at dinner, like why the president might really be from another planet.

"Her father and I are always complaining about it, but she has this thing about men dominating women. It's the way she was raised. From everything I've seen and heard, I'd agree. Her father did dominate her mother. He's a fair-minded guy when it comes to social issues but a little old-fashioned for Ava, who sometimes sounds like a socialist spy. They're always, or often, like two cats in an alley, especially when it comes to taxes and social programs. I try to stay out of it. The worst thing I can do is support her father in an argument, but sometimes I can't help it, and later, I have to take the darts out of my back.

"Now that I think more about it, she's really going to welcome you. Another female in the house to complain about the way men have ruined the world. I'm outnumbered as it is until Garson gets old enough to back up his dad. If he has the courage to, of course."

He smiled. I thought he was babbling to reduce the anxiety both of us were feeling, but nothing he was saying helped me become less tense. In fact, it had just the opposite effect. Last night, I had felt as if I was walking through a fog. Today, especially right now, I saw myself like a puppet dangling on strings that rose into the dark, heavy clouds. Fate was playing with me. I had lost control of myself completely. I was being shaped and trimmed to fit perfectly into a puzzle. In the moment, when I glanced at him, my father looked more like a stranger. I was so tempted to say, *Please, stop. I want to get out. I won't fit in here. I can't live a lie and come up with creative answers to questions about who I am.*

But I didn't. I closed my eyes and let him talk about the town, our street, his and Ava's plans for developing the backyard, and some new furniture she was considering. He wasn't going to permit a moment of silence. After a while, I wondered if he was trying to convince himself or me that this was going to be a wonderful life for everyone.

"We might put in a pool," he said. "Imagine that. In a couple of years, you and Karen will be having friends over for pool parties. Now we have to go to Saddlebrook for that."

I said nothing. I was looking out the window, but I really wasn't seeing anything. Instead, I was wondering about Mazy. What sort of funeral would she have with so few friends and no relatives? Who would care that she had died? Maybe I should have waited, but if I had, someone from some social agency would have pounced. Surely the school principal or guidance counselor would have directed them to me. What would I have done then? I had to believe Mazy would have been quite upset about it. I was confident that she would have preferred that I did what I did. It made it easier for me not to feel bad about it.

"Someday," I said, without turning to him, "we should visit Mazy's grave."

"What? Oh. Don't worry about it. I'm on it. I made some calls early this morning. Everything's taken care of, a proper funeral and burial site. Mazy donated the money from the sale of her house to an education foundation that provides scholarships to low-income families. Did you know she was going to do that?"

"No. But it sounds like something she would have kept to herself. What does it say on her tombstone?"

"Say? Oh. Just her name and dates."

"Seems unfair," I said. "She was a respected teacher, and she was my grandmother."

"Well, we can see about adding something in the future. And someday soon we will visit."

Don't promise, I thought. *Please don't promise.* Moments later, he turned into his driveway. Now that it was daylight, I saw it had been laid with the same bricks that covered the house. There were knee-high bushes along the sides. Everything was trimmed and coordinated. The lawn was so neat that a very small broken branch from one of the sprawling maple trees was obvious. The fountain gurgled. Now I could see the smiles on the children's faces. The afternoon sunlight was strong enough to make some of the windows glitter.

Do homes reveal the happiness or unhappiness of the family within? I wondered and thought about Mazy's house, how tired and lonely it looked when I had first seen it. The patches of lawn had grass the color of straw. Her porch went only a few feet to the right and left of the front door, and it had nothing on it, not even a chair. One of the spindles under the railing was split. On a cul-de-sac, it looked lost and alone, just the way Mazy was most of the time, living with only a cat and some very bitter memories, like gray and black paintings, just strokes, framed in hard wood on every wall.

"I had the garage built recently," Daddy said. "These vintage Queen Annes didn't come with them. Ours is a three-car size. Now I wish I had made it four," he added, smiling at me.

Why? I thought. *Didn't you ever imagine my living with you?*

"I had to put it next to a side door that was already there, otherwise we'd have to break a wall. Consequently, it opens to a pantry. Ava complained, but it actually works out when you're bringing in groceries."

The garage door went up. There was another car, smaller but just as new-looking, parked.

"Home sweet home," he said. He drove in. "The kitchen is right through the pantry. All the bedrooms are upstairs. The windows in yours face west, so you'll have afternoon sun, which is nice in winter if winter ever comes. The world's getting hotter and hotter."

Especially for me, I thought.

He shut off the engine as the garage door started to close. It felt like a small bird was fluttering in my chest, but Daddy didn't notice how I was feeling. Actually, he avoided looking at me. He got out and opened the rear door to get my bag and the computer. I got out slowly. He paused, but before he could say anything encouraging, I spoke.

"Did you tell your wife and daughter anything about my mother's death?" I said. "If you mentioned something, I might contradict it."

"No, no. I just said she died. We'd find out the details from you. For now, all I know is what it says in the notepad," he said in a voice barely above a whisper. "Whatever you say is gospel. You won't contradict me because I just learned the day before yesterday that your mother had died. So I don't know all that much." He shrugged. "I can or probably will say you didn't like talking about such a horribly sad scene when I had just picked you up. Besides, you have the experience now, with Mazy dying. Think of her when you answer if either Ava or Karen asks for more grisly details."

Base it all on Mazy? Yes, that was how I had thought to do it.

Did we think alike? Was it impossible for me to be anyone but his daughter? Did that mean I would always use lies as tools?

"Then I'll say she died at home just like Mazy did."

"Good."

"But why didn't you go to the funeral? She was your sister."

He looked nervously at the door.

"You ran away, and the police contacted me, right? So . . . I have to make arrangements. I'll handle it. Ava and Karen already know that your mother and I didn't talk to each other for years. I didn't even know where she lived. There's nothing to worry about when it comes to that. Just tell them to ask me. Let's go," he urged, nodding at the door. I had the free hand, so he waited for me to turn the handle.

My fingers froze around the handle. I felt like I was stepping right into a gigantic spiderweb.

"You've got to go in, Saffron. It's got to begin. We can do this," he said. He really meant *You have to do this if you want to live with a family.*

I turned the handle. My body was so tense that I was surprised I could walk, but I took only one step and stopped.

Like he had said, the garage door opened on a large pantry with white wooden shelves on which were stored canned goods, paper cups and paper plates, and boxes of basic necessities like salt, flour, and some cereals.

"Go on. Go in, Saffron," he urged, but I felt like I had frozen in place.

Because I didn't move quickly enough, he stepped ahead, and I followed him into the kitchen. It had beautiful dark-oak cabinets and marble counters, with a center island covered with matching marble. There was an arched doorway that opened to a kitchenette. I could see the paneled windows and the round dark-oak table. The kitchen

stove, range, and refrigerator were matching stainless steel. Everything looked expensive and new. It made me smile thinking about
Mazy's appliances that she said were created in the Dark Ages.

"Here she is," Daddy announced.

I had been hoping that both Ava and Karen would be unattractive
and, in fact, that everything about my father's new life would be far
less than he had described. Surely, it wasn't really that picture-perfect
as this town seemed. Deep in my heart, I harbored the hope that the
choices he had made had proven disastrous, despite how he bragged
about the Saddlebrook name and the new family he had created.

Ava and Karen looked up from the salad on the black-and-white
marble island top and gazed at me as if they'd had no idea I was
arriving. Baby Garson was asleep in a portable bassinet on the floor. I
could barely see his face framed in a blue blanket. Music was coming
from a speaker embedded in a wall in the far left corner. Later Karen
would tell me it was a song written and sung by someone named
Ed Sheeran, and she'd be quite shocked I hadn't recognized it. That
would be the initial chip in the false facade Daddy and I were creating. If there was music anywhere, it would be in California.

For a moment, as Ava and Karen scrutinized me with that femi-
nine curiosity, I amusingly imagined being in an old western movie
in which the gunslingers eyed each other before anyone would draw.
Neither had anything to fear. My clothes were drab, and my hair
needed a fresh washing and at least some brushing and trimming.
They, on the other hand, looked like some mother-daughter adver-
tisement in a fashion magazine.

Both wore short white aprons over what I would see were matching distressed-effect jeans and red boat-neck tops with three-quarter
dolman sleeves and ties. It was the sort of outfit I had dreamed
of having after I began public school and looked at some fashion

magazines. Mazy had bought me fashionable things, but on her own, listening to more conservative salesladies. My wish to see who I had hoped would be my father's plain-looking new wife and daughter collapsed like a punctured balloon.

Ava's eyes were so striking that it was almost impossible not to be caught up in them. They were almond-shaped, a deep shade of violet blue. Later I would discover she had her mother's eyes. Her graceful jawline enhanced her full, soft lips. If there was a flaw to harp on, it would probably be the sharpness in her nose, emphasized, I would learn, when she was annoyed or angry because of the awkward way her lips would turn in and the coolness that would overtake her eyes.

With what I could see was a slim model's figure, she was almost as tall as my father. Perhaps the heat in the kitchen had brought a metallic rose-colored tint to her cheeks. Her champagne-blond hair fell loosely over her shoulders into thin curls.

I fled back to my most vivid memories of my mother, who, even though she had lost the light behind her eyes, remained dainty and petite in my mind, an embossed image I hoped would never fade or be lost in the shadow of my father's new wife's beauty.

Daddy had been right about Karen. She looked just about my height and size. Not that she was unattractive, but Karen's mouth sagged more in the corners. She had fuller lips than her mother, but whether it was that she was annoyed or it was her habitual expression, her lips turned up slightly too much and took away from her nose, softer than her mother's. Her eyes were a nice shade of hazel. She had short light-brown hair and a rounder face, with dimples in her cheeks. I suspected that anyone who saw us standing together would say she was the cute one.

The way the two of them continued to stare at me almost made me do what I would do when I was a little girl, slip behind my father so he could shield me from prying eyes that made me feel so different. Strangers wanted to touch me, pet me, and for some reason, older men always wanted to tickle me.

"Saffron, this is my wife, Ava, and my daughter, Karen," Daddy said.

"Do you like Italian food?" Ava asked, instead of saying hello.

"Yes, very much."

"You're not a vegetarian or anything?" she followed, grimacing as if she was anticipating a slap.

"No, ma'am," I said.

Karen immediately laughed. "Ma'am?"

"Please call me Aunt Ava," Ava said. "We're not very formal in our house. I'm preparing some meatballs, and Karen's doing our salad."

"She makes great meatballs," Daddy said.

"It's my mother's recipe, a recipe she inherited from her mother," she said.

I smiled. Hopefully, I thought, she couldn't be that bad if she cherished family recipes. There was something more natural and friendlier in the thought, despite the way she had expressed it.

"Is that all you have?" Karen asked, nodding at my bag in my father's hand.

"Yes," I said. "It was all I wanted to take."

"But you didn't leave your computer," Ava said. She smirked and looked at Karen. "Karen would do the same. You girls today have different priorities."

"If I was leaving quickly, I would still take everything, especially my phone, Mommy."

"Right. Do you have one of those, too, Saffron?"

"No."

"She will," Daddy said.

"Of course. Then the two of them can text each other even when they're in the same room. Why don't you show her the room, Derick? We'll finish preparing dinner."

"I can show her," Karen said.

"After you've finished our salad, you're setting the table," Ava said sharply. "Remember, we're using the dining room tonight and not the kitchenette. And be careful with my good dishes and glasses, Karen. Don't be thinking of something else while you work. Derick? We'll be eating soon," she said, widening her eyes. Maybe she wasn't formal, but she was surely quite chop-chop.

"Sure. Right this way, Saffron," he said.

I smiled at Karen, but she was already in a pout and turned away.

I followed Daddy out of the kitchen. To the left was the dining room. I paused to glance at the long, dark-cherry wood table and the large teardrop chandelier. Ruby velvet curtains draped the windows. Karen entered from the kitchen carrying a tablecloth and napkins. When she saw me, she shrugged and made a face expressing her suffering as if she was doing the worst manual labor.

"Come along, Saffron. I'll give you a tour later," Daddy said. "Let's get you settled and ready for dinner. Ava likes everything ticktock. She gets that from her father," he added, dropping his voice.

I continued after him, glancing at the living room, which was on the right. How different all this would be from living in Mazy's house, with her tired old furniture. *Old* here meant valuable vintage. My family wasn't rich before the house fire. Obviously, my father had married into great wealth. How much of that was the real reason for everything?

Directly ahead was the stairway, and on the right was a short hall that led to the front entrance. I saw there was another room on the left approaching the door. The stairway had a mahogany balustrade and coffee-brown carpeted steps, only ten to a turn and then four more. At the top, Daddy turned to the west side of the house and waited for me to catch up.

"Ava and I and Karen are on the east side," he said, continuing.

He opened the only door on the right and stepped in as I entered, too. The room was easily twice the size of my blue room at my grandmother's house. And so was the size of the bed compared to what I had at my grandmother's. It had a footboard and headboard of light maple. There was a matching dresser on the right and a matching vanity table on the left, with a mirror in a square frame. The wooden floor was a dark brown, with a lighter brown area rug beside the bed. In the right corner was the closet. The two windows on the sides of the headboard had dull white curtains and faded white window shades.

"It's not much now, but wait until Ava gets started," Daddy said. "She's been looking for a reason to dress this up."

He lowered my bag to the footstool and put the computer case on the vanity table.

"We'll get a proper desk in here for sure."

I just stared, thinking I had gone from one human storage room to another.

"We don't have many houseguests," he said, starting an explanation. He could see how unexcited I was about the room.

"Is that what I am?"

"Hardly," he said quickly. He blew some air through his lips and drew up the window shades. "Good view, actually. Oh," he said, turning. "The bathroom is across the hall and on the right as you leave the room. We and Karen have en suites, so this bathroom is entirely yours. There's a bath and shower. I'm going to renovate that bathroom very soon."

"Where would I be stashed while the work's being done?" I asked dryly.

"I'm sure Karen would share." He smiled. "Hell, I bet you start sharing her bathroom and mirrors way before that."

"I've only shared with a cat, Mr. Pebbles," I said. "I might not be that good at it."

Where do smiles go when they fly off a face?

For a sheer moment, he looked angry, ready to fall into a rage, but he clamped down on that hard.

"We thought about a cat, too, but Ava read one of those stories about a cat that smothered a baby. If you ever run out of nightmares, just listen to some of the things she has read in that rag paper."

"No worries, *Uncle* Derick," I said sharply. "I won't run out of those. I have enough to share with everyone."

Maybe it came out like a threat.

Maybe it simply frightened him.

He seemed to lunge for the door.

"Put your things in the dresser drawers and wash up," he said. "I spoke with Ava before I picked you up at the Dew Drop Inn. She said she put everything you might need for now in your bathroom already. Get used to her. She's a take-charge kind of person."

"So was Mazy," I said.

He nodded and started away.

I stood there listening to him go down the stairs.

In my memory, he was carrying me with the flames licking at his heels and the heat burning my face.

And I was screaming for my mother.

CHAPTER FOUR

Daddy was right about the bathroom I would use. Ava had stocked it with everything and anything I would need, even things I would never have thought about buying.

I welcomed the new hairbrush, ties, and comb and then studied some of the jars of skin cream in the cabinet. Two had French names, each claiming to prevent skin damage and cure dry, flaky skin. There was even something I had never seen, a facial toner. There were bars of soap and bottles of shampoos I also had never seen or heard of neatly displayed on the shelf in the shower. The pink towels and washcloths were super-plush and smelled flowery-fresh. What looked like a new bath rug, white with a pinkish tint, was placed beside the tub and shower.

I had no idea what Daddy had told her about me, but neatly placed in a drawer in the sink cabinet were sanitary pads. On a shelf to the right of the sink were deodorant sticks with three different scents and a square bottle of cologne also with a French name. I held it up, vividly recalling something my mother would do with her colognes and perfumes. She would never spray them directly on herself. She would spray a cloud of whatever she had chosen in front of her and then walk through it. I used to laugh and follow her. That was when she and my father were having happier days, days that seemed to rain smiles and laughter everywhere in our home.

I sprayed the cologne in the air. The scent was unusual but not unpleasant. It just wasn't something I would have chosen for myself. It seemed more for an older woman. Was it something Ava used? My stepmother/aunt was clearly deciding how to address the most intimate details about me, including how I would smell. I really was beginning to feel like that piece reshaped to fit into a prearranged puzzle.

I put the cologne back, closed the cabinets and drawers, and glanced at myself once more to check my hair before I headed out and down the stairs to join my new family for dinner. I was trembling a little and truly feeling like an amateur actress about to step onto a stage. There would be only two in the audience for me to convince, but it might as well have been a packed auditorium of theater critics with their hands clutching knives to stab and cut up my performance.

Ava, Karen, and Daddy were already seated in the dining room. Three pairs of eyes felt like six spotlights. Even Daddy was looking at me with what seemed to be fresh curiosity. How would I behave? From where the place settings had been placed, I saw that I was being sat across from Karen and next to Ava, with Daddy at the other end of the table, a chair between him and me and a chair between Karen and him.

Why didn't Daddy feel outside of the circle to me? He did look like a man comfortably settled in his first marriage and fatherhood. I should have expected that, but it still rumbled in my heart and caused me to feel even more alienated from him. I wondered who had decided where I should sit. Was it his doing? Would it have looked too obvious if he and I were sitting closer? Would there always be a question attached even to the smallest things in this house? It was easy to fall into the dark pool of paranoia, seeing hidden motives in everything and anything.

Karen gazed at me big-eyed, Daddy smiled the way anyone would smile trying to make someone new feel comfortable, but Ava looked like she was suspiciously scrutinizing my every cell as soon as I had stepped into the dining room.

"We'll have to do something about your hair," she said. "Immediately."

"Give her a braided ponytail," Karen said. "Her hair's long enough. That's how Adele wears hers, and everyone thinks she looks great," she told me, as if I should already know who Adele was. "Adele is one of my best friends and has hair as long as yours."

One of? How can you have more than one "best" friend? I thought, but dared not ask it and immediately make her feel stupid.

"We'll see to it tomorrow," Ava said, narrowing her eyes and pursing her lips, rendering her decision like someone who could decide every breath I took. She nodded at my chair. "Sit."

It sounded like she was ordering a dog.

I glanced at Daddy, who held his smile and nodded ever so gently.

I sat quickly, trying not to appear awkward as I pulled my chair closer to the table. I could feel both Ava and Karen watching my every move. I quickly straightened up. Mazy had taught me how to sit at a formal table. She told me that someday I'd be invited to the queen of England's dinner table. Sometimes we loved to pretend. She would bring out her best china and silverware, napkins and table-cloth. Either I'd be a princess, or she'd be the queen. I often thought that pretending was easily seventy-five percent of life. It was as if people thought that if others saw you honestly for who you were, they would never like you, maybe even be afraid of you. I shouldn't really be shocked at having to be someone else here. Everyone had to be someone other than themselves more than half the time. It was as if honesty was self-destructive.

I gazed at the almost geometrically set table. The white napkins with gold trim were folded into perfect pie slices, and all the silverware was carefully lined up at each plate. I unfolded my napkin and placed it neatly on my lap. Karen, who hadn't done that yet, quickly did the same, glancing at her mother, maybe to see if my doing it first was going to bring her a reprimand. But Ava hadn't taken her eyes off me.

"You'll need a manicure if you're going to sit at my table from now on," she said, nodding at my fingers.

Instinctively, I brought them down to my lap and out of sight.

"Are you going to bring her to Renae tomorrow, Mother?"

"First thing in the morning," Ava said. "Then I'll bring her to school. We'll decide what we should do with your hair then. Derick, you make all those arrangements at school so I don't have to spend an inordinate amount of time there. I have things to do."

"Sure. First thing," my father said. I half expected him to salute when he responded to her order. Even in my thoughts, I had to keep correcting myself, or I was sure to make a mistake and call him Daddy.

"How is your room?" Ava asked.

"It's very nice," I said without much enthusiasm. I was still think-ing about my room at Mazy's.

"There'll be more done with it. We never expected it would become another family bedroom. It was expected to become Garson's room eventually. Just last week, I was looking at furniture for a little boy."

"Oh," I said. I looked at Daddy, who just stared at her with a half smile on his face. "I'm sorry. I mean, I didn't mean . . ."

"It's of no concern. What has to be has to be. Anyway, your uncle and I will now be adding a bedroom at the rear of the house, off the living room. I always wanted more personal space. We have enough property for that sort of expansion. We'll use the same contractor who built on our garage," she said.

It seemed like she was telling Daddy these plans for the first time. He nodded.

"I contacted him this afternoon just after we planned it all last night," he said. "He'll be around to give us an estimate."

"Our bedroom will eventually become Garson's, then," Ava said as if she was anticipating my question.

Karen bounced in her seat.

"Why can't he have mine, Mother? Yours and Daddy's is too big for a boy. Girls need more room," Karen declared. "You just said you wanted more for yourself."

Ava looked at her almost as if she hadn't realized she was there.

"Your room is fine for you, Karen. We just bought you a new vanity table and mirror. You have a walk-in closet and enough dresser drawers for a dozen girls. Besides, you have a nice view."

"Yours is nicer," Karen insisted. "But"—she paused, thinking—"we'll be living in Saddlebrook one day anyway, I guess."

"Your grandfather will live to be a hundred," Ava said. She thought a moment. "It's not very nice to say that anyway, Karen." Ava glared at her and then turned to me.

"Just as I expect of Karen, you are to keep your bathroom and your bedroom as immaculate as possible, Saffron. Our maid, Celisse, comes only twice a week unless we need her to care for Garson. She does the whole house both times, so I don't want her to have to spend an inordinate amount of time on your bedroom or, as she knows, on Karen's."

Ava looked sharply at Karen, who frowned.

I looked at Daddy, but he didn't come to my defense and get her to soften her tone. Supposedly, I had just lost my mother. He didn't even smile reassurance at me.

I'm on my own, I thought. *Why doesn't it surprise me?*

"I cleaned our house every day," I said. "We couldn't afford maids. Just let me know where all the cleaning materials are kept, and I'll look after my own bathroom, too."

Ava nodded, this time coming close to smiling.

"Having to do things for yourself is not something to be ashamed of. Karen will show you where we keep all that. She vaguely knows where they are."

"Ha, ha," Karen said. "I keep my room clean."

"That'll be news to Celisse. Okay. Let's start eating," Ava announced as if she was launching a ship. Salad was already on everyone's salad plate. There was a glass of water beside Karen's and mine. Daddy and Ava were drinking red wine. Ava's eyes followed my hand to the correct fork, the salad fork. She looked a little surprised.

"I don't imagine your mother set a table like this every night," she said.

"No, but we ate in a nice restaurant once in a while, and I was often with her when she worked as a waitress. Before she became a store manager at the Southcoast Plaza," I quickly added.

I hoped she didn't notice that I was glancing at Daddy practically after every word I uttered to be sure he approved.

"Did you work as a waitress, too?" Karen asked. "It's so disgusting picking up people's leftovers and having to smile even at creepy boys."

"No. I wasn't old enough yet. Also, you have to be twenty-one to serve alcohol."

"You do?"

Who had been locked away more? I wondered.

"You obviously picked up some good habits," Ava said. "That's very good. We've all got to make the most of any good opportunity in life, especially if you have so few. It's a lesson I hope my daughter learns."

"Oh, give me a break," Karen said.

Daddy smiled. I was getting compliments directly and indirectly, and it was obvious that Ava was quite thrifty when it came to that. I had yet to hear her say anything nice to her own daughter, despite how Daddy had built up their good relationship. Still, this compliment made it sound like I had come from some sort of slum life. Mazy's world was quite the opposite, but I couldn't defend it. However, it made me feel very defensive. Although Ava would never know why, perhaps, I was frustrated at not being able to defend my grandmother.

"It's not brain surgery for any young girl," I muttered instead.

"Excuse me?" Ava said.

Now Daddy was actually holding his breath.

I said nothing, but when I lifted my eyes, I saw Karen's wide smile. It was as if I had just confirmed that she would have a coconspirator.

Suddenly, we heard Garson's cry. I had almost forgotten about him. He was on Ava's left side below the table.

"He's finally teething," she explained as she reached down for him.

"I'll get his pacifier," Daddy said, jumping to his feet. I watched with surprise as he hurried out to the kitchen and quickly returned with a pacifier from the refrigerator. He handed it to Ava, who put it in Garson's mouth. He immediately clamped down on it. Daddy stood by, proudly watching, and then looked at me.

Maybe he will be the one to make a mistake, I thought. Maybe he would suddenly blurt that I started teething late, too. Or he would mention something about me when I was a baby. That would give it all away. I wanted him to be the one to make the mistake. I practically prayed for it.

Garson immediately calmed.

"Cold works the same on his gums as it does on a sprained ankle," Daddy explained.

"You didn't have to do this with me. Daddy told me," Karen informed Ava before she could respond. Sibling jealousy dripped like molasses out of her eyes and mouth. Ava bristled.

"You, on the other hand, didn't make a sensible sound until you were nearly one. Everything was one form of ga-ga or another," she muttered, gazing down at Garson lovingly. Karen squirmed in her seat.

"That's not true. Is it, Daddy?"

"Ga-ga," Daddy said, trying to joke his way out of a trap.

Karen smirked and looked at me. "What about you?" she asked. "Did you start teething late or anything?"

"I don't remember," I said. "I was so young."

Ava actually laughed.

Karen looked like smoke would soon emerge from her eyes.

"Didn't your mother tell you?" she asked sullenly.

"They weren't happy times to remember. My father deserted us soon after I was born. She avoided talking about those days."

Her face reluctantly softened.

Ava handed Garson to Daddy, and he gently returned him to his bassinet. He stood there looking down at him and smiling. I wondered if he had looked down at me the same proud way when I was that small. Ava returned to her salad.

"I'm sure they were hard times for your mother and you, even after you were older. You couldn't waitress, but did you ever babysit for extra money?" she asked me.

"No," I said, maybe with too much surprise and emphasis. She had no idea, of course, but no one back at Hurley would have trusted me with watching a dog or cat, much less a child.

Ava stiffened as if I had made her sound stupid.

"Considering what you just told us and what Derick's told me about your situation, that wouldn't have been so unexpected."

For a moment, I was lost for words. How could I explain why I was never asked to babysit?

"We moved around too much, right up to the last year," I said, "so we didn't have many close friendships, especially with people who had younger children, and my mother didn't like me walking about alone at night. We didn't live in the best neighborhoods all the time."

She relaxed and nodded with understanding.

"Yes. That was probably quite sensible of your mother. Karen has been helping with Garson."

She glared at her daughter, making it clear that contrary to what Daddy had suggested, Karen wasn't eager to volunteer.

"Oh. I'll gladly do whatever I can," I said, wishing I could add, *for my half brother.*

"That's good," Karen said quickly. "I miss stuff because I'm stuck here. You can take over sometimes, can't she, Mother?"

"We'll see," Ava said. "Problems occur when we move along too quickly in life."

"Yes, Grandpa Amos," Karen moaned.

Ava gave her a look that could shatter buildings. Karen looked down and kept eating. I glanced at Daddy, who ate as if he hadn't heard a word.

"How did your mother die?" Karen suddenly demanded. It was almost an accusation. Although Daddy had made it sound otherwise, she was obviously upset about my coming to live with them.

"It was a heart attack," I said, and continued eating, my head down. Whatever look Daddy gave her was enough. No one spoke until we had all finished our salad.

"Didn't you get the paramedics or something?"

"When I found her, it was too late."

Karen's face lost color. She looked like she couldn't swallow.

"You found her? Dead?"

Ava rose like an oil well opening. She seemed to rise to a great height. Karen bit into her lower lip and looked down.

"This isn't the time for this discussion, Karen. We talked about that."

Karen glanced at me with guilt and looked down again.

"I'll put up the pasta now. Karen will clear the salad dishes," Ava declared as if she was dictating the Ten Commandments.

"Should I help?" I asked.

Ava paused, considering.

"Tonight we'll let you be a guest," she said. "I'd like you to see how we do things first. If you do things that have to be corrected, it makes for double the work. Karen?"

Karen rose and picked up the salad dishes as if they were steaming hot.

As soon as she went into the kitchen, Daddy leaned toward me to whisper.

"You're doing great," he said. "I knew you would."

Garson started to cry again.

"Uh-oh," Daddy said, and hurried around to him.

"Derick?" Ava called from the kitchen.

"He's fine. No worries."

Daddy rocked him gently in his arms. My mind fell back through everything that had occurred these past five years as if it was all made of tissue paper. Earlier memories flashed like pictures projected on a wall. He was sitting on my bed to tell me bedtime stories. I was holding his hand as we walked through a mall. I held on to a cart as he pushed it along to choose groceries. He was lighting a birthday candle. So many small things brought so much joy back then. Now it seemed like we'd have to move mountains to have the same happiness.

And then, as if a movie had ended, I blinked away the pleasant images and instead saw him shouting at my mother, who stood looking at the floor, a soft smile on her face. His face was reddening. I thought the whole house was shaking until he stopped and walked away. She turned to me, her lips quivering, a single tear crossing over the crest of her cheek.

In my memory, I started to cry. I sounded like Garson now, only Daddy wasn't comforting me. No one was comforting me. Mama looked frozen and then suddenly crumbled right before my eyes, folded into herself, and disappeared. I thought I might have gasped at the nightmare image, but Daddy didn't hear or look at me.

Karen entered carrying the steaming pasta. She struggled to place it on the table. Ava entered with her meatballs.

"Go get the bread," she told Karen.

Did she ever say "Please," teach by example? I wondered. Was this the way she would always speak to me?

Garson was quiet again. He looked like he had fallen asleep. Daddy returned him to his bassinet.

"Smells delicious," he said. He looked at me, his expression changing as if he could see all the images I had recalled still flashing on my eyes. The worry washed over his face.

"Something wrong?" Ava asked, looking from him to me.

"I think Saffron is tired," Daddy told her, keeping his eyes fixed on me. "The traveling . . ."

She looked at me as if she had X-ray eyes. I squirmed a bit.

"You're hungry, though, aren't you?"

"Yes," I said. I was, but Daddy wasn't wrong. I was also exhausted, mostly from the emotional strain and tension.

"Well, you're not on KP duty tonight, so you can go to sleep after you're finished with dinner or just go up to your room and relax. If you look in the top drawer of your dresser, you'll find a clean pair of Karen's pajamas. I'm sure they'll fit. There are slippers in the closet for you. We have most of the morning to spend together, and we can talk more then."

"About what?" Karen asked, returning with a platter of bread.

"What she wants for Christmas. What do you think?" Ava snapped at her.

"I'm just asking," she moaned, and put the bread on the table and sat.

"Don't sit. You bring everyone's dish up, and I'll serve the pasta and meatballs, Karen, just the way we've done in the past."

Karen rolled her eyes, stood, and went around the table to get my plate.

I looked at Daddy. He was staring at Ava in the strangest way.

His eyes looked cold, and through the slight parting of his lips, I thought his teeth were clenched. The muscles in his jawbone were taut. Once again, my memories flipped like cards, and I saw him looking at my mother in a similar way. It frightened me then; it frightened me now.

For a while, we ate in silence once we were all served. When I looked at Daddy, he gestured with his eyes from the food and then toward Ava. Message received.

"This is very good," I said. "Maybe the best meatballs I've eaten."

"Thank you. Have you done any cooking?"

"Oh, yes," I said, maybe too enthusiastically. Daddy's face was filling quickly with warnings. *Slow down. Review everything you're going to say, and then say it.* "With my mother working so much, I had to help, and I enjoyed cooking."

"Really? Karen's not so much as broken an egg," Ava said. "On purpose, that is."

Karen glared at me.

Uh-oh, I thought. *In five more minutes, she's going to hate me.*

"I'd be glad to share anything I've learned with her."

"Really?" Ava smiled. "Maybe we'll have the girls make us dinner one night, Derick. What do you think?"

"Sounds great."

Karen's face folded into an indecisive smile. Then something widened her eyes.

"I hope not this Saturday night," she said. "It's Margaret Toby's birthday party."

"Thanks for reminding us, Karen," Ava said. "That would be a wonderful way to introduce your cousin to everyone."

"But she's not invited."

"She wasn't here when the invitations were sent, was she? You make it your business to get her invited. How do you think she'll feel when you go off to a party and she's left in her room Saturday night?"

Karen looked at me, annoyed.

"She's in the tenth grade, isn't she? Most everyone there will be from the ninth grade."

"Boys, too?" Ava asked, smiling.

"No, but . . ."

"It's all right," I said. "I've been left alone many, many times."

"Well, that's coming to an end," Ava insisted.

I looked at Daddy. He was nodding.

"Yes, it is," he said.

"What if Margaret doesn't want to invite her?" Karen asked petulantly.

"Well then, she's an idiot, isn't she? You don't want to hang around with idiots, do you, Karen?"

Daddy rose to pour more wine into Ava's glass. For the first time, I saw her smile at him lovingly. Even after all these years and all that had happened, it stung to see him return that look.

I continued to eat. Karen started to sulk again, eating mechanically as she glared at her food. Daddy returned to his seat.

"This is the one thing that makes your father jealous of me," he said, eating a meatball.

Ava smiled.

"He has his own chef," Karen said petulantly.

"Not the same thing," Daddy said. He sipped his wine. Ava and he were looking at each other like they were alone at the table. Karen sighed and stabbed her fork into her food.

This is like being in a movie, I thought, *and watching it at the same time.*

Afterward, I did feel bad about leaving Karen to clear the table and help Ava take care of the dishes. It wasn't in my DNA to be lazy. Mazy had seen to that. But working beside her these last two years had drawn us closer together. For some reason, it helped resurrect stories from her own childhood. Some were funny, but most were sad.

However, Daddy looked anxious and grateful that we could retreat to the living room and be alone for a little while before dessert was served. Garson was still asleep, so he thought it best to leave him.

"Sometimes moving him is like stirring up a hornet's nest," he joked, loud enough for Ava and Karen to hear.

We went to the living room.

"I have nothing to do with any of the furniture in this house," Daddy said, almost proudly, when we entered. "Ava insists I have no taste and no sense of color coordination. Some of what she chose, she chose to be sure it was quite different from her father's home. She said her father had to approve everything her mother bought for them, down to towels for the bathrooms.

"It's a comfortable-looking room, though, isn't it?" he asked.

I thought it looked unused, a room on display and far from comfortable. It was a room you'd want to tiptoe through and be sure you had clean, washed clothes before sitting on anything. Nothing was out of place. The two overstuffed white couches were juxtaposed with the marble mantel of the fireplace. Hardwood floors gleamed. The brown and white pillows on the sofas were placed identically at right angles on both. At the center was a glass table in a wood frame that matched the floor. The only thing on the table was a bowl of imitation fruit. The fireplace looked like it had never been used, even though there was real wood neatly placed within. On the top of the mantel was a single lamp that looked like an antique gas lamp. There wasn't a magazine, a book, or a piece of paper anywhere in sight. Everything appeared like it had just arrived from the showroom. Even the one painting on the far wall, with its thick frame, a mixture of lines and shapes, had no emotion. It was framed wallpaper to me. There were two miniature versions of it, one on each side. Other than that, the walls were bare.

"Does anyone ever come in here?" I asked.

He laughed. "We do spend most of the time in the den, which is off the front door, except when we're entertaining special dinner guests. The den is where we have the television set. Karen has one in her bedroom. Ava didn't want one in ours. If you want one in yours . . ."

"I never had one," I said. "Mazy would have gotten me one if I had asked for it."

"Okay," he whispered. "Try never to use that name. We'll talk about it later." He looked back toward the kitchen. "Let's go to the den," he said, clearly thinking we might be overheard.

Try never to use that name? The very idea made me cold, but it was true. All my memories of Mazy had to be forgotten or at least never mentioned. I followed him through the hall.

Although the den was as immaculate as the living room, it did look used and more comfortable, with its soft brown leather couch and a wall of bookcases interrupted by a large painting of Sandburg Creek from what looked to be the point of view of a hawk. There were two reclining easy chairs and a large center table with magazines and real flowers, or great imitation ones, in vases on the side tables. The large-screen television set was on the wall on the right.

"We modernized the sound system in here, too," Daddy said. "Subtly. Keeping the house in character is almost a religious thing for Ava to maintain its authenticity."

Just as we sat on the sofa, Karen appeared in the doorway.

"Vanilla or chocolate ice cream?" she asked me.

"Vanilla."

"I like chocolate. So does Daddy, right, Daddy?"

"Sure, but I could eat both."

I smiled, recalling how Mazy had used the prospect of pizza and ice cream to help tempt me to go home with her the night she appeared at the train station. She had asked the same question—vanilla or chocolate? Those choices seemed to separate people before anything else would.

Karen huffed and put her hands on her hips. She was a little wide there, I thought.

"I called Margaret. She says you can come to her party," she said. "Later you can tell me all about the parties you used to go to. Five minutes," she told Daddy, and left us.

I looked at him.

"Tell her about the parties I went to? I never went to any party."

"Just make up something racy," he said. "That's all she wants to hear. Something naughty. That's how teenage girls are. They like to tempt each other with outlandish things, titillate."

I shook my head. He was telling me how teenage girls behave. What did he think I was, an alien? I couldn't do this. This was not going to work.

"How could I become someone else this fast?"

He stared at me. He didn't have to say it, because I could see it on his face.

He was able to do it, and therefore, so should I.

I was his daughter, wasn't I?

CHAPTER FIVE

I took advantage of Ava's suggestion at dinner and claimed to be very tired right after we had our dessert. After all, I had supposedly flown all night and ridden on a bus for hours crossing the country right after my mother had died. Actually, I really didn't have to pretend. I felt numb with exhaustion from tiptoeing over a thin glass floor of lies. However, my real reason was to put off any more real questions and explanations. The tension was tiring. Of course, I knew that paranoia would be sitting and standing right beside me maybe forever, but I also knew that catching my breath would help me to avoid mistakes.

I excused myself and went up to my room, changed into the pajamas Ava said she had left in the dresser drawer, put on the pink furry slippers, which looked brand-new, and went to the bathroom to get ready for bed.

When I came out and returned to my room, however, Karen was sitting on the bed, thumbing through a fashion magazine she had brought with her. For a split second, I thought she knew the truth and had come up here to let me know, too. How could I live here with this daily fear? I held my breath in anticipation when she closed the magazine and looked at me with beady eyes. From the moment I had first seen her, I had scanned her face, looking for similarities with mine. In both cases, we looked more like our mothers. I was sure that I flashed some of Daddy's expressions. Would pretending he was my uncle be enough cover for all that? Did Karen already suspect something?

"Those pajamas fit you perfectly," she said, looking up at me. "They were a little too big for me up here," she said, pressing her palms against her breasts. "I'm still filling out; at least, I hope I am. I like your hair tied back like that, but be prepared for tomorrow at the beauty salon."

"It'll be fine," I said. Finally, I added, "I've never been to a beauty salon."

Would the break between my thoughts and my tongue always be wide enough?

She put the magazine aside.

"Never?"

"No money for that."

She smirked with disbelief and then nodded as the possibility became real.

"I do have friends who don't ever go, but I don't think it's the money thing. They'll go before birthdays or events but certainly not regularly."

I nodded as if I understood what it was like to be so carefree about such expenses.

Once again, she stared at me suspiciously.

"What?" I asked.

"We have to get to know each other if we're really going to be like sisters," she said.

I was hoping the irony wasn't dripping from my face. Be *like* sisters? She obviously had no suspicions. Relief washed over me in a cool flash, just the way it would for anyone who had gotten away with something blatantly obvious.

"Actually, I always wanted a sister. I don't know why they took so long to have Garson. When I ask, Daddy always says I was four handfuls, even for him."

Even for him? But he wasn't there for so much of her early years. I wondered how much of the truth she knew about herself, much less about me. Did she know she was unexpected, that she had been born before her parents had married? Did she have any idea about her parents' past, even an inkling about my father's previous life? What did she know? What had he told her, created for himself? Did she overhear him tell Ava his fictionalized account of his sister? Did she ask him any questions? How had he twisted the truth with her?

I wasn't the only one living a lie here.

This was a family built on lies.

Now that I had learned some of what had been going on while Daddy was still married to Mama, I wondered why Ava did go through with Karen's birth. How did her father react? How did my father win his acceptance? Daddy didn't really explain it very much. How much did people in this town know about it all but keep cloaked in secret whispers?

My mind was racing with questions, but I thought if I asked her even one of them, she would ask ten about me. She was probably going to do that anyway, but why bring it on tonight?

"Did you ever want a brother or a sister?" she asked.

When I was in deep thought, I could look directly at someone and never hear a word he or she said.

"Hello. Earth to Saffron?"

"What? Oh. Sorry. I guess I am just so tired. I think I'm sleeping on my feet."

"Well, you don't have anything to do until Mother takes you to get your hair and nails done, probably not until late morning, so you can sleep in. And no one will expect that much from you at school for a while." She paused, giving me those beady eyes again. "I asked my mother about your name. She said you must have been born with that shade of hair and enough of it. Who named you, your mother?"

"Yes," I said.

"So your father left pretty soon after?"

"I don't know the exact day, but I have no memories of him," I said, hiding my face as I walked around the bed and sat with my back against the pillow.

She didn't get up, but she had to turn around. I closed my eyes, but I knew it wasn't going to be that easy to get rid of her. If I tried too hard, she might get suspicious, I thought. That might be my concern over almost anything I did or said.

"So you never ever saw him?"

"Yeah . . . I don't even have a picture of him. Not that I care. He deserted us."

"Didn't it bother you not to have a father?"

I pretended I was giving something I had thought about so often new, long, serious thought.

"Yes. Especially when other girls bragged about theirs or I saw young girls walking hand in hand with their fathers. Sometimes I pretended I had a father, that his hand was holding mine. And I even read children's stories aloud to myself at night the way a real father might. You know, changing my voice?"

"Oh. That's sad."

"Just another in a long list of bad memories, most that would give you nightmares."

"Huh?"

"So what's the school like?" I asked, to get her off the subject.

She shrugged. "I don't know. A school's a school. I hear our class sizes are infinitesimal compared to public school, and everything we have is newer and cleaner. What about your school? Were your classes big?"

I thought about Hurley. Did I want to reveal that I had been in advanced classes with small class sizes? I was afraid of being intimidating. *Let her find out after I'm at school.* Careful with the details anyway, I thought, always careful. I was doing what Daddy had advised me to do, asking the question over in my head.

"About twenty-five or so, but there were some larger and some smaller. Grades were about a hundred or so in one school and nearly two hundred in another and even more in another," I said, remembering I had supposedly been to more than one and in areas where there would be large classes, bigger populations.

"Two hundred? You'll be shocked, then. We have maybe thirty in a whole grade, and that's divided into regular classes and advanced placement."

"Really? Are you in advanced placement?"

"No, and I'm glad."

"Why?"

"Those classes are so small that you can't hide," she said. "You'd better hope they don't put you in one," she added as if she knew a reason I would. "Besides, those AP kids are the snobbiest. The smartest girl in the school, Melina Forest, walks like a ballet dancer through the halls, so daintily you could eat off the heels of her shoes. She has a pretty face, but she's already five foot ten and so flat-chested you can practically see her wing bones when you look at her from the front."

"Sounds like you're obsessing about her."

"What? What's that mean?"

I thought a moment. *Why do I have to be so like Mazy and say what I think so often? That's dangerous here.*

"Does some boy like her, a boy you like?"

She pursed her lips in and out, looking like a fish breathing.

"Tommy Diamond's always with her. He's in AP classes, too, and the star of our basketball team. I'm not the only one who likes him," she said. "Some of the girls go ga-ga when they look at him, even though their mothers would never let them go out with him."

"Why not?"

"You'll see," she said, enjoying holding back.

"Oh. So is he snobby, too?"

"Not really, but if he was, I could forgive him," she said. "I could forgive him for anything," she added, and I laughed. "I mean it!"

"Okay. Sorry."

She stared at me a little too hard, feathering all sorts of suspicions.

"Did you have a boyfriend you left behind?"

"No."

I answered too quickly. Her eyes widened.

"Not even someone close to being a boyfriend?"

"No. When you have to travel about like we did, it's not easy establishing a relationship."

"Establishing a relationship? I'm just talking about a boyfriend, not a marriage."

"So what's your favorite subject?" I asked, now thinking that if I talked about school, studying, reading, I might bore her into leaving me alone and going to sleep.

"Sex," she said.

"Very funny."

"I'm not joking." She spun around completely. "And don't tell me it's not your favorite subject, too. If you really want to be more than just a guest here, you have to follow Karen's rule."

"Oh? What is that?"

"It's simple," she said, rising. "I'll tell you one of my most secret secrets, and then you tell me one of yours. We keep doing it almost every day until we have no more secrets from each other. Then we'll be more like real cousins, and I'll always stick up for you, and you'll always stick up for me. Of course, if one of us reveals one of those secrets to someone else without the other person's permission, everything ends. We don't look out for each other, we don't care about each other, and we're permitted to do anything we want to hurt the other. Agreed?"

"Sounds like a trap," I said, and she pulled her head back.

"What? What kind of trap? How's that a trap?"

"I don't know. I have to think a lot about it when I'm fully awake."

She stared at me a moment and then stepped closer to the bed so she could loom over me.

"It's not funny, Saffron. There aren't many people I've made that promise to. It's the most special thing anyone can do. The only reason I'm doing it with you is you're my father's niece and you're going to live here."

"I realize that, and I appreciate it."

"Appreciate it? Establish a relationship." She smirked as if I had said the dumbest things. "You sound like a teacher, not a student. Maybe you're weird."

I smiled. "We're all weird."

"That's a weird thing to say," she said, and started out. I could see her mind was spinning like a satellite falling to earth. She turned, squinting at me suspiciously. "Why didn't your mother ever tell my father anything about you? He claims he didn't even know your name. It's like you fell out of the sky or something and landed on our front steps. Why was that? What happened to make them hate each other so much?"

"Ask your father," I said. "I don't know it all. My mother wouldn't talk about it much, either," I added quickly.

She thought a moment, shrugged, and said, "Whatever. I'll admit that's weird. Get ready for tomorrow. My mother's going to change your whole look. You won't recognize yourself when you look in the mirror."

I don't recognize myself now, I thought, and wished I could say it.

She waited a moment as if she was anticipating what I wished I could say, and then she left, closing the door behind her.

I lay there for a few moments thinking about Mazy's last words to me: "I'm not going to tell you what to do. If you want to go back tomorrow, go back. If not, we'll keep going and ignore them. You decide."

Deep in her heart, she knew I had accepted it. I would have to decide, and whatever I did with my life was really up to me. Soon she'd be unable to do much about it anyway. But when she said, "If you want to go back tomorrow, go back," I realized now, she didn't mean returning to the Hurley public school to try to become friends with the kids my age and live there normally. What she really meant was returning to my father.

There was nothing obviously to connect me with him, forcing me to acknowledge him, as far as anyone at the school or in the town knew. After Mazy passed away, I could have gone along with the fiction she had created for the public about my parents being dead and turned myself over to some social service department, or I could have put my pack on my back, the way I had envisioned myself sitting on the train here, and become one of the invisible kids my age and around my age who disappeared into the shadows of American towns and cities. It wasn't whether I had the smarts to survive; it was what I would survive to become.

I thought that along with everything else she kept well hidden in her smiles and words was the assumption that eventually I would decide to become part of my father's new life. It must have saddened her, because she knew that to do so, I would have to swallow back all the pain, and I would have to refuse to believe the most terrible of things about him. But who forgave their parents more than their children? More often than not, all children were like me at one time or another. Hardened and full of rationalizations. Otherwise, like me, they might not survive. Many times, just like I was doing tonight and had done when I first stepped off the train in Sandburg Creek, I would question whether that survival, clinging to the thin ties to family, was worth the cost. What would I think of myself years from now?

I rose and went to the window to look out at the lights of neighboring houses. Every family in every other house was woven in their own secrets and sins. They did everything they could to avoid facing them. Life was filled with little lies. Ironically, too often the most deadly thing was honesty. It could crush you. Angels floated by in the darkness, pausing at this door or that, hoping there was a place pure enough for them to rest until morning. But there was none.

Nevertheless, they were obligated to search. It was their mission. I was sure they didn't even pause at this doorway. This house bled dishonesty into the night, all night. I really shouldn't blame Karen for looking for someone to trust, I thought. Instinctively, she knew it was nearly an impossible task. Some time or another, we all realize that. She was hoping I understood.

Could she be an ally for me, and could I be an ally for her? Wasn't that what I longed for back in Hurley, a trusted friend? I had barely spoken to Karen, barely even looked at her, but somehow I sensed a desperation. Perhaps we shared far more than the same father. She wanted to reveal things, things she remembered from the darker past we had both lived through.

In time, I would reach out to her. She would smile, placing her hand in mine, but I was certain that she then would realize what all that truth really meant and would quickly retreat to the safety of ignorance again.

I don't want to know. Thank you, but really and truly, I don't want to know . . . We'd both reach for that same mantra.

Ignorance allows us to sleep.

I returned to bed. I had to build my strength. Most of my time here, I would be learning new secrets and experiencing new distrusts and pain, and not only Karen's, either. The lies in the foundation of this family squirmed like snakes. These were snakes that could smile gleefully. When I finally fell asleep, I tossed and fretted and dreamed awful things. But I didn't dare whimper and especially not scream. Who would come to comfort me anyway?

"I'm not going to tell you what to do," Mazy had said. "If you want to go back tomorrow, go back. If not, we'll keep going and ignore them. You decide."

Mazy's words were the only words of comfort I possessed. Memories of her voice truly were what enabled me eventually to fall into a safe sleep. It was as if I was still with her, still in my robin's-egg blue room, and all that had happened had just been a long nightmare.

As Karen had predicted, I did sleep late into the morning. I had the image, maybe some wishful thinking, of my father looking in on me and then closing the door softly sometime during the night. I knew that he had taken Karen to school so he could make all the arrangements for my enrollment. Finally, because she had made the appointment for me at her salon, Ava came to the door of my bedroom and sharply told me to wake up.

"This will be the only morning you oversleep in this house, Saffron. Get washed and dressed, and come down for some breakfast. We're going to the salon in an hour," she declared. She started to back up and close the door again but stopped. "How did you sleep?"

"Pretty deeply," I said.

"Lucky you," she told me. "Garson kept me up all night with that damn teething. Fortunately, he's asleep now. Move along. In the closet, you'll find a fresh blouse and a skirt that should fit you. I have a sweater for you to wear to school, too. Saturday we'll do some shopping for a more complete wardrobe for you, including shoes and underthings."

She paused again, thoughtful, and looked at me. "You've had your period, haven't you?"

"I have."

"Well, I imagine you saw you have what you need."

"Yes, thank you."

"When are you due again?"

"Next week," I said.

"Um . . . sometimes travel and other traumatic events play havoc with it. We'll see." She returned to her stiff posture as if she had just realized that she was being too nice. "Get moving," she said.

I stared at the closed door for a moment, wondering if all that talk about my period was motherly concern or concern that I might do something that would embarrass her. I rose to wash and dress. I found the blouse and skirt she had described all the way in the left corner of the closet, as if they had been put there secretly. Everything did fit, and I hurried down the stairs to the kitchen. She had a setting on the kitchenette table for me.

"I'm scrambling some eggs," she said. "I'll put a little fruit with it and some toast. Do you want something else?"

"No, that's fine. Thank you."

"There's orange juice poured. Do you drink coffee?"

"Yes."

Apparently, my father had been careful not to tell her I did. She'd wonder how he would have known. Little blunders could explode it all instantly.

"Well, I have a fresh pot for myself as well. You can just go sit."

I knew she was preparing to ask me dozens and dozens of personal questions. Why was Daddy so confident that I could get Ava to believe any and all of this? Or was he hoping I would fall on my face and then use that to tell her the truth, that somehow if he could then get her to feel so sorry for me, she might forgive him and the lies? Then again, perhaps he was thinking that my desperation would motivate me to be as perfect a liar as he was.

As Ava put my breakfast on a dish, I really was favoring blurting it all out in one frantic breath: *This is all a lie. I am not your husband's niece; I am his daughter. I've been living with my grandmother for the last five years because he left me at a train station as part of a plan. My mother was not his biological sister; she was his wife. Yes, they did grow up as brother and sister . . . but . . .*

The madness of the explanation, the complications, choked the words. I turned and drank my juice. It was warmer than I liked. I smiled, thinking he could have messed up again by telling her to put an ice cube in it first. How many of those little mistakes hovered in the air around us? How keen was Ava? Was she a Miss Marple, too, the famous female detective Mazy always accused me of being because I was so pensive and so full of questions?

She put the plate of eggs and fruit in front of me.

"Thank you, Ava," I said.

"You can call me Aunt Ava," she replied sternly. I had forgotten. I nodded and began to eat. Ironically, she had made my eggs the way I liked them, quite well done. "Are they all right?"

"Yes, thank you."

"It's the way I like them, too," she said. "I hate runny eggs."

"So do I."

She didn't smile, but she looked less tense.

"I'd like to hear more about how things were for you, especially these last few years, and more about your mother. Derick refuses to talk about her. He gets visibly angry when I ask questions. Your arrival has been quite the surprise. I know it was for him. Why did you decide to come here?"

I ate and listened, just as he had instructed. I repeated the instructions in my mind: *only answer questions directly, and don't volunteer more than the question asks.* Were there any signs of suspicion?

"My mother died," I said.

"Yes, but you had nothing to do with Derick your whole life, from what I understand. He said he didn't even know your name or your age."

I had to swallow back the answer I wanted to give her and, again, stick to the obvious.

"Uncle Derick is the only living relative I have now," I said.

"And your mother's parents? Didn't either of them have a sister? Weren't there cousins?"

"She never said. She wasn't talking to her parents, either."

"Like your uncle," she said. "Did they ever know about you?"

"I don't know. As far as I know, they didn't try to contact us."

"And your paternal grandparents?"

"I never knew my father, much less his family, so . . ."

"How sad. Sounds like your family, my husband's family, was a constantly erupting earthquake. Parents can be burdens. Well, hopefully things will change for you here. Karen is taking you to the party Saturday night, so you'll begin to meet other girls and boys your age. I've already told her we're going to do some shopping for you on Saturday, both for the party in the evening and for things you will need. She'll probably come along so that if I buy you something so new that she doesn't have it, I'll have to buy it for her, too.

"Yes," she said before I could even change expression, "she's spoiled, but not entirely by me. Your uncle and her grandfather are putty in her hands when she starts to whine, especially if I'm not there. Sometimes even if I am."

She drummed on the table with her fingers. Maybe she was hoping I'd say something, but I didn't even breathe.

"I've ordered the family limousine for nine forty-five. Stores open at ten, so Karen will have to get up earlier than she usually does on Saturdays if she wants to come along with us. The driver will assist us with the packages. He's my father's driver, Tyson Mathis, a very nice man who puts up with a lot, you'll see. Not from me, from my father, who was born cranky. We'll be going to dinner at his estate Sunday night. He knows about you, of course. I'll prepare you for all of that."

"Prepare me?"

"I wish someone had prepared me," she added in a mutter.

I drank some coffee and tried to look away, especially so she wouldn't see the way I had reacted to hearing how my father catered to his younger daughter.

"How did you know to come here, to this exact town?" she asked quickly, almost like a police detective trying to catch a suspect off guard. "I mean, if your mother refused to have anything to do with her brother, they didn't exchange information, especially if your mother was moving so much. Had they had contact recently?"

"Not that I know."

"So?

I fumbled answers in my mind.

"The police," I said, hoping that would be enough. "Once I gave them his name, they located you, and just in time, too. Some social worker was talking about a foster family."

"I see. And then what happened?"

"Everything was taking too long. I was scared they had called Uncle Derick and he had said they should put me in a foster home. I had some money and decided to come regardless."

"So you made your own arrangements," she said, nodding.

"I just got on a plane. The woman at the desk in the airport looked up the travel route for me, so I knew about the bus to Sandburg Creek."

She nodded. "The police in California must have contacted our chief of police," she said, thinking aloud. "And he tracked your travel and told Derick."

"I don't know those details. I wasn't thinking about any of that. I thought that even if Uncle Derick didn't want me to come, I'd pretend he did just to get away."

"So you came here without being sure?"

"I guess I wasn't thinking very well about anything after I found my mother."

"Yes, you said you found her. Tell me about that."

"It wasn't like I just discovered her. We were supposed to go to eat. She didn't come out of her room, so I went and . . . I couldn't rouse her. Actually, I was more frightened at the sight of her like that than sad at the start."

"Of course. You poor child," she said. "Forget about how and why you came here. That was smart. Thinking well in a crisis is what distinguishes successful people from unsuccessful ones. You're here, and you're safe," she said.

We heard Garson's cry, and she rose.

I had finished eating. Maybe I had eaten too quickly out of nervousness, but she didn't seem to notice.

"Leave everything," she said when I started to gather the dishes and silverware. It was almost a reflex now. "I have Celisse coming in to look after Garson and do some extra work today. She'll be here in fifteen minutes. Do you want anything more to eat?"

"No, thank you," I said.

She stared at me so hard I was afraid it was all over. She was thinking about the story I had just told her and had seen through the fiction I had created. My voice, the look in my eyes, had betrayed me. I simply wasn't a good liar after all. But that wasn't it; that wasn't why she was considering me so hard.

"I hope some of your good manners rub off on Karen. Her father and her grandfather have spoiled her to the point where she looks after herself before she looks after someone else. Maybe you'll have a good influence on her. Just be careful it's not the other way around. She may look and seem harmless, but . . ."

I know I widened my eyes. She was talking about her own daughter as if she was some sort of poison.

"I'll go get Garson and start his feeding until Celisse comes. She's always on time, so don't dawdle. Oh, here," she said, unfolding a light green cardigan sweater she had draped over one of the chairs. "Wear this for today."

"Thank you," I said, taking it.

"It's actually one of mine."

I watched her leave and then released a deep breath threatening to burst out of my lungs.

Was this what she was going to do—talk about simple things, daily life, and then insert a sharp question that would cause me to stumble and look guilty? Daddy said Ava didn't like to talk about sad or unpleasant things. She was certainly pursuing them now. Was what he said about her another of his lies to distract me from worrying? And what was all this warning about her father? We were going to his house for dinner Sunday night, and she would prepare me? Why? What sort of a cross-examination would he conduct? Wasn't this something Daddy should have warned me about? He barely talked about it.

How could I live like this, trying to act as normal as I could while anticipating something or someone would jump out of the shadows and rip the cover and disguise off me?

I went upstairs quickly to get ready to leave. I could hear Ava soothing Garson in her bedroom. When I came out of my bathroom, I heard her downstairs talking to the maid. She was telling her about my arrival. I stood at the top of the stairway and listened.

"She puts on a good show," Ava told her, "but she's obviously quite shattered. She's had a miserable life. Don't ask personal questions. When she talks to you, a smile will suffice."

"*Oui, madame*," Celisse said.

They both began speaking French. Ava sounded fluent.

I continued down the stairs.

Celisse looked too petite to clean a house this big and care for a baby, too. Maybe she was an inch taller than I was, but she certainly didn't weigh much more. She couldn't have been older than twenty, if that. She had a pretty face with soft features and dark-brown hair pinned up neatly. She wore a dark-blue dress that resembled a uniform because of the pockets. She was cradling Garson, who was moving a teething ring gently around his gums and staring up at her.

"Hello," she said when I appeared.

"Hi."

"This is Celisse," Ava said.

"I'm Saffron," I said.

"Welcome." Her smile was sincere. Now that I looked at her more closely, I thought she was even younger and certainly too innocent to be in this house. She looked like a rose growing in a patch of weeds.

"Your uncle and I met Celisse during a trip to Èze, France, and we talked her into coming home with us two years ago," Ava said. "I studied in France when I was your age. Do you know any French?"

"A little," I said. "From reading." I looked at Celisse. "*Un peu.*"

"*Très bien,*" she said, smiling.

"Two years with Celisse, and Karen doesn't know that much," Ava said. "Maybe now that there are two of you here, Celisse will be more successful with her."

I said nothing. One thing was clear to me: I really could have an enemy in my half sister in a heartbeat. *Just side with her mother whenever she complains about her*, I thought, *or show her up in some way or another, Saffron. See where that gets you.*

"Let's go," Ava said. She slipped on a jeweled denim jacket and started for the door to the garage. I followed quickly, nervously expecting a more intense cross-examination to come.

Which it did the moment we backed out of the driveway and she turned to head down the street. From my walk, I recognized where we were going. We would pass the Dew Drop Inn. How did Daddy ensure that the manager would never mention me or, if he saw me, pretend he never had? Deception had to have more tentacles than an octopus, especially in these small rural towns.

"Did you recognize Derick when you first saw him?"

"I wouldn't have, but he was the only man his age waiting at the bus station."

"Didn't you even have an early picture of him?"

"There were some, but he and my mother were too young. I mean, there were certainly resemblances."

"And you left without much money?"

"I had some," I said, afraid she would see what I had found in Mazy's closet. "There might be something left in my mother's checking account."

"Well, you don't have to worry about money. Keep whatever you have for emergencies," she said. "Not that I can imagine your having any."

Emergency? Like the discovery of who I really am and my quick departure? I wondered.

"You've had a hard young life, but you've developed a strong sense of independence. I like that. My father is not terribly fond of strong, independent women. My mother wasn't one."

"I never thought of myself that way," I said. It was something Daddy had said, too, and for some reason, the word sounded evil.

"Well, think it now. You seem like a bright girl. Did you do well in school? I don't know the details. Derick's taking care of that or did by now."

"Yes."

"It doesn't sound like your mother had that much time to oversee your behavior and your schoolwork."

"No, she was always working so hard and was often very tired at the end of the day."

"I can imagine. Other girls—Karen, I fear—would take advantage of that and slum around."

I said nothing, but I was wondering why she was so negative about her own daughter. What would she be like if she discovered the truth about me?

"Have you ever been in trouble, at school or otherwise? It's best I know now."

"No."

She'd actually go wild if she ever knew I had been blamed for putting a curse on a boy who died in a car accident.

"For now, I'm going to believe everything you tell me," Ava said, "because you've given me no reason to think otherwise, but the moment you do . . ." She looked at me with fire in her eyes. "Let this be enough warning. And know this . . . Sandburg Creek is a small town. People gossip here as much as if not more than anywhere, especially when it comes to anyone involved with a Saddlebrook. Sometimes I think some are like hawks waiting for an opportunity to swoop down and seize something that would hurt us."

"Why?"

She looked at me and turned away to focus on the road. I thought she wasn't going to answer.

"It's human nature. Jealousy," she said. "You'd better be prepared for that once everyone understands who you are and where you live."

I said nothing, even though my mind was flooding with questions. She'd been pregnant without a husband, hadn't she? How did they manage that secret? She glanced at me and then turned to pull into the salon parking lot.

"Let's see what Renae suggests for your hair. She's quite good. While she works on you, her assistant will do your fingernails. Maybe we'll have your toenails done as well. They'll know the best colors. Then I'll take you to school to follow up on your enrollment. Either your uncle or I will pick you two up at the end of the school day."

"There are no uniforms?" I had been expecting it since this was a private school.

"There was an attempt to do that, but you'll see when you're there why it fell on its face. We've got plenty of fashionistas. Some parents think they're dressing their children to stand in storefront windows. You'll have nice things, but neither you nor Karen is going to be in some competition every day.

"Let's go," she said. "Nothing cheers up a woman like getting her hair and nails done. Am I right?" she asked with a real smile.

"I wouldn't know, Aunt Ava. I have never been to a salon."

Her smile fell somewhere into her face. "Who looked after your hair?"

"My mother, when she had the time."

"If you tell my father that, he'll chant how necessity is the mother of invention. You'd think he was a pauper. Okay, let's go. There are many different kinds of virginity to end, and we'll start here," she said, opening the door.

I smiled and followed her into the salon, wondering if in the end, I wouldn't somehow like her, if not respect her, far more than I did or ever would my father.

CHAPTER SIX

From the way Ava described me to her hairdresser, Renae, when we entered the salon, someone would think I had just arrived from a hidden corner in Tibet or some other place where salons, hair conditioners, shampoos, and nail polish had never been seen, not to mention running water. Anyone listening looked like she would think it was a sin not to have gone to a beauty salon to have your hair and nails done. A little panic seized me. Would Ava's descriptions lead everyone to ask personal questions that would lead me to contradictions? I tried keeping my eyes down and not looking at anyone else in the salon.

Renae did say my hair needed a lot of preparation. It was dry and stringy with split ends. Fortunately, she avoided saying "dirty," which surely would have brought a parade of questions for Ava with negative connotations. *Who did you say this girl was? Where is she from? Parents? Derick had a sister?*

Maybe most, if not all, were afraid of her. No one asked anything like that. Both Renae and Ava stood back and studied me as they flipped through pictures of hairstyles. All other eyes were on them, too. Every once in a while, they'd pause on one page, and Renae would bring the picture up beside my face.

This one emphasized my eyes too much to the detriment of all my other fine features; this one exaggerated my jawbone and distorted my otherwise good looks. It was taking so long that I thought they wouldn't find any that worked, and they'd give up and just have my hair washed and brushed. I was almost hoping that would be so.

Suddenly, they both agreed on one.

"Which one is it?" I asked. The whole salon was waiting to hear and see, but Ava didn't tell anyone anything.

"Relax. Just leave it up to Renae," she told me. "Better it's a surprise."

Renae's ebony eyes brightened with excitement. Someone would think she was really re-creating me. Moments later, she was washing my hair as vigorously as she would if it was crusted with soot. I thought she'd make me bald. After she blow-dried it, the manicurist started on my nails while Renae began snipping and brushing. To me it felt like she was taking an ax to it. Gobs fell. With both the manicurist and Renae at me, I was afraid to move, practically to breathe. Ava stood in the background, thumbing through fashion magazines and occasionally looking at me and nodding at the progress. I watched in the mirror as if I was looking at someone else on television. Gradually, the hairstyle took shape.

"What do you call this?" I asked. I think the sound of my voice surprised both the manicurist and Renae. Until then, I was more like a seated statue, a mannequin, something used for training hairdressers.

"It's the new bob," Renae said. "As you see, you have a voluminous crown and a neat nape. I'm working on elongated wedges now."

As Mazy might say, that was Greek to me. But it did seem like my face was changing, too. My eyes looked bigger and my lips softer, fuller. I glanced at my nails after they had been neatly trimmed and cleaned. Ava had chosen the color, which the manicurist agreed was the best match for my complexion, Sandy Nude. She would do the same for my toenails.

My whole look was altering, but it occurred to me that I shouldn't be surprised. I was becoming a different person in so many ways. Why not look different, too? It was almost supernatural, slipping into a new persona in a new family in a new world. Even my memories had to change, of course. Past feelings were to be forgotten or at least put into storage.

For the last five years, I had spent most of my life in one house, seeing the world through Mazy's eyes. She had shaped my opinions of almost everything, including myself. Now cutting and washing my hair, buying me new clothes, and enrolling me in a new school was a new leg of the journey taking me away from the person I thought I was and creating someone I had yet to know myself. Was I happy to be here? Did I like all this and want all that was promised? Indecision married to fear made me so vulnerable, so helpless. With all that had happened to me and the little I came with, what else could I be but clay to be formed by both Ava and my father?

Suddenly, a really frightening thought occurred. I wondered, when my hair was completely shaped and the features of my face highlighted, would Ava look at me and instantly realize that I could be no other than Derick Anders's daughter? Would my true identity jump out at her? I was feeling so naked now, even with the shadows lifted away. What would I say if she made the accusation?

Even the most successful and efficient liars crumbled when they were confronted abruptly with the truth.

However, nothing like that happened. When everything had been completed, all the other customers and other hairstylists congratulated Ava as if she were Pygmalion bringing a statue to life. Apparently, to them, I hadn't had much of an identity when I stepped into this salon anyway. Clearly implied was that before all this, I was so plain, so ordinary, that I was no better than someone carved poorly in stone, a resting place for birds. People would have passed me by, barely noticing I was there. Now I had been touched by the good fairy's wand. How could I be anything but grateful?

Everyone interpreted the look on my face as I gazed at myself to be a look of pleased wonder. Some laughed at my surprise. Others wished they had my raw material. I listened to them and looked at them poke and paw at themselves as they gazed longingly into mirrors. I realized that the pool of jealousy in beauty salons could drown you.

Sandwiches and drinks had been brought in while Renae brushed and trimmed my hair, but I couldn't eat or drink while they worked on me. Ava handed me a sandwich and a bottle of water as I stepped away from the chair.

"You can munch on this on the way to school," she said. "I want to get you set at school today. There's no time to go to a restaurant with me still having time for some of my own errands."

She shoved it at me, and we left the salon. Even though it had taken hours, it all seemed fast to me. I was happy we weren't going to a restaurant, where the menu would convert to another list of questions, another interrogation. I had been so nervous that now I didn't have much of an appetite anyway.

When we got into her car, she paused and then looked at me, sitting there, staring ahead. I hadn't even unwrapped the sandwich.

"I'll take your silence to be a result of the shock at how good you look and not your dissatisfaction. Am I correct?"

"Yes," I said, although there was far more to it that she must never know.

She smiled and nodded, the look of self-satisfaction rippling through her face.

"Your mother must have been an attractive woman. I venture to guess you look more like her than you do your ghost of a father?"

"I couldn't tell you. I didn't even have a picture of him, and neither did my mother," I said. It had the effect of damming up what I was sure would be a sea of potential questions about my father and his family, each another threat to this fiction Daddy and I were creating.

"Didn't your mother ever talk about him?"

"Not pleasantly, so I didn't ask questions."

"Did the other children at school tease you about not having a father?"

"No. Most were too interested in themselves to care about me," I said. "And there were plenty of children who had divorced parents. Most had only a mother; some had only a father. I used to pretend that was me, too. My parents were divorced. It felt better than having a father who didn't want anything to do with you. It's painful to think of your father as someone who never had or has you in his thoughts now. I could meet him on a street and not know it, and vice versa. And you know what? I'd love that. I'd love to walk right past him, realize who he was, and then turn and call to him. 'Hey, Daddy,' I'd say. 'Hi.' I'd just want to see the expression on his face."

She looked at me as if some power had put everything on pause, our movements and our breath, and then she burst into a laugh that nearly brought tears to her eyes. I had to smile. It was a relief to hear it, even though I had no clue why she was laughing so hard. She was quiet for a long moment afterward, deciding what to tell me, I thought. She nodded like someone answering herself.

"You remind me more of myself at your age than Karen does," she revealed. "You and I grew up in different worlds, but we might have been shaped by similar demons. Mine must remain buried. I'm jealous of your honesty. It's refreshing, hopeful. Don't lose it."

Honesty? Hopeful? I thought, surprised. *I'm being anything but honest.* Was I really that good of a liar? Daddy would be proud. And then I realized how incredibly crazy that sounded. What father would take pride in his daughter's ability to be false? And what were Ava's demons? Of course, I was too terrified to ask. Once you ask someone else questions, you give her permission to ask you endless questions.

"However . . ." She paused and looked at me. "Although we don't know each other that well yet, I will give you some advice. You're about to be enrolled in a school I venture to say will be quite unlike the ones you've attended. All the other students here come from well-to-do families. It's like too much cream in your coffee. For the first few days, even weeks, I advise you to keep your opinions to yourself, especially about any of the other girls. Just listen and be as neutral as you can be. Put honesty on the back burner for now. At least, until you feel more secure, and at this stage in your life, that's the most important thing. Sometimes it takes a lifetime to realize how to best juggle your need for the truth."

When I had entered Hurley's public school, Mazy had given me similar advice about being too honest. "Everyone," she had said, "likes to be lied to about themselves, even if they know that what you're saying is completely false."

"You'll discover soon that many of Karen's friends are quite superficial," Ava said now. "We're an important family in this town, and I ascribe most if not all her friends and invitations to that. You don't snub a Saddlebrook. My family's tentacles, my father's, I should say, pierce and poke just about every business in this community, one way or another. As I told you earlier, he spoils Karen, and she knows how to take advantage of that. He's taught her well, despite me. Karen can be a bully, just like her grandfather can be. Understand?"

"I've read Charles Dickens and Jane Austen novels," I said. "I know how families can damage themselves and how powerful people can get away with almost anything."

Ava looked at me with surprise again.

"I wouldn't have thought someone who lived the life you've lived would be as studious as you appear to be," she said. It was the first hint of suspicion and sounded a little too much like an accusation. I was really afraid to speak or explain, but I thought it through carefully as I spoke.

"I wasn't able to become that sociable with other girls at school, and I wasn't up to hanging out in malls or something, so I spent my time reading. It was just a way . . ."

"Just a way?"

"Out. Escape," I said.

She widened her eyes. I could see that she liked that. I breathed relief. How many times would I be in a little crisis like this, and how many times would I make as clever an escape?

"We'll have more talks like this," she promised. Then she nodded. "That's the elementary and high schools just ahead."

It was time now for my eyes to pop. It appeared more like someone's estate. This was no official, government-looking building with the usual austere front. Although it was already mid-October, it was warmer than usual. Leaves had not changed colors, and the grass was still rich green, even greener than it was at my father and Ava's home. Sprawled over beautiful grounds with an enormous front lawn, recently mowed, was an enormous classic building with dark-green vines growing around the front windows of what was obviously the main building. Added-on connecting structures led to an adjoining smaller building on the right with the title "Administrative Offices" over the arched front door and to what looked on the left like more classrooms and then a glass-enclosed modern building, which Ava said was the gymnasium her father had built. She described the athletic fields behind the buildings but said the population of the school was too small for a football team. There was a girls' and a boys' basketball team. At the moment, only three groundskeepers were outside the building. I kept thinking this was too picturesque to be an elementary and high school. It was warm, attractive, and inviting.

Ava glanced at me and smiled. "Not like the schools you attended?"

"No. If it weren't for the sign revealing what it is, I'd drive right by looking for a school."

She nodded with obvious pride. "It was originally a billionaire's estate," Ava said. "My father was instrumental in getting it all for a private school. But believe me, he worked out ways for himself to claim big deductions by donating the property."

She smiled.

"Rich people look out for each other more than poor people do. Less desperate. Sometimes they make money just to prove they can. Remember that. I'm not often as honest about my world."

That didn't amaze me, but I was thinking too hard about the

school. It seemed to reek of privilege and wealth. To the right was a smaller parking lot clearly labeled for teachers and administrators only. The parking lot for everyone else was on the left side of the building and farther from any entrance. Ava went to the right and pulled into a space marked for the high school principal.

"It's something of a secret that there are two reserved places for the principal," she said, winking. She started to open the door and then stopped. "Oh. Your uncle was supposed to buy you school supplies with a backpack and leave it at the office for you. Hopefully, he didn't forget. Lately, he's been my absentminded professor. My father keeps him too busy."

We got out and walked to the entrance of the administration building. Everything looked just built, polished and cleaned better than a hospital ward. The gray and black tile floor glistened, as did the dark-brown panel walls. The hallway had bright but warm lighting. But what struck me the most was how quiet it was. There were no sounds of students. Anyone blindfolded would never guess he or she was in a school, public or private.

We turned into the first door on the right, a double glass door that opened to a secretary busy on a computer at her half-moon, dark-cherry wood desk with a vase of mixed fresh flowers on the right corner. The moment she saw Ava, she nearly rose to attention. A plaque on her desk indicated that her name was Mrs. Hollingsworth and she was the principal's secretary. She was gray-haired and matronly, like someone's sixty-odd-year-old grandmother.

"Oh, Mrs. Anders, I have everything here for your niece," she said, lifting a large manila envelope. "And her backpack is right here, too."

"Where's Dr. Stewart?" Ava asked with her characteristic tone of demand.

"Oh, she's on the monthly tour of the facilities with the head custodian, Mr. Hull. She should return momentarily."

"I have no time to wait for that," Ava said. When something annoyed her, there was enough fury in her widened eyes to make the president shudder.

"Of course. I'll let her know you're here." She reached for an intercom.

"That's not necessary. My niece is far from an idiot. She'll peruse the school packet and wait for Dr. Stewart. I assume my husband signed any required documents."

"Oh, yes, yes. She's ready to get started," Mrs. Hollingsworth said, smiling at me. "You can sit right there, Saffron." She nodded at the dark-brown leather settee on the right. There was a glass table in front of it with a half dozen pamphlets neatly displayed.

On the wall on the right was the portrait of a distinguished-looking elderly man with thick gray hair.

"Is that your father?" I asked, practically in a whisper.

"Actually, my grandfather. My father's little joke," she muttered.

"Huh?" I thought and uttered.

"Get your things," Ava told me. I stepped to the desk, and Mrs. Hollingsworth handed me the packet and a gold foil backpack. A small nick on the strap revealed it was the same one, the one I had left in Hurley, the one my grandmother had bought me. Had my father gone there and fetched it? When? Had he had it sent to him? Why? Did he want me to feel more at home? Was that why he did it? Or did he want to be sure no one had discovered any connection to him in Mazy's house? Did he want to convince anyone in authority that I had run off?

Whatever the reasons, wasn't that dangerous? What else of mine had he brought back?

Concerned, I glanced nervously at Ava. Although it was quite unlikely she'd realize anything from looking at it, it still seemed somewhat risky to me for him to have done it.

"I don't anticipate any problems, Mrs. Hollingsworth," Ava said, "but you know how to reach me should you have any reason to."

"Oh, of course. I'm sure all will go fine."

Ava turned to me, deliberately speaking loudly and firmly enough for Mrs. Hollingsworth to hear.

"If anyone is capable of handling new challenges, I'm sure it's you, Saffron. Compared to what you have endured, this should be child's play. Good luck. Follow the rules, and remember my advice."

She gave Mrs. Hollingsworth a look that would have resulted in a strike at any bowling alley and then walked out. Mrs. Hollingsworth offered me a fragile smile and sat. I went to the settee and opened the backpack to see if anything from the Hurley school was still inside. It had been completely emptied. I sighed with relief and began reading the information in the manila envelope, familiar rules and threats with an added full page on cleanliness and proper dress, specifically forbidding certain types of T-shirts, short skirts, and jackets with inscriptions and images. Any form of profanity or even a suggestion of it was practically a capital offense resulting in suspension, if not expulsion. Heavily emphasized between the rules and suggestions was the fact that it was costly to go here and there were no refunds if you were expelled.

I wondered what the tuition was and found a page with the numbers almost too tiny to read. Grades 9–12 cost $60,000 a year. The penalties for late payments were on a rising scale that quickly doubled the tuition.

I looked up when a tall, surprisingly attractive woman wearing a khaki two-button jacket and skirt entered. She had a white tie

loosely tied over the white blouse beneath. I couldn't imagine her
to be older than her mid-thirties, if that. Her coffee-brown hair had
been cut to fall in curls about her neck, no longer than the arch in
her shoulders. She wasn't an African American, but she was clearly
not a white Anglo-Saxon. She had startling sapphire eyes, soft full
lips, and a nose fit for a beauty queen. Maybe she had been one as a
teenager. She was at least five foot ten or so, with narrow hips, a small
waist, and a bosom in perfect proportion to the rest of her. She was
the sort of woman people looked at and immediately thought *movie
star*. Her smile at me seemed to brighten every perfect feature.

"You must be Saffron," she said. There was something foreign in
her accent. She spoke with the clarity and sharpness of what Mazy
called "the King's English," but she didn't seem British. She spoke
more like Grace Kelly, the actress who did become a princess. Mazy
and I used to watch her old movies together.

"Welcome." Dr. Stewart extended her right hand. I thought she
was wearing the same nail polish that had been put on me. Her fingers were long and thin but firmly took mine when I stood. "You look
as frightened as I was my first day," she added, widening her smile.
Then she turned to Mrs. Hollingsworth and changed her expression
so dramatically, it was scary. Rage seemed to flood up from her neck
and into her face. Her voice deepened.

"Weren't you supposed to follow up on Mr. Hull's report about
the hot water heater in the girls' locker room, Mrs. Hollingsworth?"

"I did," the secretary said, and started sifting through papers on
her desk. "Yes. They were sending someone either yesterday or today."

"Well, no one has come. Follow up again, but more sternly. I want
someone here before the end of the day."

"Yes, Dr. Stewart," Mrs. Hollingsworth said, and pressed a button
on her phone to get an outside line.

Dr. Stewart turned back to me, her warm smile returning.

"I know your schedule. You have advanced world history this hour. Mr. Leshner is your teacher. I'll introduce you. I've assigned Melina Forest to be your 'big sister' for the remainder of the week. She shares every class with you and is one of my more responsible students. She's anxious to help. Shall we?"

Melina Forest? That was the girl Karen didn't like.

I picked up my book bag and the manila envelope.

"Why don't you put your school pamphlet in your bag now?" she suggested. I did it quickly. "Your uncle told me a little about you," she said as we walked out of the office. "I'll schedule a meet-and-greet for us during one of your study periods, or perhaps we'll have lunch together in my office and get to know each other better, okay?"

I nodded, amazed at the suggestion. Was it just for me? A member of Ava Saddlebrook Anders's family?

"I have one with every student here. I like to know everything I can about my students, including their ambitions. You look a little surprised, but we have a relatively small high school population. I'd be remiss if I didn't know as much as I can about my students. And they should know as much as is proper about me. Is that okay with you?"

For a moment, I couldn't even nod. She was another adult to fool, to lie to, another pool of risk to swim through. I hoped, expected, Daddy would first tell me exactly what he had told her. Did he add any details? Surely she wouldn't be easy to deceive.

"Yes," I managed.

She laughed the sort of laugh that makes you want to like someone. She squeezed the top of my left arm gently.

"Don't be so frightened," she said. "You're about to begin the best educational experience of your life. You'll even get to regret weekends."

She laughed again and then turned almost as serious as she had with Mrs. Hollingsworth.

"From the information your uncle has provided us, I can see that you're a high achiever. I expect that here you'll surpass everything you've achieved previously. I know my student body is a highly sociable one. Some are satisfied just gliding along, but from what your uncle has told me about you, about your challenges, I don't expect you to be one of those."

She leaned toward me as we left the administration building and entered the high school corridor.

"For most of these students, practically everything's come easily, but I know that's not true for you. What you don't know is, it didn't for me, either, despite how it might appear. That, I hope, will convince you to be honest with me. *N'est-ce pas?*"

I know my mouth fell open stupidly. She laughed again.

"Your uncle told me you knew some French."

"No, I don't. I mean, just some expressions I've read."

"Nevertheless, Mr. Denning will be excited to have you in his French class," she said.

We walked on.

Ava had to have called my father, maybe when we were in the beauty salon and I was too occupied to notice, and told him about my tiny exchange with Celisse.

Was every word I said at the house recorded? How would I be able to keep track of every little detail that came from my lips? I felt as if some power larger than us all had put a great magnifying glass over me.

When Dr. Stewart opened the classroom door, it was as if everyone inside froze; even the words in the air stopped dead. It was unexpected to see so beautiful a woman as Dr. Stewart command so much obvious fear. Now that I saw what I would call her power, the prospect of having heart-to-heart, honest talks with her was more daunting.

Daddy, Daddy, a little voice inside was crying, *what are you doing to me?*

Dr. Stewart introduced me to the class of nine, but from the looks on their faces, she didn't have to bother. *Karen,* I thought. Karen had probably been talking about me all day. Mr. Leshner gave me the textbook and I took my seat, left available for me, it turned out, to be next to Melina Forest. I turned to the chapter they were discussing, a chapter on China. It was all quite new to me. What if everything at this school was miles ahead of Hurley public school and even all that Mazy had taught? The first assumption about me could fall flat on its face. I wasn't as advanced as I thought and as Daddy had surely led everyone here to believe.

Melina gave me a big smile, and before Mr. Leshner could show me where we were in the textbook, she leaned over and turned mine to the right page. Dr. Stewart left, and Mr. Leshner continued the discussion as if I were merely a breeze passing through the classroom. However, when the bell rang, he stepped over to wish me luck and offer his personal services anytime I needed them.

"We'll get you caught up pretty quickly," he assured me.

When I stepped out of the classroom, Melina practically blocked anyone else from approaching me, not that the rest of them looked that excited to meet me. Had Karen described me as her poor, despondent relative?

"We're off to Introduction to French," Melina said. "You've got to tell me all about your last school. I know you came from California. I've been to Hollywood and Universal City. Did you ever see a movie star? Oh, let's go," she said before I could even start to answer. She took my left arm at the elbow, and we walked out.

A tall, at least six-foot-three-inch African American boy in a light-blue shirt and jeans stepped up beside us.

"Hey," he said to me.

"I haven't even formally introduced myself to her, Tommy."

"Well, let's get going," he said, smiling. "So we can talk about me."

For a moment, I thought he was serious, and then he laughed, and she elbowed him hard enough for him to cry out.

"I'm Melina Forest, and this egomaniac is Tommy Diamond."

"I'm Saffron," I said, mostly to him. So this was what Karen meant when she suggested some parents wouldn't be fond of their daughters going out with him. He was an African American. I couldn't help staring at him, because he had brown eyes with a bluish tint. His smile brought out the tint. He was lean, but he had impressive shoulders.

"Hi," he said. "Welcome to Cloud Nine."

When he put his hand out to shake mine, I saw how big his hands were.

"You're the basketball star," I said, recalling what Karen had told me.

"Just a member of the team," he replied. He had the most impish smile I had ever seen, especially when he looked at Melina.

"His middle name is Narcissus," she said. "Take it from there," she added, and he laughed.

"Believe everything she says," he told me. "She likes being brutally honest."

We all turned when we heard my name. Karen was hurrying to catch up.

She immediately moaned, "I could have been your big sister."

"You're a class behind, Karen, and you're not in AP," Melina said. "Your not realizing that simple and obvious fact is probably a good reason you're *not* in AP."

"Ha, ha. Hi, Tommy," she said.

He put up his hands. "I didn't do it," he said.

"What?"

"Whatever anyone told you I did," he said, and he and Melina laughed. I did, too.

Karen looked at me as if I had become best friends with the two of them in an instant. I shook my head.

"Did my mother choose that hairstyle for you?"

"She and the beautician. Do you like it?"

She grunted. "It's all right. I'll meet you outside at the end of the day," she told me. "My father is picking us up," she said, stressing the words *my father*, seemingly more for Tommy's benefit than mine.

We watched her trail off, attaching herself quickly to two other girls who surely wanted gossip.

"Are you positive you want to move here?" Melina asked, looking after Karen and her friends.

"I didn't have a choice," I replied.

Tommy's smiled faded. What had he already heard about my fictional past? How much did Karen embellish what she had been told?

Melina nodded. "Actually, few of us did," she said dryly. "*Allez, ma chère.* I'll tell you what to expect of Mr. Denning. By the end of the semester, you'll be speaking nothing but French in his class or else."

"See you later," Tommy said, turning. "I'm in AP Spanish."

"Because it's easier for you," Melina yelled after him. He held up his hand and kept going.

"And his mother's Spanish," Melina told me. "Minor detail he left out!" she shouted in Tommy's direction. He raised his hands but kept walking. She turned back to me.

"I'll be happy to study with you and catch you up, but have your aunt and uncle bring you to my house. Karen's not my favorite Saddlebrook. Oh," she said, stopping. She dug into her bag. "Here." She handed me a business card.

"What's this?"

"My card. Everyone has one. Your aunt will probably have some made for you."

"Card?"

It read "Melina Forest," with her address, phone number, and email.

"*Allez*," she said. "Mr. Denning gives demerits for lateness, ten a second."

I hurried to keep up with her long strides, clutching her card in my right hand, wondering even more where the train from Hurley had taken me.

CHAPTER SEVEN

Karen was waiting for me in front of the school, looking as if she had been waiting for hours, her arms crossed, her face full of huffs and puffs of impatience. Two of the girls from her class were standing beside her, all turning with similar expressions on their faces as I hurried along. Melina had kept me for a few minutes, explaining more about the school campus and describing the teachers I had yet to meet. She wasn't rushing to go home because she was staying to do some work in the library and watch Tommy in basketball practice. I pretty much concluded that they were really just good friends. She had invited me to join her, but I thought I'd better not do too much this first day. And I sensed how jealous Karen would be.

"I have to show my face at practice," she explained. "I'm his lucky charm. Not that he needs one. You'll see when you come to a game. Call me tonight if you have any questions. You have my number on my card."

I thanked her for helping me and started away. Two other girls in our class, Vikki Summers and Liona Wesley, had given me their cards as well. Even one of the boys, Bradley Kadinsky, gave me a card, too. Did everyone really have one? I wondered why Karen never mentioned having one or why Ava didn't mention that she would get one made for me. It couldn't be that she didn't know about them.

"Lucky for you that my father's never on time," Karen said as I approached. The girls with her smiled. "You'd have to walk home."

"Sorry. I couldn't help it. Melina had some more things to tell me, and some of the other students in the class wanted to give me their cards, like business cards. Do you have one, too?"

"No. If someone here doesn't know who I am, too bad," she said.

"Well, Melina told me—"

"Melina." Karen interrupted as if it was profanity. She raised her eyes toward the other two, who nodded. "She thinks she's student government president or something. She'll twist her ears over, telling you about herself. She'd keep the president waiting until she's finished."

The other two laughed.

"I was also on the other side of the building," I said.

Karen shrugged. I looked at her friends. I was about to introduce myself when Karen finally spoke up.

"This is Adele Scholefield and this is Margaret Toby, whose party you're going to Saturday night."

"Hi," I said. "Thanks for inviting me."

"Glad you're coming. New kids are always a headline," Margaret said.

"Believe me, I'd rather not be a headline."

Karen groaned, maybe afraid that I would dramatize my life the way she dramatized hers and become the center of attention.

"Karen says your mother died recently, and she was her father's sister," Adele said. There was a pause when I didn't say anything. "We're sorry," she said.

"Thank you."

I looked at Karen, wondering how much more she had told them. Did she explain why I had come here and why she never had known me? Other kids my age would have the most questions to ask, especially at a party, and that was only two days away. Daddy and I should talk about this, I thought, as well as about what he had told Dr. Stewart. The problem was, it was difficult for us to have private talks at the house.

"We'll see you at my party," Margaret said as a Mercedes sedan was pulling up.

"It's not too soon for you to party, is it?" Adele suddenly asked me.

"Yeah, maybe it's too soon," Karen said, and looked at me hopefully.

"Everything's too soon for me. One more thing won't matter," I said. I looked at Karen. "Besides, Karen wanted me to meet all her friends."

"Huh?" Karen said.

Her two friends laughed.

"Love your hairdo," Adele called.

"Me too," Margaret said. They shouted goodbye and hurried to the Mercedes. The moment they were too far to hear us, I turned to Karen.

"What else did you tell them about me?" I asked.

She shrugged. "What else could I tell them except your mother

died and you showed up unexpectedly? You don't share secrets yet."
Before I could respond, she cried, "There's my father!"

We watched *our* father drive up. Karen quickly got into the front
seat, and I got into the rear.

"Your hair's very nice, Saffron."

"Thank you . . . Uncle Derick."

"I should get my hair done for the party, too," Karen said.

"Talk to your mother. How was school?" Daddy asked me as he
started driving off.

"She only had two classes, Daddy," Karen answered for me.

He ignored her and waited for my response.

"It's great," I said. "How lucky everyone is to have a school like
this. It's beautiful, and the two teachers I met were very nice. So is Dr.
Stewart, who told me she gets to know every student," I emphasized.
He glanced at me quickly in the rearview mirror.

Karen turned to me and widened her eyes as if I had said something that betrayed her and every other student.

"Dr. Stewart is very nice?" she asked, her eyebrows raised.

"She was to me."

"Because you're new. Wait until you're here a week," she said, and
turned back around quickly.

"Don't discourage her, Karen. I'm glad to hear you had a good
start, Saffron," Daddy said, and started away. "Don't forget to
mention that to Ava's father, Amos Saddlebrook, when you see him
Sunday night."

"I told my grandfather that lots of times," Karen said.

"He never hears it enough," Daddy said.

"You'd better not just give him compliments to get him to like
you," Karen warned me. "Mommy says he has a built-in bullshit
detector."

"Karen. Watch your language."

"I'm sure she's heard worse, haven't you, Saffron?"

"And seen worse, too," I added, glaring back at her.

Her smile quickly faded. "Well, don't describe anything disgusting about where you've been and what you've done when you're with my friends at the party. They all gossip and exaggerate. It's like that game you told me about, right, Daddy?"

"It's known as telephone. A message is passed along through a group and usually is quite changed when the last one repeats it."

"Exactly. Especially things *you* might describe," Karen told me.

I might describe? I thought. *Oh, there is plenty to tell that you won't want to hear.* I caught Daddy's eyes in the rearview mirror. *Shut up* was written across them.

I looked away. To have to sit quietly and listen to Karen basically tell me to avoid talking to people about myself while Daddy sat silently was shredding my heart. Maybe he was thinking it was better to ignore Karen's snide remarks than to come to my defense. The more he did protect me, the more suspicious she would become. He and I would never stop tiptoeing on the thin ice.

"And what about you, Karen?" Daddy asked her, obviously eager to change the topic. "How was your day at school?"

"Pretty good. I got an eighty-five on my English test today," Karen said. "And I hardly studied for it."

"Really? Well, now that you have an AP student living with us, maybe she'll help you get a ninety-five," he said.

Karen's shoulders rose as if she had felt a chill run through her body.

"Right, Saffron?" Daddy asked, looking at me in the rearview mirror.

"We'll help each other, Uncle Derick," I said. "Going to school isn't just taking tests. There's a lot else to learn, and I'm sure Karen can teach it," I said, making it sound like what there was to learn was unspeakable and she was the expert when it came to any of that.

Karen spun around to look at me. Maybe she thought I was joking or making fun of her. I was, but the expression on my face was enough to convince her I wasn't. Ironically, she looked pleased.

"That's great," Daddy said. "You can help your mother shop for Saffron on Saturday. Mom might not be up on what's cool now and what isn't."

"Won't Saffron know that herself? She's from California. I'm from Sandburg Creek."

"Fashion wasn't at the top of my list," I muttered.

She looked at me suspiciously. "Still, you saw what other girls were wearing in school, didn't you?"

"Why look in the windows of jewelry stores if you can't afford any? You're just torturing yourself."

"Huh? What's that mean?"

Neither Daddy nor I answered.

She sighed deeply. "Oh, I'll go shopping with them. I need some new things," she whined. "Mother hasn't bought me anything new since my birthday."

"Well, lucky for you that Saffron needs some new things," Daddy said, and laughed.

I knew he was trying to be funny, but I couldn't even smile, watching and listening to him being so kind and loving to another daughter. I never wanted to face a crisis in which he had to choose between us. Karen would always come first. After all, I was only his niece.

Besides, when it came to him choosing me over his own happiness, my success record was not too good.

In a real sense, I felt trapped now that I was really here. I had to avoid serious conflicts with Karen at all cost, with anyone, for that matter, and I feared there were plenty of possibilities for conflicts here at this school for privileged kids. The more spoiled someone was, the less compassion she had for others. Karen was climbing to the top of that list every passing moment we were together, most likely out of jealousy and fear that I would steal whatever spotlight she lived in at this school.

Would I, could I, ever get to like her or get her to like me? Did I really want that?

"Yeah," Karen said. "You mean how fortunate for her that I'm here to help her get the right stuff," she said.

We were both waiting for Daddy to say something, but he just looked forward and drove. I had been hoping he'd turn to her and at least say something like *She's really far from lucky, Karen. She lost her mother and has had a very difficult time of it. We should all help her as best we can.* I longed for him to say something like that, but it was clear in the silence that he wouldn't. My orders were just as clear: stay away from bringing up my past because of the danger that I would confuse things. The safest option was to pretend I was just reborn here. I had no history beyond yesterday.

We drove in that uncomfortable silence all the remaining way. When we reached our street, Daddy slowed down to almost a crawl. I saw a police car in front of his house.

"What's that?" Karen asked. "Why are the police here?"

Daddy said nothing. We pulled into the garage. When we all got out, Daddy looked at me and spoke so low that he was practically only mouthing the words. "Don't say anything. I'll do the talking."

Ava called to us from the fancy living room the moment we had entered from the garage.

"In here," she said.

Karen looked at me with an impish smile. "Did you rob a store or something on the way here?"

"No," I said. "I robbed it here."

"Karen," Daddy said sharply, the worry written in capital letters all over his face. "Maybe you should go upstairs and start your schoolwork."

"After I say hello," she said defiantly. She was obviously very curious about why the police were here. "Mother doesn't like me dissing guests, you know. Besides, why didn't you tell Saffron to go up to her room, too?"

"Just behave your . . . selves," he said.

We entered the elegant living room. Ava was seated across from a policeman whose highly decorated uniform loudly announced he was the chief of police. He had his hat in his lap. His golden-brown hair was cropped military-short. To me, he looked quite young for a chief of police, maybe thirty. He had wide shoulders, but he was a bit chubby, with soft round cheeks nearly swallowing up his jawline. He stood up immediately and was clearly over six feet tall, with bright hazel eyes. I was sure that the mature and commanding look he sought was compromised by the freckles on the crests of his cheeks.

"Hello, Chief," my father said, and smiled.

"Mr. Anders. Karen," he said, nodding at her. "How's school?"

"Long," Karen replied, and he laughed.

Then he looked at me. "You must be Saffron, then."

"Yes, sir," I said.

"Chief Siegler was cruising our neighborhood when I came home," Ava said. "I invited him in for a cool drink. He wanted to see Garson, too."

"Going to be a big guy," Chief Siegler said.

"Once he gets those teeth," Daddy said. "Sit, Sam. Girls?" Daddy looked at us both. He looked very nervous, but maybe only to me.

"I'm going up to take a shower," Karen said. Fortunately, she was bored already.

"You might stay a while, Saffron," Ava said pointedly. "The chief was asking about you, how you were fitting in. It's better if you speak for yourself."

Karen grimaced.

More talk about me? Boring.

She left after looking at Ava and saying, "Nice to see you, Chief."

Daddy nodded at the sofa Ava was on, so I moved to it. Chief Siegler looked at Daddy and sat. Daddy didn't move. The chief turned to me.

"Everything working out all right for you? I know it's only been a little while, but I know how hard these things can be for kids your age, going to a new school, making new friends, and learning the ropes. And that's without the unfortunate circumstances that brought you here."

"Yes, sir," I said. "Everything is fine. It's a beautiful school."

"Quite a trip you took to get here?"

"Yes, it was."

"How was your flight?"

"It was my first, but I thought it was okay. I slept most of the way, even on the bus."

He nodded but looked keenly at Daddy, who smiled. Was it all going to collapse right now in front of Ava? Would the police chief ask me more detailed questions, like the name of the airline, or when exactly the flight left?

"She's an AP student, you know," Daddy said quickly. "She'll graduate early."

"No kidding? Did you fly out of LAX?" he asked. Before I could reply, he added, "My wife and I have always wanted to go to Los Angeles? You lived close to L.A.?"

"Yes," I said. I was glad he had said "Los Angeles." I didn't know where LAX was or what it was.

"You ever been to Hollywood?"

"No, sir."

He laughed. "It's like people in New York City who've never been to the Statue of Liberty."

"I've never been," Daddy said.

Ava looked sharply at him and at me.

"It's a big country and lots to see, especially for a hometown boy," the chief said. "The only time I left Sandburg Creek was to join the army. My wife and I are always talking about doing a cross-country trip, too. I hear a train might be fun," he added, looking at me. "You ever go on a train?"

For a moment, I thought the lie would choke me. I didn't try to swallow.

"No, sir. I never traveled anywhere, any way, for enjoyment," I said, trying not to sound surly.

"I see." He held his gaze on me for just a beat too long. I had to look away and then back at him. "Sure. I understand." He looked at Daddy. "Anything in particular you need for Saffron, Mr. Anders?"

Why would a police chief ask that? I wondered.

"We're okay. I think we've made a good start. As you said, Chief, a change, under her circumstances, is not easy, but she's doing fine. Proud of her."

"Glad to hear it. Well," he said, standing. "They got me checking out some potholes in the neighborhood. Someone on the street is quite persistent about it. I think you know who I mean."

"Shouldn't that go to the highway department?" Daddy asked suspiciously. He glanced at Ava, too.

Chief Siegler nodded. "You know how it is. Everyone looks to someone else. Everyone's too busy. Thanks again for the chat and the Coke, Mrs. Anders." He put on his hat.

"I'll walk you out," Daddy said. He looked at me with a bit of concern. I knew the warning in his eyes. *Don't offer up any information. Just answer questions directly.* It was the mantra that greeted me in the morning and that I feared would follow me forever here.

As soon as Daddy left with the police chief, Ava turned to me.

"And really, how is school so far? Did anyone give you any trouble? Any of Karen's so-called friends?"

"Oh, no. Just the opposite."

I described everything about my half day that I could. I told her how nice Dr. Stewart was and how a girl named Melina Forest had been assigned to help me adjust. I even brought up the business cards.

"A stupid affectation. I won't permit Karen to do that, nor will I allow you."

"Not anything I care about having, Aunt Ava."

I laughed to myself recalling how Karen had defended herself for not having one, claiming to be above all that, when the truth was, her mother wouldn't permit it.

"Good." She looked toward the front of the house. I could see out the window, too. Daddy was in an intense conversation with the chief. Of course, I knew exactly why. The question tormenting my stomach was what had the chief of police told Ava? As part of the fabrication Daddy had given her, the police supposedly had informed him I was on my way. Did Ava ask him, and did the chief deny that?

"You can go up and change, Saffron. Do you have much homework?"

"Yes. Melina Forest had my other textbooks from the earlier classes I missed and marked where the classes were up to in the books. She was quite helpful. I have a lot of catching up to do. Some of the subjects are brand-new for me."

"I'm sure you'll do just fine," she said, looking out the window at them again. I didn't think she had heard a word I said. Hopefully, she had not seen how much I had been trembling in expectation of her questions.

I quickly rose and went up to my room. Was all of this going to come to an abrupt end now? I went to my window and looked down to see the chief of police drive off. Then, feeling my insides still trembling, I sat on the bed and listened to every sound in the house, anticipating the roof falling in. Garson started to cry, and that was followed by footsteps on the stairs and in the hall. I waited, half expecting to hear Ava shouting. Another set of footsteps grew louder and closer. There was a knock on my door.

"Yes?"

Daddy slipped in, not opening the door fully.

"I know you're worried," he began, almost in a whisper. "He didn't give anything away."

"Are you sure?"

"Absolutely. His contract renewal is coming up. He played Ava well, looking out for me. He doesn't know why or anything; he just thought it was a good idea to go along with what I had told her happened. We're fine."

"Ava's not suspicious?"

"Not a bit," he said.

"I'm worried about going to this party, the questions. And this

Dr. Stewart. She wants to have a private get-to-know-you session. What did you tell her? What could she ask me?"

"I followed the notes I gave you to a T. You can elaborate on anything you want. Don't be nervous about any of it. Just do as I told you to do. Your story is always that you don't want to bring up troubling memories just yet. Just go with that and stick to the general facts in the notebook. Dr. Stewart will definitely not be a problem."

"You've been married a long time, and you're part of the family business, Daddy. Don't you think the truth might be better now?"

He drew closer, a cold look in his eyes. "Try to avoid calling me Daddy, Saffron. And no, it would, as I told you, be a disaster for us both."

He paused, waiting to see if I would say anything, and then he slipped out the way he had come in.

I let out a breath that seemed to have originated from the bowels of the earth and then began preparing for a shower and changing my clothes. As soon as I stepped into the shower and closed the curtain, I heard the bathroom door open and saw Karen come in wearing her bathrobe and sit on the closed toilet seat. She sat back and began filing her fingernails.

"What do you want?" I cried.

"Just take your shower," she said. "I'm not rushing downstairs to look after Garson because Celisse is leaving or to help with dinner."

I saw her stand up, turn, and undo her robe to look at herself in the mirror, running her palms over her developing breasts.

As soon as I stepped out, she turned to look at me. Not anyone but my mother and Daddy when I was little and Mazy ever saw me stark naked. I reached quickly for my towel, fearful that she would declare I wasn't as old as I claimed. If anything, however, it was just the opposite.

"You're so well developed already," she moaned. "Look at me. And you have the ass of a grown woman, too."

"Sometimes it all happens practically overnight," I said, putting on my robe after drying myself. "Don't obsess over it."

"Every other girl in my class is more developed than I am."

"Not Melina Forest."

"She's not in my class, and I don't compare myself to her for anything. She's from another planet."

She thought a moment, staring hard at me.

"What?"

"Do you masturbate? Adele thinks that makes you develop faster. Is that what you did?"

"You share everything with your friends, even stuff like that?"

"With best friends. That's what they're for. I told you about sharing our secrets before we became best friends." She paused and looked at me askance. "You sound like you never had even one?"

"I wasn't as trusting as you are," I said. "Even with the short time I was at school and the few girls I met, I wouldn't be so eager to do it now, either, after meeting some of those girls."

"Well, are you going to share secrets with me or not?" she asked, with her hands on her hips. She did look a lot like Ava, especially when her temper flared. In my heart of hearts, I wished she was practically a clone and my father just happened to be here.

"I have masturbated," I admitted. "But that's not why I've developed and continue to," I said. "It's a ridiculous idea. Probably some stupid thing on the internet. Some suckle on the internet like a baby on its mother's breast."

"What?"

She smiled. Her little rage calmed, and she followed me to my bedroom.

"Suckle on it?"

"That's how it seems," I said.

"You don't have to put on your old clothes," she said when I started to reach for the clothes I had brought with me. "Just wait. I'll get you something nicer."

"Thank you."

I smiled to myself, remembering Mazy telling me you get more with honey than with vinegar. About a minute later, she returned with a long-sleeved dark-blue sweater dress with rib-knit cuffs. She handed it to me, and I held it up.

"It's very nice. Thanks."

"I think I wore it twice since my mother bought it for me. I have clothes that still have tags on them," she confessed. "My mother forgets what she bought me."

"Really?"

I slipped on the dress and looked at myself.

"It fits you better because you're more filled out," she said in the tone of a moan. "Your mother must have been pretty. Don't you have any pictures of her?"

"I do," I said, and took out the envelope of pictures Daddy had given me.

She seized them like a starving animal and plopped onto my bed as she sifted through them.

"There's none recent?" she asked, looking up from the last one.

"We were both too busy to take pictures."

"Even on your phone?"

I looked down, playing on the ashamed bit.

"Remember, I said I never had a phone."

"I didn't believe it. Why not?"

"We had to budget our expenses, especially this past year."

She stared at me as if I had really just landed on earth.

"Oh," she said, looking like she had swallowed sour milk. She didn't even want to hear about people who were less fortunate. "Well, I'll ask Daddy to get you one. You need it," she said firmly, even angrily. "We have to stay in touch all the time."

"I guess," I said. "He did say he would."

"Well, I don't guess. We sneak texts in class. I'll show you how to hide your phone and put it on vibrate so you can feel a message without the teacher knowing."

She glanced at the pictures and then put them back in the envelope.

"Your mother was beautiful, just as I thought," she said.

"Yes, she was."

"How many boyfriends did she have after your father left?"

"I don't know exactly. Too many."

"You never liked any of them?"

"No."

"Any you hated more?"

I looked down. *I'm onstage*, I thought.

"What?"

"One was a little too interested in me."

Her eyes widened. "You'll tell me all about that, right?"

"What I can. It makes me sick to remember."

"I bet. Yes, when you can."

She looked so happy that I nearly laughed.

"I'm getting dressed for dinner. Afterward, we'll do homework together and talk. In my room," she added, like someone driving nails into the wall.

"Okay."

She marched out. I looked at myself in her dress again. *I'm sure it looks better on me*, I thought. *But I'm sure I should never let her know I think so.*

Almost as soon as I entered the dining room, Karen emphasized my need for a phone. "I know you said you were getting her one, Daddy, but make sure it's just like mine. It makes texting and exchanging photos easier."

He looked at her across the table, got up, and left the room.

"Derick, what the hell . . ." Ava called after him.

When she shouted, Garson moaned in his bassinet but didn't wake up.

A minute later, Daddy returned with a new phone in its box.

"I forgot I got it today. It's all set up, and it's just like yours, Karen," he said, and handed it to me.

"Let me see it," Karen demanded.

I took it out, glanced at it like someone who's never seen one, and handed it to her. She immediately began entering numbers.

"We'll do all that after dinner," Ava said. "You know how I feel about phones at the dinner table, here and especially at a restaurant."

Karen ignored her, finished what she was doing, and handed it back to me.

"You have my number and the other girls who are important," she said.

I looked at Ava, whose eyes were flaming, and put it quickly back in the box.

"Thank you, Uncle Derick," I said pointedly. He nodded.

"I swear," Ava said, shaking her head. "Sometimes I feel as if I'm all alone here."

No, I wanted to say. *That describes me, not you.*

Later, Ava calmed enough to give Karen and me compliments on our cleaning up after dinner. Karen worked hard and fast, looking forward to our retreating to her room. I knew I had to become quite creative quite quickly. I only hoped that the stories I was about to invent would be ones I wouldn't forget in a week and get caught having lied.

There was one clear realization that would never be a lie: the only truthful moments I'd spend in this house were the hours I slept.

Now I'd have to worry that I might talk in my sleep.

CHAPTER EIGHT

"My mother chose my bedroom furniture two years ago without me even knowing anything about it," Karen complained as soon as we entered her room. "She said she wanted to be sure it fit the house. I hate it. It's a wonder I can fall asleep in that bed. I hate bringing my friends up here, too."

I looked at it, amazed at what she was saying. It was a king-size cherry wood bed with a high headboard and plush, oversize pillows. The top of the mattress looked a good two and a half, three feet off the floor, with wide bedframe sides and a beautifully matching arched footboard. It looked like a bed for a queen. There were nightstands on both sides, the one on the right with a pinkish-white phone on it. The one on the left had a picture of Ava and my father and Karen when she was ten or eleven, standing between them and looking lost and uncomfortable. It looked like Ava had her hand on the back of Karen's neck, making sure she stood straight. I could almost hear her in the picture saying, *Posture, posture.*

There was a cherry wood dresser with three drawers. The mirror above the dresser was shaped exactly like her bed's headboard. To the right on entry, she had a large vanity table with drawers and a square mirror and a chair. On the left was her oversize computer desk, also in cherry wood. The door to her walk-in closet was to the right of that, and to the right on entry, directly across from the center of the bed, was the door to her en suite bathroom.

I would have to agree that the pictures of country scenes, lakes, and forests on the light-coffee walls and the artificial plants and other decorations were not what anyone would expect to find in a teenage girl's bedroom. Only her pictures of rock stars, bands, and handsome actors or models crowdedly displayed on her computer table suggested that someone younger than thirty slept here. Her pink pajama gown was neatly spread on the bedspread. Slippers were on a small step stool at the left of the bed. The room was quite large, however, at least twice the size of the room I was in and probably four times the size of the room I had at Mazy's house.

"My mother won't let me put anything on the walls. Daddy promises that when we move to the estate someday, I can choose my own furniture and redecorate my own room. Of course, the way Grandpa Amos is, that might not be until I'm in my twenties and maybe married myself. Well?" she said when I didn't confirm her complaints. "What do you think of my room or, I should say, my mother's idea of a room for me?"

I walked to the bed and sat on it.

"This is very comfortable."

"Oh, spare me," she said, rolling her eyes. "The room! It doesn't look like me!"

I nodded. "Not what I expected, I admit."

She looked more satisfied. "So what was your room like?"

I wasn't going to describe my room at Mazy's. That was really a girl's room and had more warmth. But I did remember a room description in a novel I had read last year.

"The last one, you mean? A quarter of this size, a single bed, not even a double. The tables beside it didn't match, and I didn't have a dresser. I had an old armoire and a small closet hardly wider than me. Most of my stuff was in cartons on the floor. Which was worn gray wood with no rugs. I think it must have been flooded once. It had that musty, moldy smell no matter what I sprayed," I added, thinking that was a good touch. "Oh, I had a mirror on the closet door, but it wasn't full-length. There was no desk like that," I said, nodding at her computer desk. "I did everything on my bed."

"Really? Ugh," she said. From the expression of disgust on her face, I might as well have told her I had just come from a bombed-out building. She quickly returned to herself. "Well, I still wish I could have picked out my own furniture, at least."

She sighed and then brought another chair over to her desk.

"I hate homework," she moaned, and sat. "Do you really like our school, or did you say that just to please my father?"

"The last school I was in had to be closed for a few days to kill rats."

"You're kidding?"

"Anyway, this school is beautiful to me, but I'm not sure how many friends I'll make," I said. She liked that. I sat on the other chair and put my books on the desk. "So what's really your favorite subject?"

She stared down at her books. I thought she was giving real thought to my question, but it was more like she didn't hear it.

"I really don't have that many real friends," she confessed. "What about you? I know you moved around, but I bet you made friends fast. It's hard to believe you didn't have a boyfriend, too. You're not exactly Miss Piggy, and now, the way my mother had your hair done . . . you'll need a fly swatter to keep their sticky little fingers off you. So?"

I could see that she wouldn't open a book or start a homework assignment until I told her more about myself.

"I did have sort of a best friend at the last school," I said.

This "almost a real revelation" brightened her eyes. It was almost real because I hadn't had enough time to become close friends with Lucy Wiley, who lived a few houses down from Mazy and me. Lucy had leukemia. I had no doubt that if there was enough time, we would have become best friends, and none of what I could make up would have been an exaggeration. Mazy told me that Lucy's death was the sort of thing that made her happy that she had become more of a hermit: "Once you get to know and care about someone, you add his or her suffering to your own, and your own is enough, in my opinion."

"Are you going to ask your friend to visit? I'll make sure my mother says it's all right. You want to call her? You have a phone now. Might as well use it. Call her now," Karen urged.

"I can't call her," I said.

"Why not? Oh, the time? But isn't she in California? I think the time is earlier."

"She's not there anymore."

"Well, where is she? Nearer?"

"She died," I said. The stab of fear those words put into her eyes nearly stopped me from talking about Lucy any more. I felt a little guilty using what really had happened to her to help lend credence to my fabrications.

"Died? What happened to her?" she asked, her voice breathless.

"She was sick, and she got sicker, and they found out she had leukemia."

"That's . . . I forgot what it is."

"It's cancer, Karen," I said. "She died shortly before my mother died and I had left."

I could almost see the sheet of white fear fall over her. For a few moments, she sat speechless, staring. I wondered if rich people thought less about death. All their money insulated them from confronting what was ugly and painful in this world, at least suggesting they were further from the grip of who Mazy called the Grim Reaper.

There was probably some truth to that. Even though I was quite protected in Mazy's world, homeschooled and confined for most of my life with her, I knew about the violence in the inner cities, the pain of the poor when it came to their health care. We watched it together on television. Mazy always had a personal story to add to what we had seen on the news, stories that had come from her years as a grade-school teacher.

"To the rich," she said bitterly once, "all this is just on television. They make sure their chauffeurs take detours."

After she had said it, she snapped out of her moment of anger and smiled at me. "But don't let that stop you from becoming rich," she said, and laughed.

Because of the death of a boy in high school who was in a car accident and Lucy's tragedy, I already had seen how strange, almost impossible, death seemed to young people. You couldn't reduce the pain by saying and thinking, *Oh, well he was ninety. He had a good life.* The boy and Lucy hadn't had that chance, that way of rationalizing the sorrow.

So Karen's reaction wasn't unusual. Even our story of my fictional mother's recent death didn't affect her like my telling her my best friend died. This was about someone our age. Death had managed to sneak in despite *it can't happen to me* thoughts.

"Couldn't they do anything to save her?" she asked.

"No, it was too late and very bad," I said. "I don't like talking about it," I quickly added. "It still gives me nightmares."

She nodded, nearly in tears herself.

"I'd rather think about the here and now and pretend I never existed before I arrived. I don't have that many good memories anyway, Karen. That's why I don't like talking about any of it."

"Right. Right," she repeated, her eyes brightening. "That's a good idea, actually. Let's pretend you always lived here. Don't worry. I won't let my idiot friends drive you mad with questions. They just want to be entertained and feel superior anyway."

"Thank you."

I was surprised at how honest she was about them. Did she mean herself as well? I smiled to myself. With a bodyguard like her, I'd probably be all right.

"Unless there's something you want to tell them, something that's important for everyone to know," she said on second thought.

"Unless there's something I want to tell? Right, but don't worry about it. I'll tell you first. For now, let me see where you are in math. I was good in math especially," I said, eager to move off the topic of my past. She looked just as eager, if not more so, to do the same now and showed me her math text.

For almost the next two hours, we worked on school assignments, and I started catching up in the history text. Every once in a while, she'd insert a story about this one or that at school, but I didn't keep her talking about any of them.

"We've got to concentrate," I'd remind her.

"You are like one of the teachers," she said, and said it so seriously I had to laugh.

"I mean it. You talk funny, too."

"Why funny?"

"It's just . . . you use words my friends don't use, even Melina Forest doesn't use. And you're very responsible. And so serious most of the time!" She thought deeply a moment. "It's like you grew up only with adults."

Was it that obvious? She didn't know me long. What did I have to do to change it? Imitate her? Her friends? I thought of what I had told Ava.

"It's because I read a lot, I guess."

"Yeah, maybe. I hate reading. I don't even read the backs of cereal boxes at breakfast. I don't like to read anything longer than a tweet."

I laughed just as her phone rang. It was Adele, eager to gossip, mostly, I thought, about me, but Karen cut her short. I could see it didn't please her girlfriend.

"I'll see you tomorrow," she said abruptly. "I said I'll see you tomorrow, Adele. I have to finish this homework," she added with her eyes on me. She ended the conversation without saying goodbye.

I pretended I wasn't listening.

"Sometimes my friends can be so immature," she said. Suddenly, she wanted to be grown-up, maybe in her mind as grown-up as I was. The irony was, I would rather switch places with her any day. To have a mother and father and live such a privileged life rather than the life I had would not be a hard choice to make.

Who really wanted to be forced to age beyond your years, to lose your youth so quickly, to seem like you had grown up with only adults anyway? More responsibility wasn't something to rush achieving, especially when it was responsibility that stole your innocence. Everyone my age, even younger, was in a hurry to get older. Mazy taught me that later, when you were responsible for yourself entirely, you would yearn for the days when "you breathed bubbles and heard only laughter."

Right now, someone else had to make sure you had enough to eat, enough clothes to stay warm, and a safe place to sleep. But I was inches away from having to do all that for myself and still might be. Karen could go to sleep dreaming of lollipops. I had to first shut away the nightmares, the main one being Ava coming to my room in the middle of the night and saying, *I know who you really are.*

"When you want to, you can tell me more about your mother," Karen said with a lot more softness in her voice than anything she had said up to now. "I can't imagine all the pain and sadness you've endured."

She said "endured" like a terrible actor in a soap opera. She was trying to impress me with how well she could understand. Could she ever understand being left at a train station at night when you were only eight? Being taken away by a strange elderly lady and practically imprisoned in her house? I doubted she could even imagine it happening to her. I was jealous of how protected and spoiled she had been all her life. And yet something deeper inside me wanted me to be different, to hold on to what was true about myself.

"Yes, I'll tell you more when I can," I agreed. "It just takes time." I recalled Mazy telling me that time was the only real cure for anything sad or painful.

She nodded. I paused. Were those actual tears in her eyes? Maybe I was missing something here by being so judgmental. It suddenly occurred to me that Karen was emotionally much younger than I was assuming she was. She wasn't spoiled as much as she was frightened. What had she seen? What had she heard? For a moment, I sat there realizing that from the little Daddy had told me, Karen's early life might not have been that great. It sounded like she and her mother, mostly she, were walled into the Saddlebrook estate until Daddy had finally married Ava and they had their own home. What had he done to win over Amos Saddlebrook, or was that his problem and the only reason he remained with my mother and me for Karen's early years? It took him that long to get Amos Saddlebrook to accept him as the father of his granddaughter.

Ironically, perhaps, there was almost as much to learn about Karen and her life as there was for her to learn about mine. We both lived under the umbrella of a grandparent, but the big difference, of course, was that she hadn't lost her mother. I had.

"Your watch looks pretty old for someone your age," she suddenly said. "It looks like one of my grandmother's."

"Actually, it was someone's grandmother's. My mother got it for me at a pawn shop for my birthday."

"Really? She had to go to a pawn shop to buy you a birthday watch?"

"It was what it was," I said. "Every dollar was important to us."

She stared, thinking, and then burst into a smile.

"I have a few watches. I have very nice earrings and a few nice bracelets and necklaces. Sometimes when my father went on a trip, he brought something back for me. He doesn't do that much traveling anymore, but he still buys me something from time to time, even though my mother says he's spoiling me. Come look."

She went to her jewelry box on the small marble-topped table just outside the door to her en suite bathroom.

"Take a look," she urged.

I rose and peered into the drawer. The drawer had a black velvet bottom, so all the jewelry was highlighted.

"That is a lot."

"Some of it was my grandmother Saddlebrook's, but my grandfather doesn't want me wearing those things until I'm older. He's a bit of a fossil."

"What?"

"Old-fashioned that way. To tell you the truth, a lot of this is old-lady-like anyway."

"Why didn't he give those things to your mother first?"

"I don't know. She and him fight over him spoiling me, too."

"He," I said.

"What?"

"Not 'him,' subject pronoun 'he.' She and he."

"Oh, brother. I do have a teacher living with me now," she moaned, and then smiled. "I'd like to see you do that to my mother one of these days. She thinks she's so perfect, you know. She hates being corrected about anything."

"Being afraid of being corrected is a sure sign of insecurity," I said.

"Huh?" Karen shook her head as if she had water in her ears. She stared and thought. "Better not talk too much with my friends for a while."

"What? Why?"

"They'll think you're a spy or something. Here," she said, handing me a pair of emerald earrings. "You haven't had your ears pierced, so I can't loan you any of the others. These are the only ones that clip on. I don't wear them at all anymore. Take them," she insisted.

"Thank you."

"That was a big fight, by the way," she said, returning to our work on her computer desk.

"What was?"

"When my father let me get my ears pierced. He had taken me to the mall to get some shoe boots I wanted, and I begged him to let me do it. When we got home and my mother saw, she had what Grandpa Amos calls one of her shit fits. She didn't talk to my father for days.

"Hey," she suddenly said, "you should ask him to take you to do it. Then I could share more, or maybe he'd buy you a pair of your own."

"I think I had better wait a few more days before I'm the cause of a fight between your parents," I said.

"There," she pounced, poking her right forefinger at me. "Only a teacher would say something like that."

The shocked expression on my face made her laugh.

Whatever it was, it broke the wall of distrust she had thrown up between us. She said she was even willing, when we had time, to read me some of her diary. She claimed she had begun it when she was only seven.

That, I thought, I did want very much to hear.

Reluctantly, especially for her, instead we finished our homework, and I went to my room to catch up some more in the history text before going to sleep. I heard Garson crying and Ava complaining. Whatever Daddy said was mumbled, and then it grew quiet.

The next day at school, Karen was around me as much as Melina Forest, but I thought it was more to flirt with Tommy Diamond, who, according to Melina in a whisper, looked to be flirting more with me. Was I oblivious to it because I had so little experience with boys? Karen said nothing about it, maybe because she was so intent on flirting with him herself.

On Saturday, Ava was quite surprised at how eager and excited Karen was to help buy me some "desperately needed" clothing and something nice to wear to the party.

"I can help her choose what girls in our school favor, Mother. We can't let her look stupid."

From the look on Ava's face, however, I wasn't sure she was all that happy about it. I knew she had been hoping I would be that "teacher" when it came to Karen, that I'd have more influence on her than she had on me. The irony wasn't lost on me. I, the girl who was confined and had almost nothing to do with real-world experiences, was seen to be the wiser one.

I couldn't come out and say it directly, but I wasn't here to save anyone besides myself. At least, that was what I had thought when I arrived. I believed the part Daddy had cast me in was exhausting and fraught with danger enough. My relationship with Karen, who was really my half sister, was delicate, even without all the true details revealed. There were so many undercurrents crossing beneath us, driven by her early childhood history and my own. Having the same father meant their merging seemed inevitable, a crashing of ocean waves driven by winds coming from opposite directions. Despite Daddy's confidence, I knew deep in my heart that this imaginary world he had created for me would eventually collapse into itself. In the end, I would find myself standing outside our front door again, only this time it would close sharply and with a finality that clearly sent me off into a new world of darkness.

These thoughts lay silently but constantly behind every word I spoke, everything I did in this house, and everything that was done to and for me. It was probably no different from having a persistent headache like Garson's persistent teething. Ava surely saw the stress in my face but for now blamed it on my difficult early life. I had no doubt that eventually, because she and Daddy were providing so much for me, she would begin to wonder if there wasn't more.

Celisse had arrived to take care of Garson, but Daddy didn't come along with us to shop for me. I recalled how much he hated shopping and how Mama would accuse him of rushing us so much that we always forgot something important. A few times, he did have to go back for something, mumbling and complaining like a madman out the door. Nothing, however, had prepared me for the shopping Ava would do. Karen wore a smug smile on her face, because she knew exactly how her mother would behave once we entered the mall and walked into the more high-end department store. Ava attacked the search for my wardrobe from the feet up.

Once a size was established, be it for shoes or jeans, she had to choose a half dozen of this or a half dozen of that. When I showed some amazement at the quantity, she let it be known in no uncertain terms that she didn't intend to be shopping for me or even for Karen that often. She always claimed to have better things to do with her time, whatever that was. Eventually, I learned it had a lot to do with her father's business empire here and, of course, whatever time she had to devote to her baby.

The one thing I did appreciate at the department store was her turning to me to make the choices of colors or styles. But I wasn't confident about it, and I didn't want to make fashion mistakes in front of Ava. I looked to Karen, who eagerly jumped in to help. She ended up with two new pairs of shoes, two new pairs of jeans, three new blouses, and, on the way out, another pair of earrings. Ava insisted on buying my winter coat as well. The prices of everything practically made me stutter. Mazy would have been quite shocked. I tried to keep track of it all and lost count somewhere after three thousand dollars.

I was suspicious of Karen's choice of jeans and blouse for the party. The skinny-jeans style seemed too tight, and the blouse as well, but Ava didn't voice any objections. In fact, once we chose the color of the blouse, she plucked a jean jacket off the rack and tossed it at me to try on. Karen complained that hers was getting ratty, so she bought her one, too.

Because there was now so much for the two of us, most was to be delivered, but, arms loaded, Karen and I headed for the exit behind Ava. The driver hurried to pack everything, and we were on our way home. Looking at my watch, I realized we had shopped for over four hours. Mazy wouldn't last more than a half hour at most, and Daddy ten minutes.

Once home, Karen threw her things, still in boxes, into her room and came to mine to help me unpack, hang, and fold the clothes I had carried. I suspect because it was Ava Saddlebrook buying, the complete order was delivered less than a half hour after we had arrived.

"I'm glad I have something new to wear tonight," Karen said. "When I was with you yesterday at school, did you see how much Tommy paid attention to me? He's flirted with me before," she claimed. "But Melina gets in the way all the time. Guess what, though?"

"What?"

"Tommy's invited tonight, but Melina isn't. I'm going to look extra special." She fluffed her hair, looking in the mirror, and then looked at me.

"What do you know about makeup?" she asked me.

"Very little," I said. I thought for a moment. "I don't even have lipstick."

"I noticed. Well, what do you think we're going to do between now and leaving for the party? Homework?"

"No. What?"

"We'll do your face," she decided. "Makeup done well will highlight all your good features. Any cousin of mine has got to look as good as I will. Attaching yourself to something or someone ugly and blah will affect how people view you. My mother's exact words. So? Ready?"

I had to confess to myself, I was excited about doing something like this with her. Cousin? Maybe, just maybe, we could become sisters without her realizing it.

"Come on," she said. "To my room."

I thought she was even more excited about it than I was, and it was my face.

"Everything I know my mother taught me," she announced as she pulled out the chair at her vanity table. "And you can see how pretty and put together my mother always is. I helped Adele with her makeup, too. Her mother is sort of . . . plain and disinterested in fashion. Adele is always moaning about it and wishing she was my sister instead of my friend. But a lot of girls at school do."

She opened a makeup kit. I knew she was imitating Ava when she spoke now. She had that same arrogance in her tone.

She put her hands on my shoulders and looked at me in the mirror.

"You have a pretty nice complexion, but it's a little dull."

"Dull?"

"We'll start with this," she said, opening a jar. She plucked a small brush out of the kit and began applying the slightly tinted cream. "We call it foundation," she said, as if she belonged to a special species of female "we." She brushed it on. "I'm going to use this bronzer," she said when she was finished doing that. "My mother says it adds warmth." She did, and then she stood back as if she really was a makeup artist. "Let's put a little blush on your cheeks."

"Isn't it too much?"

"It's nothing yet," she said. "And then let's get some eye shadow, just a single shadow across your eyelid."

I squirmed when she did this.

"It's good. Stop being so nervous," she said.

"What's that now?" I asked when she picked up a pencil.

"Wait a minute," she said, finally realizing my reactions. "You act like you've never done this for sure or seen it done. Didn't your mother wear makeup?"

"Yes, but I never paid attention to it, and she didn't want me to wear any yet."

"Why not?"

I was silent, thinking. Mazy never even thought to mention it.

"She wanted me to stay a little girl forever," I offered, and waited while she digested the thought.

"Oh. Well, maybe because of the way you lived . . ." She shrugged. "Let's see how some lip liner works. Watch me, and then do it yourself."

I did.

"That's good," she said.

She displayed an array of lipsticks.

"This one goes well with the lip liner," she said, choosing a bright ruby tint. "Try it. We'll wipe it off if it's too much."

I started, and she seized my wrist.

"Don't dab it on like that. It won't be even. And you'll miss the corners."

I followed her instructions and demonstration, and then we both studied my face.

"I think I'm pretty good," she declared. She grabbed my hand to pull me up. "Let's go show my mother."

She practically tugged me through the hallway to the stairs. We could hear Celisse singing to Garson in his cradle. Ava was in the formal living room by herself, sipping a martini and just staring at the wall like someone in deep thought. I wondered where my father was.

"Mother, look at Saffron. I just made up her face," Karen declared.

Ava turned slowly, looked, and then nearly burst blood vessels in her eyes.

"She looks like a clown. That's all too heavy, and that's definitely the wrong shade of lipstick. Are you an idiot? Get that off your face immediately," she ordered me. "Or I won't let either of you out of this house."

"I thought it looked good," Karen moaned.

Ava smiled coolly. "Did you? Go on," she told me. "You don't need more than the right lipstick, Saffron. I'll bring you the tube after you're dressed."

"But . . . she can use what I have," Karen said. Apparently, her mother giving me something of her own disturbed her.

Ava turned away. The conversation was apparently over.

"Where's Daddy?" Karen demanded, obviously hoping he would contradict Ava's orders.

She turned slowly again, that same cool smile. "He's been summoned to Saddlebrook," she said. "The king calls. Don't forget, we're all going to dinner there tomorrow night, so don't sleep late tomorrow. I want your homework done by early afternoon. Well," she said, turning again to me. "Go wash your face. You look ridiculous."

I turned and hurried away, Karen walking slowly behind me, mumbling how wrong her mother was and how good I looked.

But all I could think about was Daddy being summoned to Saddlebrook soon after the police chief was here. Surely the chief was more indebted to Amos Saddlebrook than to Daddy.

Once again, I wondered, was all this about to explode?

But in a strange, almost self-destructive way, I secretly hoped it would, no matter what the outcome. Being someone else was truly exhausting.

CHAPTER NINE

Sulking, Karen went to her room and remained there with her door shut tightly until it was nearly time for us to go to the party. I was afraid to knock. One look at her after Ava's tirade, and I knew she was casting most of the blame on me. With her being so bitter now, I wondered if I even should attend the party to meet her friends. If anyone gave me a compliment, I expected she would complain about her mother, claiming she could have done more for me. I could easily see her turn to me and say, *You should have said you wanted to look like I helped you to look. I felt like such an idiot after spending so much of my time on you.*

Eyes would widen and turn to me, and even though they might not come right out and say it, they would blame Karen's bitterness on me. I was already inciting discord in the community's most perfect family. Her doting friends would have it written large on their faces: *When you bring someone who is practically a stranger into your house, and your mother seems more protective and concerned for her than for you, trouble surely is starting, like mold behind a wall.*

Just before my grandmother Mazy had died and I had begun public school, I experienced what it was like to be singled out and held responsible for something really terrible, which in this case was the death of a boy in a car accident. I supposedly had put a curse on him, done something "witchy" that Mazy had taught me how to do. When your classmates isolate you, whisper about you behind your back, and follow you every moment with eyes of accusation, you're lonelier than someone alone on the moon. I saw how that could easily happen to me here. Karen was the Saddlebrook. If she breathed fire in my direction, I'd have to walk through fire at home and practically anywhere else in this community, especially the school. Why would anyone side with me?

Of course, this was a precarious way to begin the journey through a new life anyway. This would be the first party with kids my age and hers that I had ever attended. I was unsure of myself as it was, not only worrying that I might say something to contradict the story Daddy and I, reluctantly, had concocted but also worrying that anyone who looked or listened to me would realize how long I had been isolated and how limited my contact with kids my age had been. Everyone at this party would surround me and likely rain down a storm of pelting questions. I was under some suspicion as it was, simply by being someone new, especially with the background they believed I had. Should I act very shy or simply troubled and sad? I could get away with that. After all, as far as Karen's friends knew, I had recently lost my mother and came here out of desperation.

From the first day here, Daddy had given me advice that was really a map to how to safely lie. "When you're asked a question, ask yourself the same question before you answer. I find that to be a very helpful technique."

But how was I going to do that at a party where everyone would be interested in the new girl? Even if I repeated the questions in my head, that would not guarantee a safe response. And my hesitation would surely telegraph that I had something terrible to hide. Maybe I needed more time to emerge slowly, like some creature crawling out of a cocoon, in this case a cocoon not of my own making, I thought. Was this party worth the risk? I could go to Ava and say I was feeling too sad to go to a party after all. Her answer could be, *In that case, getting your mind off it might be the best way to help yourself.* How hard could I protest?

I did want to do here what I had failed to do back at Hurley, make friends, be invited to parties, and enjoy hanging out with girls my age. The conflicts inside me felt like they were tugging on both sides of my heart. Leap in and become the teenager I used to dream about being from the window of Mazy's house, or withdraw like some creature and bury myself in sadness? I wanted to do the former very much.

But Karen had pounced on me the first day for not knowing who Ed Sheeran was. What other faux pas would I commit? What other questions would I stir up with my vague replies? I could easily find myself once again the big topic in a school. I'd even be more dependent on Karen than I was now, and she wasn't exactly worried about my happiness at the moment. Her promise to be my ally seemed thin and forgotten, a bubble Ava had popped with a single harsh breath.

It was as if sibling rivalry had found its way through a keyhole into this house, even though Ava and Karen did not know it could exist because they didn't know who I really was. But right now, Karen was suffering just as any sister might. How was I supposed to blend into this family if Ava continued to use me as a tool to teach Karen? I practically could feel Karen's gloom across the hall and through the walls. She was probably wishing I had never appeared.

Certainly, now there would be none of the preparation Karen had promised, the social chatter and rundown of the girls and boys I'd meet. What if I liked someone she hated, or vice versa? All this walking on thin ice was already churning me up inside. If I was ever concerned about being a stranger in a strange land, I was surely that now. But before I could plan something, Ava came bursting into my room with a tube of lipstick as she had promised, holding it up like the torch held by the Statue of Liberty.

"Here. This is the proper lipstick for your complexion, your hair, and what you're going to wear."

I took it and thanked her.

"Now, let me see your new phone," she demanded.

I hurriedly gave it to her. What did she expect to find? I had yet to use it. Was she going to take it back? Had Karen said something about me calling someone nefarious from back home? How could I continue in this house, sitting on a time bomb, anticipating disaster with every new look and every new word? I actually glanced at the door, thinking that any moment I might just run out of this house and this world. I wouldn't even say goodbye to the father who had not said goodbye to me.

Ava pressed some numbers and letters and then handed it to me.

"My number is now in your phone under Aunt Ava. Your uncle will be taking you and Karen to the party," she said. "I'm telling Karen that you'll both be picked up at eleven thirty. If something disturbs you, don't hesitate to call me, even if Karen disapproves."

Disturbs me? Even if Karen disapproves? Was she appointing me as someone to spy on her daughter?

"What would disturb me?"

She ignored me, looked at her watch, and then changed her expression completely from concern to annoyance when she looked at me again.

"What are you doing? You should have started to dress. I specifically bought you what you wanted for tonight, but you don't simply throw everything on. I bet you haven't even cut off the tags. On more than one occasion, Karen left home for an event with tags still dangling from her new clothes and embarrassed me."

"I'll make sure they're off," I said, almost too low for her to hear.

"You don't sound too grateful about it. Don't you want to go to this party?"

"I don't know anyone well enough yet to party with her or him, so I'm nervous."

"Really?" She shook her head. "Yes, I believe you. Something is really missing in this generation, especially when it comes to socializing. Having a conversation without a phone between you and someone is almost like being in a foreign country where no one speaks your language."

"I didn't have a phone before now," I reminded her. "I never had a personal cell phone."

"I know. I was thinking how odd that is, especially since you were on your own so often."

"It's not odd. It was expensive for us, and I wasn't into gossiping and small talk."

"Um," she said, still looking suspicious. "Your mother was a little too aloof, perhaps."

"She wasn't aloof, Aunt Ava. She was overwhelmed. This is not an easy world for a woman alone, especially one with a child."

She stared at me, her eyes shifting from annoyance and anger to a softer, more sympathetic look. It occurred to me instantly that at one time, for years, in fact, she was the same sort of woman. The difference between her and my fictional mother, of course, was money. Perhaps that didn't make it all right after all. Maybe it never did. Could I ask? Would I dare? Daddy would surely be very upset.

"Well, still, how do you expect you will make new friends if you don't socialize? Karen thinks she's a social butterfly, Miss Sandburg Creek. Just float alongside her and try not to drown in her ego. However, try to be a little more particular about those you choose to confide in than Karen is. And don't let Karen's judgment sway your own about what to do or whom to like. Her judgment about people isn't exactly stellar, unfortunately."

It was on the tip of my tongue again to ask why she was so critical of her own daughter. What else should I know? But I didn't have the courage, and maybe Ava's telling me those things would only drive a wider wedge between Karen and me.

"Considering what you've been through these last few days, being bubbly, chatty, and silly might make you uncomfortable, I know. It's understandable, but I don't want to discourage you from going. Distraction is sometimes the best cure for unhappiness. It doesn't cure it, but it puts it on a back shelf for a while."

Just what I had anticipated her saying, I thought.

"Okay," I said.

I could see that prolonging this conversation only skirted the border of Daddy's and my deception. I shouldn't have told her I never had a phone. What teenager didn't? Even poor people in India, the Middle East, and Africa managed to have cell phones. I could have simply forgotten it in my haste to leave or accidentally left it on the plane or the bus. But I certainly didn't want to keep talking about it and my fictionalized past. Right now, fortunately, she was more interested in fashion and appearance than truth.

"Go look in the mirror and put on the lipstick. I want to see if I chose right for you."

I did it exactly the way Karen had instructed and then faced Ava. She nodded.

"I was right. Put it in your purse," she said.

I hesitated

"What? You don't like how you look?"

"No, I like it. I . . ."

"What?"

"Really don't have a proper purse to take to a party."

"Why didn't you mention that when we went shopping?"

"I didn't think of it. Sorry."

She sighed deeply. "Follow me. I'll give you one of my own," she said. "Well. Come along. I have other things to do," she snapped from the doorway.

I hurried to follow her. Celisse was still here with Garson downstairs. I could hear her singing something in French to him. We walked past Karen's closed door and into Ava and my father's bedroom. It was my first time seeing it, and the perfection in the decor was almost breathtaking.

The Victorian-style king-size bed had an upholstered headboard with a blue tufted look in the pink frame. There was the same tufted design on each side of the bed, framed and set in the wall. The large area rug matched the designs on the comforter and the blue bench at the foot of the bed, along with the nightstands that coordinated with the bedframe and the dresser, framed mirror, and curtains at the large window to the right. One of the nightstands had been moved to make room for Garson's cradle, which was also the same color blue. I wondered if that was Ava's side of the bed or Daddy's. Somehow I believed that he would have to be the one to get up in the middle of the night and not her.

"Your room is beautiful," I said.

"I designed it myself. Your uncle is like all men, color-blind when it comes to furniture."

Yes, he told me what you thought of his taste, I thought. I vaguely remembered my mother saying something like that about Daddy. She believed that everything would be stark, white, ghostlike to him.

"It all seems brand-new, not even used once," I said, thinking of their formal living room. I thought it wasn't an obsession with cleanliness so much as it was with perfection. I never recalled this being so important to Daddy. It was almost a military dedication to Ava and how her house would be viewed. I suspected it might have something to do with what her father would think. So many currents of emotion and rage ran under the floors of this family home.

Careful, Saffron, I thought, *or you'll be swept away.*

There was a nook on the right that encompassed the large vanity table, which boasted shelves neatly stocked with what looked like anything and everything a woman would desire for her hair and makeup. All of it lined up perfectly. The chair was the same light blue. To the right of the nook was a door that I could see opened to a marble floor and counter in the large bathroom.

"Let's get what you need."

Ava turned left to the practically wall-to-wall walk-in closet. I followed slowly, not sure she wanted me to go in with her. At the door, I nearly gasped aloud at all the clothes and the shelves of shoes. It looked like enough to be a store's inventory. At the end of the closet, there was another full-length mirror, table, and chair. The closet ceiling had a skylight, and the same dark-brown wood floor ran the length of the closet. She plucked a purse off a shelf and handed it to me.

"I don't think I've used it more than twice," she said.

"It looks quite expensive."

"It isn't. It's a little overstated, but it will complement what you're wearing," she said. The denim blue purse had a knitted top handle and shiny rhinestones. "These are called butterfly buckled flaps, easy to close and open, so keep your eye on it. You can put your phone and wallet inside and . . ."

"My wallet is kind of . . ."

"What?"

"Manly and beat-up," I said. "My real father left it behind but with nothing in it."

It had been Mazy's father's wallet, actually.

"Your mother never bought you a wallet of your own?"

I didn't answer. Another drop of suspicion trickled out of her eyes like invisible tears.

She sighed. "You sound more like you were a homeless person. You have to speak up when we're shopping and you need things," she said in a tone suggesting I was exhausting her with my needs. Her expression grew stern again. "I know you've been here only a short time, but you're part of the Saddlebrook family now. Despite Karen's disinterest from time to time in her appearance, we do not look raggedy and disheveled, especially in public. People here actually look to me to make decisions about their own fashions and other important things. Presentation is at least half of the impression you will make, on strangers especially. I don't know why your generation is so unaware of that."

She paused, aware of how harshly she was lecturing me. I was a little terrified. Someday she surely would tear the wrapping off the fictional life Daddy had created for me.

Her face softened. "I realize all this was not a priority for you and your mother."

"No. Our priority was more like survival," I said, maybe too sharply, but I didn't like standing in a pool of purple fear. Almost every other minute since I had arrived, I wanted to run.

Her eyes seemed to snap with ire and fury at my defiance. They calmed slowly like the flames on a stove being gradually reduced and turned off.

"Well, thankfully, that no longer need be your priority here," she said. "Your uncle should have made that clearer to you. You'll realize it all soon enough," she said softly. "I hope."

"What are you giving her now?" we heard.

I turned to see Karen in the bedroom doorway, her hands on her hips.

"Why didn't you see that she had a proper purse?" Ava demanded.

"Well, I didn't check through everything she brought," Karen whined. "And she didn't tell me. How was I supposed to know?"

"You make it your business to know. You're presenting your cousin to your friends. She's part of your family now," Ava reminded her, and then reached down to produce a zippy wallet.

"That's one of your Louis Vuittons!" Karen cried. I looked from her amazed expression to Ava. I didn't know exactly who Louis Vuitton was, but from the tone of her voice, I knew it was something very expensive.

"Well, make sure she doesn't lose it, Karen."

Karen stood there with her mouth still open. I took the wallet and put it in the bag.

"I don't even have something that expensive," Karen moaned.

I felt like I should suggest I'd give this one to her and take one of hers.

"You just get what you need and put it in that wallet," Ava ordered me.

"I don't see why the lipstick you gave her is so much better," Karen said, folding her arms under her breasts.

"I know you don't," Ava said sadly. "Despite everything I've taught you." She turned to me. "Go on. Do what I said. Get your things. Your uncle is waiting for the two of you downstairs in the den. Your curfew is eleven thirty, Karen."

I hurried out, smiling at Karen, who was still glaring at her mother. In my room, I transferred money and my ID from Mazy's father's old wallet to my beautiful new one and zipped it closed. I put it in the purse along with my new phone, dressed, and put on my new jean jacket. Then I took one last look at myself with the purse off my shoulder. My appearance did excite me. I hurried out. Karen silently joined me on the stairs. At the foot of them, she turned.

"When we get there, I'll introduce you to the ones I think you should talk to. Don't start talking to anyone unless I've introduced you, especially any of the boys, no matter how they look or smile at you. I'll try to be at your side as much as possible."

I couldn't laugh at her tone of superiority. Maybe I wouldn't recognize the dangers. I had so little experience with boys, and yet something inside told me Mazy had shaped my instincts well, so well that they were much better than Karen's.

"Thank you. You look very nice," I said.

She grunted. "Not as nice as my mother thinks you look. DADDY!" she screamed, squeezing her hands into fists at her sides and closing her eyes with the effort. "WE'RE READY TO GO."

My father came up the hallway. He appeared tired, even a little shaken, more like how he was the night I had arrived.

"You guys look great," he said. "Remember, no—"

"Drugs or alcohol," Karen recited. "We're the Saddlebrooks. We can't be seen doing human things."

"Your name is Anders, not Saddlebrook," Daddy told her sharply. He glanced at me, looking like he was afraid I might say something about my name.

"Yeah, well, I know that, Daddy. You need to remind Mommy," she said, and turned to go out to the garage.

Daddy stepped closer to me. "You really do look nice, Saffron. But you'd better keep your eye on her," he warned.

He started toward the garage.

Why was I suddenly the adult in the room? I thought. A whole new list of responsibilities and things for which I could be blamed rolled out ahead of me. I got into the rear of the car. I wondered if I would ever sit up front with my father again if Karen was with us. I was always to be the girl in the back, the unfortunate relative searching for crumbs of love and kindness.

"What did you do at Grandpa's so long?" Karen asked him as we drove out of the garage. She could so easily sound like her mother, demanding answers, not asking questions.

He looked at her, surprised. "Business," Daddy said. "Why?"

"Didn't he want to know about Saffron? Isn't that why he summoned you?"

"Summoned me?"

"That's how Mommy says it. So?"

"Of course he wanted to know about your cousin. Tomorrow night's dinner is going to be special," he added. "To help make her feel like part of the family. Don't forget about it."

"How could I? Mother will probably be kneeling beside my bed tonight while I'm sleeping and whispering in my ear how I should behave and dress."

There was a long moment of silence, and then Daddy laughed and laughed, hard. Karen turned back to me, revealing how surprised she was at his reaction. I had no idea why he was laughing. He was behaving as if he had drunk too much alcohol or something. Maybe my going to this party was making him more nervous than it was making me. Or perhaps there had been a great deal more to his meeting with Amos Saddlebrook concerning me.

I smiled back at Karen, but inside I was really shaking as we continued on. This party would be a bigger test than my going to a new school. There would be eyes on me the way there were at school, but there would be no respite, no bells ringing to break up the day and give me a chance to recuperate and review some of the things I had said. It was funny how I thought, maybe feared, that kids my own age would see through all the fabrication faster and more easily than Ava or Dr. Stewart. My hope was that most of Karen's friends would be like Karen . . . more interested in themselves.

If that was true, I'd be safe.

As soon as Daddy slowed down and turned, I knew this was going to be quite the special place. All the houses on this street in this part of Sandburg Creek were quite big, with most having private gates. We paused at the entrance to the driveway of one, and the gate, as though it had eyes, began to open.

"Margaret Toby's father is president of the Sandburg National Bank," Karen told me. "They're even snobbier than we are."

"We're not snobby, Karen," Daddy said. "We're just . . ."

"Snobby," she insisted.

Another car had just parked, and Tommy Diamond and a

slightly shorter but much stouter boy, with hair down to the base of his neck that was so blond it gleamed in the front lights, stepped out and started toward the front entrance. As soon as Daddy stopped, Karen opened her door and shouted to them. She slammed the door behind her.

"Hey!" Daddy shouted. "Wait for your cousin, Karen."

"Hurry up!" she shouted back at me.

I opened the door.

"What happened at Mr. Saddlebrook's? Did the chief of police tell him anything?" I quickly asked.

"No. Everyone believes everything we've told them. The police chief isn't about to stir up a family problem for the Saddlebrooks. No worries. You're doing great. Have a good time, Saffron," he said.

I looked at him. He was so casual about this. Why was he so confident in me? Didn't he understand how hard all this was for me?

"Be careful," he added, just as I closed the door behind me.

Careful?

I watched him drive off and then joined Karen to meet up with Tommy and his friend, a boy named Chris Loman who was also on the basketball team.

"You guys look great," Tommy said.

Karen stepped a little in front of me. "My mother and I have been helping Saffron with her clothes and makeup and stuff."

"Good work," Tommy said, smiling at me and not looking at all at Karen.

"Well, she came here with practically nothing," Karen emphasized. "I had to help her buy what was in fashion and choose what to wear tonight."

I looked at her. She hadn't, of course.

"Lucky she had you," Chris said. His words hung in the air as both Karen and I were trying to decide if he had been serious. "You're such a fashion expert."

He laughed, and Karen punched him.

"Hey, that's a foul," Chris moaned, rubbing his shoulder vigorously, exaggerating how hard she had hit him. Both he and Tommy laughed and went ahead to open the front door for us.

"Queen Karen," Chris said, with an exaggerated theatrical bow.

"This is probably what you'll do after high school," she said. "Doorman."

She smiled at me, and we entered, but as I passed closely, I glanced at Tommy and saw how hard he was looking at me. It wasn't exactly a chill that it sent down my spine; it was more like a hot flash that settled around my heart and had me rush ahead as if I was afraid he'd read my thoughts or feel the slight trembling in my body.

"Everyone's in the basement," Adele said when we entered the hallway. She was waiting for us at the door to the stairway. "Margaret's parents just left, but her brother is up in his room, and we're supposed to check on him every hour. Hi," she said, as though she just realized I had come with Karen. Before I could respond, she saw Tommy and Chris, who had entered but were talking softly to themselves, probably about us. She yelled to them. "Down here!"

"Hi, Adele," Chris said.

Karen raised her eyebrows and leaned in to whisper. "He likes her, but she can't stand him."

I saw Adele's smile and didn't think it was that false. Karen seemed jealous of everyone. I wondered how she kept any friends or, as Aunt Ava had suggested, if they were really her friends. We all started down the stairs, the music and laughter flowing up at us.

The basement was large. It looked like it ran the length of the house, with a bar, tables, and chairs. The walls were all in a dark paneling, and the coffee-white floor consisted of wide wood slats. There was an actual jukebox on the far right and funny vintage late-twentieth-century posters on the walls. One wall had plaques of some sort and a small glass case with some trophies in it. At the moment, there looked to be about fifteen other kids. Four boys were playing darts on the left side of the basement.

Tommy stepped up beside me as I looked toward the case of trophies.

"Margaret's father was a star quarterback on his college football team."

"Oh," I said. I didn't look at him. His lips were so close to my ear I would swear he kissed the words to me.

Karen seized my left forearm to pull me away and start introducing me to girls and other boys I had not yet even seen at school. Her introduction began with "This is my cousin from California who had to come here to live." Some began to ask where exactly I was from and how I liked it here. I started to answer, but if they showed interest, Karen pulled me to meet someone else. I didn't resist. In my mind, it was working in my favor.

Out of the corner of my eye, I saw boys ripping beer cans out of a case and handing them out to anyone who wanted one. Margaret, Adele, and Vikki waited for us to make the rounds. They were sipping something suspicious from paper cups.

"My parents won't return for a good three hours," Margaret told us. "You'd better sample the punch now so you can sober up in two and a half hours. And no one better throw up!" she shouted over the music.

There was lots of laughter. Some of the boys poked and pushed each other, obviously accusing them of not being able to not throw up or reminding them of some previous occasion when they had. I had no really accurate way to judge them, but I thought they were all acting a little immature. When the beat of the music changed, a few kids started to dance, and voices grew louder.

"You'd better not tell my parents about the punch," Karen warned when I refused a cup Margaret offered.

"Maybe you'll tell her yourself," I said.

"What?" She looked at Adele, who shrugged. "Why would I do that?"

"Maybe you won't be able to help it."

The other girls laughed. Karen smirked and gulped the cup of punch she had. She turned to get another. The moment she stepped away from me, the girls began their questions. They sounded like Karen had dictated their dialogue.

"Why weren't you ever here?"

"How do you like our school?"

"What was it like where you were?"

"Did you ever see movie stars?"

They were asking so many, so fast, I barely got out an answer to the first question. Rather than bring up the fiction of my family feuds, I told them we didn't have money to travel. More of the party-goers were drawn to the circle around me. I could feel the panic pooling in my chest, especially when Karen poked her head in to reveal that my mother and her father didn't get along.

"They didn't talk to each other for years, but we're trying to make her feel comfortable. I mean, she has no one else, really."

Their looks of pity actually made me feel sick. I resisted the urge to charge up the stairs, call Ava, and go home.

Suddenly, I felt someone grab my right hand and pull me away. Tommy wanted to dance.

I had never danced with a boy, of course, except in my imagination. When I could, I played music in my room and, following the way kids my age and a little older danced on television, imitated their steps and moves and, I thought, became better and better at it. One night, Mazy watched without my realizing she was standing there. When I finally did, I stopped as if I had been caught doing something illicit. She stared at me a moment, and then she smiled.

"You're very good," she said. "When the time comes, you'll stand out for sure."

Her comment had surprised me, but because I no longer felt that I was doing it in secret, I danced more, occasionally getting up while we were watching television together and dancing to the music. She smiled and clapped and then grew very sad.

"What's wrong?" I asked.

"It's almost time for you to be out there," she said, nodding toward the front of the house. It was a good year or so before she would enter me in the public school, but I never forgot the look on her face, a mixture of joy, pride, and deep fear.

Well, I was out there now. Would her fears be realized?

Tommy was a very good dancer. I stood there practically not moving when he began.

"I'm not very good," I said.

"Then I'll get you to be better," he replied, and tugged me to step out farther, away from the others. I glanced at Karen. She looked like she wanted to rip out my heart. She was sipping the punch quickly, more like gulping the second glass, too.

Maybe I was simply tired of seeing her jealousy; maybe I just wanted to feel free, loosen up, and forget about the image and the story Daddy had created for me. Something clicked inside me. Tommy's eyes were electric, daring. I slipped into the rhythm and the music like someone stepping into a lake or a pool to swim. In seconds, I was fully submerged, my body moving as if it had a mind of its own, all caution scattered like grass seeds in the wind. I could hear the cheers and encouragement and saw the look of delightful amazement on Tommy's face. After a few more moments, I didn't look at anyone else. No one else dared to join us. It was as if we had risen above them. I no longer heard anything but the music. When it ended, everyone except Karen applauded. Now they were pouncing on her to get more information about me.

Tommy reached for my hand.

"C'mon," he said. "Let's get something cold and soft to drink."

"You don't drink beer or loaded punch?"

"I'm an athlete," he said. "A serious athlete. I have a good shot at a scholarship. We don't need the money," he added. "I want the acknowledgment."

"That's great, Tommy."

I noted that he had to make the point about his family being well-off. Around these kids, I guessed that was quite important.

At the bar, he poured us both glasses of a fruit soda. Our dancing had encouraged others. We sat on the stools and watched them. I saw Karen was talking at her friends rather than with them. Chris was teasing her.

"What do your parents do?" I asked Tommy. I didn't want to add, *since you don't need college money*, but it was clearly underlying the question.

"My father's a corporate attorney, and my mother is a family doctor," he said. "I have two younger brothers, twins, eleven years old."

He waited, expecting me to tell him about myself, but I said nothing. He sipped his drink and smiled.

"I like it that you're a mystery," he said. He leaned toward me. "All the other girls are open books, especially your cousin."

Oh, Karen wouldn't like to hear that, I thought. She and Adele and Vikki were heading toward us.

"Uh-oh," Tommy said. "The Three Musketeers."

"Everyone is asking me where you learned to dance so good," Karen said. I was going to say, *Dance so well*, but I might as well light a stick of dynamite between her legs, I thought.

"In my room," I said casually.

"You said you didn't know who Ed Sheeran was," she said.

I looked at the other two and some of the kids who drew closer to hear. Why was she doing this to me? She had promised to keep everyone from picking on me. Ava had really driven a wedge between us, I thought.

"We had this CD player and my mother's discs, which were mainly music from the seventies, eighties, and nineties. It was her collection. You know I didn't have a cell phone, so I didn't download any up-to-date stuff."

"Didn't you ever go to a party?" Adele asked, her eyes wide with amazement.

Everyone around us was waiting for my answer, especially Karen. I had been hoping to concoct something in private so she would help me avoid this moment in front of the other kids. But right now, I no longer trusted her anyway.

"Because my mother and I traveled and lived in many different places, I didn't make friends as easily as you all have."

"So you didn't go to parties?" Adele pursued like a trial attorney.

"No," I said.

"You had a computer," Karen charged, her face lighting up with the clue. "You could listen to music on that."

"I just got it recently," I said. "One of my mother's boyfriends bought it to get her to like him more. It didn't work. She dumped him a week later, but I kept the computer."

They all stared, ironically amazed at what appeared to be my honesty. Karen sipped her drink. She was struggling with what to say next. Everyone's looks turned from amazement to sympathy.

"Maybe you'll help me get more up-to-date now," I told Karen.

"Good idea," Tommy said. They were all nodding as if his words dropped down from the god of happiness or something.

"I'll send you some good links," Vikki said. "What's your email?"

"Oh, I haven't set that up yet. Karen will help me," I said, smiling at her. "Right?"

"Right. Let's get something to eat," she told Adele, and the three walked to where the food was spread out on a table.

"Well, that was like walking on hot coals for you," Tommy said.

I shrugged. "I'm not looking for their sympathy. My life was harder than all theirs, but I'd rather not dwell on it."

"Makes sense to me. You want something to eat?" he asked. "Just sit here. I'll get a plate for you."

"You will?"

"I'm a team player. Didn't you hear? Besides, I've got to get you some fuel to keep dancing."

He brushed his hand over mine and went to the table. I took a deep breath and looked at some of the kids who were staring at me. I smiled. Some smiled back; some quickly turned away. When Tommy returned, we ate and talked, mostly about school and his ambitions.

"Whatever hardships you went through, you kept being a very good student. Melina filled me in on you. She was very impressed with you, and she's not easily impressed with anyone."

"Really?"

"I'm sure you'll do something great."

"I haven't been that ambitious. Reading and studying kept my mind off other, not-so-nice things," I said.

"Must be like being on another planet now."

"There *are* aliens here," I said, looking around and nodding. He roared and clapped.

Every once in a while, he touched my hand, mostly at the end of something he had said. It was almost as if he was trying to be sure I remained beside him. He had nothing to worry about. I felt safer, since most didn't want to interrupt us.

We danced some more. Despite Karen's muttering, no one was really nasty to me. I did notice Chris spending more time with Adele, and because of that, Karen reluctantly talked to a nice-looking red-haired boy named Billy London, who I learned was the student government president. He was paying lots of attention to her. Maybe she wouldn't be so jealous now, I hoped. However, I had the amusing suspicion that the kids here wanted to talk to her more because of me. They were hoping she had greater, maybe even uglier details to share.

Toward the end of the evening and that eleven-thirty curfew Karen and I knew was coming, Tommy took my phone number.

"Maybe you'll be able to go out with us after the big game next Tuesday night," he said. "We're playing for the division championship."

"Really? Where's the game?"

"Home court," he said. "We played these guys a month ago, at their place. Long bus ride, but we beat them by four points. Chris made a big basket that night. Amazing hook shot."

"That's great. What team are you playing? Karen might not remind me, and I don't want to look totally stupid."

He laughed. "I'll tell you all about them, our strategy, everything, this week," he said. "It's Hurley."

"Excuse me?"

"Hurley. They're pretty good. Going to be a big game. Lots of fans on both sides. The gym will rock like it's in one of your California earthquakes, believe me."

I felt my whole body tighten.

"Hey, don't look so worried. I'm just kidding. Besides, we're going to beat them for sure," he said, and took my hand.

I smiled.

Hurley.

Inside, I was crumbling like an iceberg on an unexpectedly super-warm day.

CHAPTER TEN

Fortunately, Karen had stopped drinking the spiked punch in time to prevent herself from getting sick before Daddy arrived to pick us up, but she was moaning about a stomachache and looked pale to me as his arrival became imminent. I told her to keep drinking water. Tommy suggested she and I go out a little earlier and wait to be picked up.

"Fresh air will help," he whispered, and he and Billy London went out with us. Billy held Karen's arm as we walked around the driveway. She moaned and complained, but for now, it seemed to help.

I thanked Tommy for his help.

"I like that you didn't drink any of that junk," he said when we paused in the shadows. "You have a look that tells me you're some-thing special, Saffron."

"I don't feel like something special."

"Oh, someday you will. Maybe someday soon," he whispered. We were inches apart. Slowly, he brought his lips to mine. I could hear Karen complaining about the "junky food and punch." She wasn't looking our way. When Tommy pulled his head back, I wondered if he could tell that he was the first boy I had ever kissed like that. Did I do it right? Was I stupid?

He smiled.

"You're special, Saffron, because you make me feel special."

I was excited, and I felt good, but I was suddenly overcome with a rush of fear. Someday surely he would find out the truth about me and what he thought now was special he might just decide was only weird.

The headlights of Daddy's car appeared, and we all moved quickly to greet him. Both boys said hi.

"Big game coming," Daddy said. "Don't you guys stay out too late. I have my life savings bet on it."

They laughed.

Billy opened the door for Karen, and Tommy opened the rear door for me.

"Night," I told Tommy.

He mouthed, "You're special."

Karen didn't even look at Billy.

After she got into Daddy's car, I was sure he would realize that she had drunk something alcoholic. I could smell it almost as soon as the doors closed, but if he did, he ignored it. When he asked how the party was, she said, "Good," closed her eyes, and leaned against the door. He glanced back at me through the rearview mirror.

"Did you have a good time, Saffron?"

Karen came to life. "She had a great time."

The jealousy was dripping from her lips.

"Oh?"

"It was very nice," I said quickly, maybe too quickly.

He drove away. I glanced back at Tommy, who stood there watching us until we turned a corner.

"The party's not really over, Daddy," Karen said. "Most of my friends are still there. They can stay out until midnight or later. Their parents don't treat them as still being children."

"Take it up with your mother," Daddy said. "Good food?"

"Ugh," Karen said.

"It was fine," I said.

"To you, anything would have been. Did you know Saffron hadn't been to a party before? That's pretty weird, isn't it?"

"Well, she's giving you a fresh perspective on it, then," Daddy said, still eyeing me carefully in the rearview mirror.

Karen grunted and leaned against the door again.

"You don't look like you have the energy to go much longer anyway, Karen," Daddy told her.

"Because I'm bored now. When you're bored, you look tired," Karen countered.

"How about you, Saffron?"

"I'm fine. Tired, not bored," I added.

Daddy kept trying to catch a glimpse of me in the rearview mirror. I was sure that he had heard something in my voice. I was still a little shaky after hearing about the upcoming basketball game. It wasn't easy to hide my nervousness, even from my father, who hadn't seen or heard me for years.

After we pulled into the garage, Karen got out quickly, mumbling about being treated like a baby. She charged through the door.

"You should say good-night to your mother, Karen," Daddy shouted after her.

She didn't hesitate. The door slammed behind her. I thought she might be close to vomiting now. Daddy deliberately walked slowly, so he and I could linger for a few minutes. Ava was in bed. He had mentioned that Garson had been having another bad night and had finally fallen asleep.

"How did it really go?" he asked me while we were still in the kitchen.

"The party was fine. I mean, I was asked lots of questions, but I kept my answers vague enough, except the one about not ever being at a party like that. It's not easy to check every word at your lips first."

"I know. I realize how difficult it must be for you, but it's best for now, Saffron, believe me."

What choice did I have? When he said it was best for now, I thought, *Best for you, not me.*

"Karen seemed to think you had a good time," he said, obviously fishing for more information. "She sounded a little jealous?"

"I made friends with Tommy Diamond. That's what Karen meant."

"I saw how he escorted you out. You know he's the school's star basketball player?"

"Yes."

He was thoughtful. I imagined it was because Tommy was an African American, and maybe Ava wouldn't approve. Maybe he didn't approve. Suddenly, his eyes lit up.

"We're playing for the division championship this Tuesday."

"Uh-huh," I said. "It's the home game he wanted me to attend, but . . ."

The expression on his face told me he didn't need me to say it. The realization lit his eyes. "It's against Hurley."

"Yes, and if their fans come in large numbers and anyone sees me . . . It was a village half this size. Unfortunately, I became too well known. If some of them approach me, they'll want to know what I'm doing living here. Karen could overhear the chatter."

He nodded, thinking.

"Don't worry about it."

"I don't see how I can go. Karen will find it very strange that I don't, since Tommy and I became such good friends. He'll be after me to be there, too. What should I do?"

"I'll figure out something," he said. "Go on up to bed. You're meeting my father-in-law and seeing Saddlebrook tomorrow. Just think about that."

Just go to bed? Did he think I could simply fall asleep? Was he really this oblivious to my feelings and fears?

I left him and went up to my room. Before I could undress and get ready for bed, Ava surprised me by coming to my room. She was in her nightgown. Without any makeup, she looked older, angrier. She stared at me so hard for a moment that I stopped breathing. Had she found it all out? Had Daddy confessed because of the game with Hurley? Was it over? This could be his solution to my attending the game, and indeed my whole future here, but I felt like I was running over a bed of hot coals to get there. I was afraid, but I also let a feeling of relief seep in.

"I've looked in on Karen. I just wanted to see how you were," she said. She stepped deeper into the room to get a closer look at me and smell for alcohol.

"Just tired," I said. "I danced a lot more than I expected I would."

"You'd have to be absent the sense of smell not to know Karen's had something alcoholic to drink. Your uncle either is the most oblivious man on the planet or would rather ignore it. That's frequently his choice when it comes to problems, especially with her. You didn't drink anything alcoholic?"

I shook my head.

"Couldn't you stop her?"

I looked at her askance. Was she serious?

"I know she thinks that because of your hard life you're somehow street-smart, cool."

"I've done or said nothing to lead her to believe that, Aunt Ava. She sees what she wants. I'm not corrupting her, if that's what you think."

She nodded. "Anyway, I know Sid and Marilyn Toby very well. They'd never have permitted anything like that. What went on there? Was everybody else drinking? Did they use the Tobys' liquor? Anything get broken? Was it worse?"

I pressed my upper lip over my lower as if I was preventing myself from blurting out information. Ava had a way of staring right into you, I thought. How could she not see all the deception in my father? Or was she doing the same thing she accused him of doing, ignoring it?

"Well?" she asked. "How much did my daughter drink? Did anyone use any drugs?"

"I don't want to get you angry, and I don't want to lie to you, Aunt Ava, but Karen and I are just getting to know each other. I have no way to know for certain, since I didn't have the experience, but it seems to me it is difficult for a daughter, especially a teenage daughter, to have another teenage girl suddenly become part of her family and have to share her parents with her. If you force me to be the tattletale and get her into trouble, what do you think the chances of she and I ever having a good relationship will be?"

Her eyes stopped piercing me with darts and widened with more surprise. She nodded slowly. "Karen also was complaining that you're too adult. The word 'adult' to her is not favorable at this age. All it means to her are more restrictions on her behavior. I can see she was right about you, however. Your hard life has forced you to be wiser than others your age. Okay," she said. "Let's leave it for now."

She started out, then stopped at the door and turned back. "What was your overall opinion of the kids you met at this party, Karen's friends?"

"They're just . . ."

"What? Well?" she pursued when I hesitated.

"Lucky," I said, and she gave me the warmest smile since I had arrived.

"Have a good night's sleep, Saffron. My father is looking forward to meeting you tomorrow, but he can be quite judgmental."

"What does that mean?"

"He has strong opinions . . . about everything. And he's never shy about offering them. He's a man who is used to getting his own way. For my father, 'compromise' is a fancy word for surrendering. He is, however, one of the, if not *the*, most successful men in the state."

She didn't sound like a loving daughter should, I thought, and nodded.

"And yes," she said as she was leaving, "he does regret never having a son."

And yes?

I hadn't said anything. Did she believe everyone assumed that, or did her father do something to make it obvious?

She left, leaving my door opened enough for me to hear Garson starting to cry. When she closed her bedroom door, it was muffled. I closed mine completely and moved quickly to get myself to bed, but when I did, I didn't fall right to sleep. I tossed and turned as if I were sleeping on abrasive straw. However, it wasn't because I was worrying about meeting Mr. Saddlebrook or how I would handle the upcoming game between our school and Hurley. Those images of potential disaster weren't the images I was envisioning. What I was revisiting were Tommy Diamond's smile, Tommy Diamond's laugh, and Tommy Diamond's intense perusal of my face before we had kissed. I wanted the memory and feel of his lips on mine to be there until I fell asleep.

Favorite movie love scenes and my own fantasies rushed the birth of my sexuality like some impatient bird pecking holes and cracks in the egg that lay between it and the experiences that awaited outside. Right now, lying here and staring up at the ceiling, I could think only about how Tommy and I danced. The feelings I recalled when he had touched me and the way his whispered breath caressed my ear, my cheeks, and once, face-to-face and so close, my moistened lips, all that and especially that good-night kiss made the nipples of my breasts tingle against the top of my pajamas. My fingers pressed softly on the insides of my thighs. I subdued a moan and quickly turned to press my face against my pillow to smother the thoughts, but they were not easily pressed away.

What's wrong with me? I should be terrified, I thought, *not lovesick*. How could I become close and intimate with anyone right now? He would surely see through all the lies eventually. Honesty has to be a blood relative of affection. The stronger and the deeper my feelings for someone else and his feelings for me became, the faster deception would be peeled away until that moment would arrive when I would have to say, *I am not who you have been told I am.*

Then what? The world of lies would tumble, cascade, dropping me into oblivion. Why would someone on a rocket ship to success want to tie on such dark and foreboding weight?

Get back, I ordered my romantic feelings. *You're too soon. There isn't a safe place for you yet here.*

Maybe there would never be, I thought.

I closed my eyes and clung to the darkness for safety and sleep.

Surprisingly, Karen rose before I even opened my eyes in the morning and came into my room. I was anticipating her having a hangover and complaining, somehow finding a way to blame me for it.

"What?" I asked, looking at her standing beside my bed and glaring down at me.

"Did you say anything to my mother about the party? I'd like to know before I get dressed and go down into the pit."

I sat up. "I didn't say anything, but she came in here to question me because she smelled the alcohol on you. Did you get sick?"

"No. She came in so quickly after I stepped into my room that I had to swallow it down. She didn't start screaming or anything. Just her usual 'we'll talk about this in the morning' threat, but I got a text already from Margaret."

"A text?"

"You get it on your phone, stupid. Messages?"

"Oh. Right. Well, what was the message?" I said, sitting up.

"No one knew it, but Paul Martin and Lee Burton thought it would be clever to give her brother some of the punch so he'd sleep and not bother anyone. He threw up in his bed. Her mother is bonkers. Margaret can never have another party, and she is grounded for a month. She can't even go to the championship basketball game."

"I was wondering why nobody said anything about her brother. I remember Adele said someone was supposed to check on him all the time. Is he still sick?"

"Forget about her brother. Don't you get it? Marilyn Toby's going to call my mother for sure, if she hasn't already. If she asks you again about me, just say I had a little. That's what I'm going to say. I had a little, and I didn't like it. I can't be blamed for what other kids do. When we found out, you and I both thought it was terrible, but we couldn't stop them. Got it?"

I stared at her a moment before replying. Either everyone in this family knowingly lies to each other, or they're all just as oblivious as Ava accused my father of being.

"I haven't known your mother that long, Karen, but she's not someone easily lied to. And," I decided to add, "I'm not a good liar."

She raised her eyes to the ceiling. "I know that. Just . . . don't offer much. I'll take care of it. Okay?"

"Whatever," I said, shrugging.

"If we both get grounded, you won't be able to go to the game, either, and that won't make Tommy happy. I know you'd like to make him happy."

She waited for me to confess it, but I didn't move a muscle in my face. What she was threatening was actually something of a solution for me. I was very tempted to get us both into trouble. It would certainly simplify things for both me and Daddy.

"Jeez," she said, blowing air through her lips. "Just do what I told you to do." She turned and left to get dressed.

She waited for me in her room at her door before going down. As soon as I stepped out of my room, she stepped out of hers.

"Let's face the firing squad together," she said. "That way, we'll make less mistakes."

She walked ahead of me. As I followed, I realized I had yet to spend a minute in this house without being deceptive.

Daddy was holding and rocking Garson at the kitchenette table. Apparently, Garson was asleep. Ava turned from the stove and glared at us. One look at her face told me Mrs. Toby had called and given her two earfuls for sure. Her eyes looked like they could burn holes through walls.

"Just sit," she ordered.

There was more fire in those violet orbs than ever. Frightened, Karen hurried ahead to the table. We sat and quietly started to serve ourselves juice and coffee. Daddy said nothing. He glanced at us and continued rocking Garson. Only the sounds of Ava preparing scrambled eggs broke the silence.

"I don't like eating with anger," she said, bringing the eggs in and serving us each a portion. "So we won't talk until we've all finished."

Daddy lowered Garson carefully to his bassinet and took his seat as quietly and as obediently as another child. We were all in a silent movie, waiting for someone to turn up the volume. Karen looked at me, probably to confirm I would do exactly as she had prescribed, but I simply ate and stared ahead. When Ava put down her fork, I thought it was as if someone in another room had begun a drumroll.

"Marilyn Toby called me this morning. She was quite beside herself. I'd like some honest answers," she said, speaking with great control and patience. "Do either of you know who fed Ben Toby the spiked punch that turned his stomach?"

"No," Karen said, much too quickly.

I shook my head.

"Did you know such a thing was happening?"

"No," Karen said.

"No one bragged to us that they'd done it, Aunt Ava. Most of us were dancing and talking and didn't think at all about her brother."

For me, that was the truth. I wondered when I sounded more honest, when I lied or when I told the truth, since the latter was so rare for me right now.

"And most of you were drinking that garbage," she said, looking at Karen. "I'm sure more than just little Ben Toby were sick from it."

"I just had a sip, and it was nauseating. It nearly ruined my night. I don't know how others drank so much of it. Right, Saffron?"

I looked at Ava. I wasn't even going to try it.

"I'm not looking for alibis, excuses, or half-truths. Margaret's been grounded. I don't want to hear about any parties for the foreseeable future," Ava said. "School parties included."

"That's not fair," Karen moaned. "We can't tell everyone else what to do. Why are you blaming us? If we win the championship, there'll be a celebration party. Parents will be going, too, so there won't be anything going on anyway."

Ava curled her lips and looked at Daddy, obviously ordering him to respond.

"If there is a school celebration party, your mother and I will attend. We'll have Celisse watch Garson that night. But until things settle down, that will have to be it for now, Karen. No friends over and no going to friends' houses."

"And don't tell us you just sipped it, Karen," Ava said. "Neither of us was born yesterday."

"That's all I did!"

Ava stared hard at her. Karen had to look down.

"I have told you many times, Karen, that lying about something you've done wrong is like adding a poison frosting to a bitter cake."

Karen continued to stare at her plate.

"Fine example you're showing your cousin, Karen, and the first time at a social event, too. I can just imagine the gossip going on in homes all over Sandburg Creek. You know all eyes are on this family," Ava said.

Karen looked up, nearly in tears, and gathered her defiance, something I was sure she had inherited from the Saddlebrook side of her family.

"Showing my cousin? You don't think she's seen worse just because she doesn't talk about it? Besides, we're not royalty, Mother. You're not inheriting a throne. This is a democracy."

"Royalty in America comes from exemplary behavior, from success and influence. Now, after you two clean up after breakfast, I expect you to spend the rest of the day doing your schoolwork. We'll be leaving for Saddlebrook at four. Be sure you dress properly. Choose a casual dress, and Karen, do not load yourself up with jewelry. You know your grandfather isn't fond of that, nor is he fond of young girls with heavy makeup. A touch of lipstick will do. Your father and I are going to the den to discuss some business concerns. If Garson wakes, tend to him. His bottle is prepared."

She rose, and Daddy got up instantly. Karen kept her head down, but I locked eyes with him. His were full of warnings. He nodded and followed Ava.

"Well, that's better than I expected," I said.

"What?"

"We're not grounded like Margaret is," I said. "We just can't attend parties. That's how I interpret it."

"How you interpret it? What are you, a lawyer?"

Her eyelids narrowed with suspicion. I feared her next question would be *Who are you really?* But she was thinking of something else.

"My mother didn't direct anything toward you. She blamed me for setting a bad example for you. Did you tell on me? You did, didn't you?"

"I said nothing negative about you, Karen. Like I told you at the party. You telegraphed it all yourself."

"Negative? Telegraphed? Interpret?" She shook her head. "You're weird."

She started to clear off the table, making more noise than necessary. Garson woke and immediately began crying.

"Go on," she said. "Get to know your cousin."

She went into the kitchen. I looked at my half brother, who was squirming uncomfortably. I had never held a baby. I rose and carefully lifted him out of his cradle. His eyes searched my face, and he suddenly stopped crying. *Does he sense who I really am?* I wondered. *Do babies have unfettered instincts and feelings?*

"You know me, don't you?" I whispered.

He looked like he was smiling.

Karen returned to continue clearing the table and paused. "What did you do, hypnotize him?"

I shook my head. "Just doing what Uncle Derick did, rocking him."

"Good. He likes you better than he likes me. You can take care of him most of the time when we have to babysit."

"That's no problem," I said.

She groaned. "Stop trying to be so damn goody-goody. The more you look like an angel, the more I look like the devil."

"I'm no angel, Karen, and I'm not trying to be one."

"Yeah, but they don't know it," she said.

Garson started to squirm and cry.

"You think he needs his bottle?"

"I don't know. I'll warm it, and you feed him. I want to get back up to my room and call some of my friends to see how fast all this is spreading. You feed him and rock him to sleep," she ordered.

"Doesn't Celisse come on the weekends?"

"Sometimes. She's not a live-in nanny. My mother likes pretending she's a mother," she said. She paused, her frustration and anger disappearing. "My grandmother wasn't much of a mother. Mom claims her mother missed her birthdays often to attend social events. She says she was brought up by her nanny, Victoria Austen, who was only in her twenties when she started working for my grandparents. Supposedly, Victoria was real royalty, but her family went bankrupt, and she had to work. You'll see her picture at Saddlebrook. My grandfather practically worships it."

She paused, and then in a whisper, with her eyes on the door, added, "I think he might have had an affair with her. The house is so big you could set off a bomb in one room and no one would know in another. My mother wasn't brought up in a happy household despite how rich they were."

"I understand," I said.

"You do? Well, I don't," she said. "Why do I have to suffer because she wasn't loved enough?"

Garson started to cry harder, so Karen went to get his bottle. I didn't think I'd ever pause to feel sorry for Ava, but it was as if a discordant note had been sounded on a piano. This so-called envied world of power and wealth had rips in its seams. They were covered over or ignored, perhaps, but nevertheless they were there threatening to tear it all apart. Had Daddy known all this when he stepped into it? Right now, I didn't know if he had, and I couldn't tell if he knew how serious it all was now. Maybe I would learn more at Saddlebrook about this family and his place in it. I'd never approve of what he had done, but I might understand why he had done it.

The truth was, he was really still more of a stranger than he was my father. He was more comfortable living in the fiction than I was. Was it only because of his fear of Ava and her father? Or had he written me out of his life that day at the train station and hoped it would stay that way forever? Surely I reminded him too much about what had come before, especially my mother. I had been noticing it in his face more and more, especially when he didn't think I was looking at him. It was like a mixture of anxiety and anger seeping into his eyes, turning them into pools of white and gray, the color of bones.

"Here," Karen said, thrusting the bottle at me. "Go for it."

I sat and fed Garson. As he suckled, his inquisitive eyes continued to search my face.

"I'm going up," Karen called from the kitchen.

I didn't move; I didn't speak. Her steps died away on the stairs, and it was so quiet I could hear only Garson's little grunts of pleasure as he fed. After a while, he just stopped, closed his eyes, and fell asleep. I lowered him gently into his bassinet just as Ava and Daddy reappeared. I didn't know how long they were standing there and watching me, but they both looked very pleased when I turned to them.

"That's very good, Saffron," Ava said. "He doesn't do as well with his sister. Maybe there's something else you can teach her."

I looked at Daddy. There was no expression of irony, no regret, and no urge to be honest. I imagined him saying, *Well, to be truthful about it, Ava, she is his sister, his half sister.*

Silence, even for a moment, felt like ice dripping down my spine. I forced a smile.

"I'm sure she has things to teach me," I said.

Ava rolled her eyes. "I hate to think what. Go on up and do your work, and make sure she does hers."

"I've got a few errands to do. See you all later," Daddy said, and hurried off just like someone effecting a quick escape.

When I entered my room, I heard the phone ringing and for a moment didn't realize it was my own, my new cell phone. This would be the first time I had used it. I pressed *accept* and said, "Hello? Who is this, please?"

I heard Tommy laugh. "Didn't you see my name on your screen?"

"What? Oh. I just answered quickly without looking. I didn't know it would tell me that."

He laughed again. "Word is this is your first cell phone. Is that true?"

"It's complicated," I said.

"That makes it more interesting. So I'm calling to see if I can take you to lunch today. I can—"

"Didn't you hear about Margaret Toby's brother? All the parents are on the warpath."

"Yeah, but you didn't do anything wrong. Neither did I. No one's accused either of us. And besides, none of these parents wants it advertised. We're safe."

"Karen's mother wants our social activities on hold for now."

"Oh."

"Besides, I couldn't go anyway. We're visiting Saddlebrook for dinner. We're leaving at four, and both Karen and I are confined to our work so we'll have nothing to do when we come back tonight."

"Saddlebrook. Most impressive estate in the area. Probably see you in school, then," he said, sounding quite down.

"Of course," I said.

"Maybe you can come to watch practice. I'll take you home," he quickly added.

I knew my hesitation was discouraging, but I was thinking ahead to his disappointment when I didn't go to the big game. Every moment of my life now seemed to be tied in a knot.

"I mean, that's not really socializing."

"I'll try," I said. "We'll talk about it tomorrow."

"Sure. Have a great time at Saddlebrook."

"Thank you."

"Don't give any other boy at school your phone number," he said quickly, before ending the call.

I started to answer but realized he was no longer there.

Still, I had a smile on my face. The first boy I had a crush on and who had one on me appeared to be the heartthrob of a number of girls at the school. It all happened to me very quickly, too. Probably, after what had happened at Hurley, no boy there would have asked me out, ever. Mazy used to say, "Dig deep enough even into bad news, and you're bound to find something to give you hope."

These seeds of romance were making it difficult for me to do my reading. I told myself that I'd surely have some time before I went to sleep. For now, to distract myself, I went to Karen's room to help her with her homework. She hadn't opened a book and was still on the phone with friends.

"I'll come to your room," she told me, with her hand over the phone. "I'm on a conference call."

"Oh, sorry," I said, and returned to my room. *I guess I will read after all*, I thought, and went right to it.

Karen didn't come into my room for a good half hour or so and didn't bring any of her books with her.

"This whole thing is a big disaster," she moaned. "Parents are bigger gossips than kids. Practically everyone is grounded . . . no home parties, and some can't go out for a month. You'd think we'd robbed the bank Mr. Toby runs."

"Tommy told me they wouldn't be talking about it, that they didn't want to advertise it."

"Tommy? When?"

"Just now. He called me to go for a ride."

"Are you going?"

"We can't do any socializing, remember?"

She stamped her foot. "It's not fair."

I sighed and shook my head.

"What?" she asked.

"When something unpleasant happens and you dwell on it, you only make it worse. Let it settle down," I said, and thought to myself how small this was compared to what had happened to me in Hurley—my neighbor dying, a boy being killed in a car accident, and Mazy's suddenly dying. Karen's biggest tragedy would be losing cell-phone service.

"Let it settle down? You talk like someone older than my mother."

"You lied to your parents. All your friends lied to theirs. Stop being so dramatic about it. What if that little boy had been hurt? What if someone who could drive had left the party and gotten into a serious, maybe fatal accident? Mr. and Mrs. Toby could be sued or something."

She stared at me. "The school's guidance counselor and therapist has moved into my house," she said finally.

I laughed.

"It's not funny."

"Relax. Everyone's going to live," I said. "We'd better get on to the schoolwork."

"No."

"No?"

"Adele and Vikki have come up with a plan, and so far everyone agrees," she said.

"What plan?"

"No one is going to do schoolwork, and no one is going to speak in class. Our parents will find out instantly. If they can gang up on us, we can gang up on them. You'd better close those books and join us," she said. "Even Billy London and Chris Loman agree. Chris is going to tell Tommy. And don't mention it later at Saddlebrook. We want it to come as a surprise."

"That's a mistake," I said.

"Oh, yeah, why?"

"If the basketball players join your protest, the principal could suspend them from the team. You want to be responsible for that?"

She stood there blinking. "She wouldn't do that."

"Who has more influence on her, you and your friends or the parents, especially Mr. Toby?"

"You're weird. If you don't do like the rest of us, you'll never have a friend in this school," she threatened, then turned and hurried out of my room.

I was in a crisis with my father; I was in a crisis in this house and with my half sister. Soon I'd be in a crisis at school.

The prospect of packing my old bag, taking only the things I came with, suddenly loomed large.

I would get back on that train.

Right now, I thought that whatever awaited me at the next stop or two could not be worse than all this.

Eventually, I thought, I would get on anyway.

What difference would it make if I did it sooner rather than later?

"Mazy Dazy," I whispered. "What do you think I should do?"

CHAPTER ELEVEN

As difficult as it was, especially after hearing Karen's threat, I returned to my school assignments and finished them all before considering how to dress for our visit and dinner at Saddlebrook. I was more nervous about this than I had been about attending a new school and facing questions from my peers at a party. The way my father, Ava, and even Karen spoke about Amos Saddlebrook created the image of a king who would be seated on his throne when we arrived. Suddenly, every decision I made for myself, no matter how small it would seem to someone else, grew in importance.

What would Amos Saddlebrook think about me if I chose this dress or that, these shoes or those? It was as if I'd be introduced not only to a king but to a man who had two microscopes for eyes. I could hear Mazy saying, *Stop worrying. He puts his pants on like everyone else, one leg at a time.*

In the end, I decided to be more like Mazy and not let myself be intimidated. My choices would be for myself, not for him.

I settled on the fishnet fit-and-flare dress. It was wine-colored and knee-length, sleeveless with a round neckline. I recalled Ava calling it casual chic and thought that was what I should want tonight. I was putting it on for the first time since I tried it on at the store. My new double-breasted vegan wool coat to wear over it seemed perfect. The black boots Ava bought both Karen and me completed my look.

Ava had made it crystal clear that we, perhaps especially I, should not wear makeup. For me, that was no big sacrifice. I turned and looked in the full-length mirror. With my hand on my hip, I turned slowly to scrutinize myself from this angle and that. Dare I think I was really attractive? Was it really a sin to admire yourself so? I recalled Mazy telling me that little girls were mostly selfish by nature, and "some never lose that characteristic and become selfish women. Their prized possession is a mirror."

"Why not boys, too?" I'd asked.

"They're usually not aware of their looks until they're teenagers," she said. "I used to wish I could wash the boys in my classes before they took their seats."

"You're overdressed," I heard Karen say now, and turned to my opened door. How long had she been watching me?

"It's my first time meeting your grandfather, Karen. It's very important to everyone, so I think I'd rather be overdressed than underdressed."

She was wearing a pair of jeans and a light-blue sweater with scuffed running shoes. Was Ava going to let her go like that?

"I told you. Grandpa Amos can tell a bullshitter immediately."

"Good. I hate when I'm mischaracterized."

She twisted her lips into her cheek and then rolled her eyes. "Whatever," she said. "I'm going to finish brushing my hair, get my new jean jacket, and go downstairs. And I'm wearing a little lipstick," she added defiantly.

"I'll meet you downstairs."

She paused, her eyes beady, suspicious. "You've been doing your homework?"

I just looked at her. The answer was quite clear in my expression.

"I'm not going to defend you tomorrow," she threatened.

"I'm sort of used to having to defend myself," I said.

She turned abruptly and went to her room. I gazed at myself one more time and started downstairs. Despite how brave and defiant I had played it in front of Karen, my heart was thumping so hard that I was sure someone could hear it without a stethoscope.

Daddy was the only one downstairs. He was standing by the kitchenette window gazing out, his hands clasped behind his back. He wore a dark-gray pinstripe suit, and I saw that he had had his hair trimmed today. For a few moments, I stood there gazing at him, my childhood memories rushing in to flood my thoughts.

So often back then, he was in a similar posture standing by a window. I recalled that when my father was in this sort of deep thought, it seemed like the whole world had been put on pause. I remembered that I was afraid to move, to make a sound, because when I did and he turned to look at me, he looked like he didn't know who I was. It took a few moments for his face to produce a smile. Those few moments were frightening for me. Now, when I thought about it, I realized he was behaving as if I had been able to hear his thoughts, thoughts I was sure he didn't want heard, especially by me.

"What's up?" he would say. I'd have nothing to ask other than *Why have you been standing there so long? What are you looking at?* But I wouldn't ask. Behind us in the living room, Mama would be sitting and staring at nothing. It was like they were doing everything they could not to look at each other. They were even looking through me.

I would shrug and run off.

I stood there now, waiting.

He turned slowly to face me, just the way he did back then, but he didn't smile. He glanced toward the stairway and then took a few steps forward, beckoning me to draw closer to him.

"What's wrong?" I asked in a voice just above a whisper.

Something wasn't right. I raked through my recent memories. Did I reveal something, make some factual error?

"The nurse who was Mazy's friend reported you missing," he said. "The police consider you a runaway because of your age."

"Oh. Someone saw me on the train? Are they going to come looking for me here?"

"Eventually, they might. There are so many runaways these days that I'm sure they're overburdened, but it's a concern nevertheless."

"What should we do?"

"There is one simple solution to end all the tension and worry. I tested it out on Ava, even though she doesn't know the real reason why. She's not opposed. Ava and her father, as I've told you, are often at wit's end with each other. It's complicated, but despite their disagreement, even about something as inconsequential as the color of a bath towel, she wouldn't do anything involving legal issues or business issues without his blessing. So I'll be looking for that tonight."

"Legal issues? What legal issues?"

"I suggested we formally adopt you," he said.

"What?" I started to smile. *My own father is going to adopt me?*

"We're pretty connected to the judiciary system here. I think we could put it on fast track, as long as Amos Saddlebrook doesn't throw up any roadblocks."

"But you'll have to tell the truth in a court, won't you?"

He smiled. "It will be handled by a family court judge who is actually Amos's best friend's son. If there's an inquiry and we've done that, it will be the end of it. So," he said, glancing toward the stairway when we heard a door close upstairs, "just win the old man over tonight. Put on that Anders charm. I'll handle the rest."

"Win the old man over? The first time we meet?"

Daddy smiled. "You can do it. Look at all you've done in so short a time already."

Karen appeared and looked from Daddy to me and then back at him. The expressions on our faces surely lit up her suspicions.

"Did she say something about me?" she demanded. I breathed relief. She was totally off the mark.

"What? No. What could she say? We were just talking about Saddlebrook."

"Oh," she said, but still looked at me distrustfully. I couldn't even begin to imagine what her reaction would be to my officially being her sister now, albeit an adopted one. "Garson is crying again. Celisse is having trouble, and Mother's upset."

"Okay. I'll see what's up," Daddy said.

He hurried back to the stairs.

"What did he tell you about Saddlebrook?" Karen asked the instant he was gone.

"He said it's very big, so big that your voice could echo in some rooms."

"I already told you that. It's the biggest house in the county, with the most land. In it there's a room just for parties, a ballroom, Grandpa's office, which is bigger than the president's, and six bedrooms. One is reserved for me anytime I want to sleep over. It used to be mine when I was very little. Grandpa Amos doesn't let anyone else sleep in it or in Mother's old room, either. The ballroom is in the rear of the house and has its own small kitchen just for parties. I'm going to have my graduation party there, maybe even my Sweet Sixteen. It will be the most important invitation of all that year."

She opened the refrigerator and looked at me.

I was tempted to ask her about when she lived at Saddlebrook and when Daddy wasn't here most of the time. What did she remember? Did he always call himself her father? How did he explain his long absences? People remember things differently, especially young children. She might not have the vivid memories of her parents that I did, especially since she didn't see Daddy daily. She had yet to mention anything significant about that time. I was filled with curiosity, but I was afraid of opening up a jar full of angry bees.

"You want some white wine? If I pour it quickly . . ."

She took out a bottle less than half full.

"No, thank you," I said.

"No, thank you," she mimicked, and poured herself some. I watched her gulp it down.

"That's not the way to drink wine," I said.

I remembered when Mazy and I had discussed it, and she showed me how to enjoy good wine and how to tell if it was good or not. We'd been going to have something special on my next birthday.

"I drink with my mouth. What do you use?" Karen said.

"No one's ever shown you how to smell wine, check its color, taste it correctly? Besides, you sip it, not gulp it like water."

"Yes, yes, but that's all boring," she said. She took a breath.

"Grandpa Amos showed me how to tell good wine. Listening to him go on and on about the vineyards, the weather, all of it, you can fall asleep before you take a taste. He'll have it at dinner, I'm sure, and we'll hear a small speech about the wine, where it comes from, how old it is, or what big, important person gave it to him."

"So he lives alone in this big house?"

"No. After Victoria Austen died, he hired a new live-in house-keeper who's almost as old as he is, Rebecca Johnson, who we call Miss Becky, his chef, Tommy Edwards, who was a chef in the navy, an army of grounds people there every day, and his limousine driver who lives above the garage, the guy who took us shopping for your tons and tons of things."

"Tons? You got quite a bit, too."

"Not half as much as you."

"But you didn't need as much as I did."

"Whatever," she said. She gulped some more wine, just to annoy me, I thought. She couldn't be enjoying it.

We heard a door close upstairs. She put her glass in the sink after rinsing it out quickly.

"What did you get out of gulping that?" I asked, just before Ava and Daddy appeared.

She grimaced. "A lot more than I would from water," she said. "You'll wish you had done it when you get to Saddlebrook."

"Wish you had done what?" Daddy asked as soon as he appeared.

"Smoked pot."

"What?" He looked at me, and I looked away. "Celisse got him to sleep," Daddy said. "Poor thing's suffering with that teething."

"Poor *thing*?" Ava said, coming up behind him.

Daddy reddened. "Just an expression. Speaking of things, let's get these two moving," he added, smiling at us.

Karen spun dramatically toward the garage door, acting as if she was making a great sacrifice of her precious time.

Ava looked me over closely. "Very nice," she said.

"Thank you."

Karen had already gotten into the car in the garage. We followed her. Daddy opened the door for Ava, but she stood there looking in at Karen.

"That's what you chose to wear to Sunday dinner at Saddle-brook?"

"Grandpa doesn't care as long as I don't wear my ripped jeans."

"Well, I do," Ava said. "If we weren't going to be late, I'd have you change."

She got in.

Once we drove out, Ava turned and looked at us. *She's going to say something now about their adopting me,* I thought, and braced myself for Karen's reaction.

"I don't want Grandfather Amos knowing anything about this disastrous event at the Tobys' house last night, so don't bring it up in an effort to get him to reduce your punishment, Karen."

Ava looked at me and nodded to emphasize it applied to me as well, even though I hadn't yet met her father. How could I ask him for anything?

"It's unfair," Karen muttered. She folded her arms, looked at me, and turned to stare out the window.

Once we left the village of Sandburg Creek, we drove a few miles down a nice two-lane highway with houses on both sides, most with one or two acres of property, many quite modern-looking ranch-style homes. We passed a dairy farm on the right, and then Daddy turned left on a much narrower road with thick woods. The unusually warm fall had kept the leaves from drenching the ground beneath them. It was as if we were parting a sea of yellow and brown around us. After a mile or so, the woods just suddenly ended and opened to flowing fields of fading fall green, rolling small hills, and then Saddlebrook seemingly rising on the right as we drew closer. A driveway of what seemed to be another mile led to the large house with a four-door separate garage on the right.

The house itself looked long enough to be three houses joined. It had two stories in a rectangular shape with a gabled roof. The arched black front door was right at the middle of the house, and all the windows on both floors were in pairs, evenly spaced. It had redbrick facing, with two white columns at the entrance. There was a decorative pediment of curves and swirls above the large front entrance.

If there was ever a house with adjoining property that looked like it belonged to the lord of a manor, this was it, I thought, as I gazed at the well-manicured hedges with fountains of all shapes and sizes spaced along the front. The small army of grounds people Karen had mentioned were scattered over the property, raking, trimming, and doing some digging to clear ditches. There were two tall oak trees on each side of the house, their golden leaves barely lifting in the soft breeze. Stone benches, more to be decorative than used, were placed between the trees on both sides.

In the distance, the mountains loomed against a darkening afternoon sky. I imagined the forest had been pruned years and years ago to fit the needs of the home some earlier owner had envisioned. Later I would learn that Amos Saddlebrook's great-grandfather had purchased the property. He'd had a small home that Amos's grandfather tore down to build the heart of what Amos would expand into his mansion.

I saw a barn in the rear of the house when we made the turn into the wide circular parking area. And off to the left was a swimming pool with a cabana and what looked like a bar. Chaise lounges were stacked neatly on one side. Behind the barn was a corral.

"Does Mr. Saddlebrook have horses?" I asked when I saw it.

"My grandfather did. My father has no interest in having any," Ava said.

"He was going to buy me a pony," Karen said. "But you told him not to."

"It would need constant care, and you wouldn't do it, Karen," Ava said.

Boy, I sure would, I thought.

"About a half mile down on the right, there is a natural lake fed by waters from Sandburg Creek," Ava said. "My father used to stock it with fish. There's still some. When I was Karen's age, I used to fish with my father and sometimes my mother."

"Boring," Karen sang.

After we parked, Daddy winked to boost my courage as we walked toward the entrance. Seconds before we got there, the large door was opened, and a short woman, with gray hair speckled with the remnants of her darker brown and swept up in a neat bun, smiled at us. She wore a light-blue ankle-length dress with heavy-heeled black shoes that added another inch or so to her height. Her grayish-blue eyes were warm, brightening her smile that nestled so gracefully in her circular face with puffy cheeks. Her smooth complexion looked resistant to age.

"Saw you pulling up in that security camera he's so proud of," she said, stepping back. "Used to be we enjoyed a surprise visitor now and then."

"Times have changed, Miss Becky," Ava said. "Dramatically. Surprises are more often dangerous or annoying than not."

"Ain't that the sorrowful truth, though," she said, and gave me a wider, friendlier smile. "And you're the poor lost little lamb."

"*Baa*," Karen said.

"Oh, dear." She gave Karen a stern look and then smiled at me. "I'm Miss Becky," she said, offering me her hand.

"Saffron," I said, taking it.

"What a beautiful name. For your hair, of course."

"Someone told me it's something you eat," Karen offered.

"Yes," Miss Becky said. "Saffron oil. Mr. Saddlebrook is in the study," she said, and we entered the house, immediately confronting the grand stairway with its thick mahogany banisters and red carpeted steps, which were wide enough for three people to walk up side by side. What appeared to be a newly laid dark-oak floor ran off the entry carpet. It was so polished it looked like you could skate over it. The stairway seemed to have been placed to separate the two sides of the first floor, as the hallway ran left and right in what were equal lengths. Ava turned right immediately, and we all followed her to the study.

My eyes were instantly drawn to a large painting. The gilt-framed portrait of a beautiful, elegant-looking woman whom Ava resembled was hung above the fireplace, one of the largest field-stone fireplaces I had ever seen, even in pictures, even in pictures of castles. The woman in the portrait was looking off slightly to her left so that the artist could capture her beautiful profile while still highlighting her violet eyes. She was holding a bouquet of white and red roses and looked to be in her late twenties at most. She wasn't wearing a wedding dress. It was an off-the-shoulder, lead-silver dress with an embroidered bodice. It had a tiered skirt. Her light-brown hair was brushed to her right side and lay softly over her shoulder and breast.

At first, I didn't realize anyone was there. My eyes drifted down to the man seated in a coral shell–colored oversize chair with rolled arms and nailhead trim. He looked like he sat comfortably, but he kept his back firmly against the chair so that he sat very straight, his arms placed on the rolled arms with his hands palms down. On his left hand was a large gold pinkie ring with an oval diamond that glittered in the light dropping from the two large teardrop chandeliers. His thick, clear-plastic-framed glasses rested on the bridge of his chiseled nose. They magnified his steel-grayish blue eyes. His full, masculine lips were poised to fold into a smile, but probably a tight one because of his narrow cheeks and almost embossed jawbone outlined in his light complexion. His silvery hair was sharply trimmed and, I imagined for a man in his eighties, still quite thick.

I would never have guessed he was that old anyway. His eyes looked lit with interest and the curiosity of a man much younger, and even seated, he looked slim, tall, and athletic. His black, highly polished shoes sat flat on the white, fluffy area rug that covered that part of the same dark-oak wood as in the hallway.

Everything about him seemed perfect, from the crisp knot in his light-blue tie to the sharp crease in his pants. He sat so still that for a moment, I imagined him drawn and painted there, the portrait of the Saddlebrook patriarch, as regal as any king. There was an air of immortality and power about him. And yet I felt nothing terrifying and angry flowing from him the way Ava often portrayed him.

So this was why Karen thought her grandfather would live forever, sometimes regretfully so, I thought. There was nothing really elderly or infirm in his appearance. He had the ruddy complexion of a man half his age.

"You two never looked more like parents of teenagers," he said, his lips forming the smile I was anticipating, although this smile was somewhat impish.

As we drew closer, I thought he was a good-looking older man. There was something confident and refined in his face, and with that youthful touch, it created a subtle sexiness. Some of the firmness I saw in Ava obviously had come from him, but I felt he could flash it on and off with almost a flick of his wrist.

"Being that we are," Ava said, "that's not much of a profound observation, Daddy."

"You'd be surprised at how many people don't look like what they really are," he replied. "So this is Saffron," he said, not waiting for an introduction. He nodded at me, and although no one had asked me to, I felt drawn to step forward quickly.

"Hello, Mr. Saddlebrook," I said. "I'm in awe of your house and the grounds."

He stared for a long moment like someone trying to see if I were really sincere.

"The result of many years of tender loving care," he said. He looked at Karen. "So, granddaughter, how are you two getting along? It must be nice having someone your age sharing your home."

"She's all right," Karen said, looking at me. "And will be better once she learns how to be a teenager."

Her grandfather laughed. "I don't know as being a teenager provides any advantage these days, eh, Derick?"

"Too much static," Daddy said. Amos Saddlebrook nodded as though they shared some secret about my generation.

"Well, everyone get comfortable." He nodded at the half-moon sofa across from him. "I had Miss Becky open one of the bottles of Veuve Clicquot champagne the French ambassador gave me for my birthday last year."

"Ugh. I hate champagne," Karen said.

"You're not drinking it anyway," Ava said.

We crossed the study to the sofa. There was another easy chair on the right. The floor of the study was covered with a large rug woven in hues of bright sage green and light orange. Ava sat in the far right corner of the sofa, and Daddy sat beside her. I waited for Karen to sit next to him, but she was practically moaning with boredom and struggling to move forward, so I did.

"What a beautiful rug," I said.

"It's Moroccan. My wife bought this on one of our trips," Amos Saddlebrook said. "I'm surprised you noticed. Most of Karen's friends move through here as if they wore blinders. This was quite the exciting buy."

Karen rolled her eyes and plopped down beside me.

"Might be another long, dreary story," she warned.

Miss Becky brought in the champagne in an ice bucket. A young African American woman followed her with a tray of champagne glasses and some dip and crackers.

"May I introduce Molly Carter?" Amos Saddlebrook said. "Just hired last Tuesday to assist Miss Becky with her duties."

Molly smiled at us. She looked no more than seventeen.

"Would you like to taste the champagne, Saffron?" Amos Saddlebrook asked me.

I was surprised. I looked at Ava, but she was looking down as if she were trying to control her anger. Was there always rage dancing around her when she confronted her father? She had made no attempt to greet him warmly, kiss his cheek, anything. He could be any stranger.

"Yes, please."

He nodded at Miss Becky, who started to pour five glasses.

"None for me. I'll have a Coke," Karen said.

Miss Becky nodded at Molly, who turned quickly, obviously to fetch it. Then Miss Becky brought glasses to Ava, me, and Daddy before she brought one to Amos Saddlebrook. Molly must have run to the kitchen. Before we had a chance to sip our champagne, she hurried back with a glass of Coke for Karen.

She took it, and a good beat went by before she said, "Thank you."

"Okay," her grandfather said after Miss Becky and Molly left. "Let's toast Saffron's arrival, not under the best circumstances but hopefully the right place for her to be at this time."

I sipped the champagne.

"Thank you," I said.

"How's Garson?" he asked Ava.

"His teething is not getting any better, and he's had bouts of diarrhea and vomiting. I'm taking him to Dr. Ross tomorrow."

"You'd think all the pain and trouble we have coming into this world would convince us not to," he said. He looked at Karen. "You helping with your brother?"

"He's got Celisse, but I help whenever I'm asked to, Grandpa."

"Helping has more meaning when you do it before anyone asks you to," he said.

She groaned. "Did Grandma have anything to do with making Mommy? She's more like your clone, or what's that character who popped out of Zeus's head?" she asked, looking to me. "My class just learned about it in literature class."

"Athena," I said. "She became his favorite child."

"Yeah, well, Mommy never had any competition. It's harder when you have competition."

I stared at her. Was she referring to herself and her baby brother? Once again, I wondered what was going to happen when she learned about her parents' intentions for me.

"How do you like our school, Saffron?" Amos Saddlebrook asked, ignoring Karen.

"It's the nicest school I've ever seen. It's beautiful. I like my teachers, too."

"That's good. I heard you're an honors student."

"I hope I'll continue to be."

"If you were capable of it in more unfortunate circumstances, you surely will be here. What do you favor, math? Science? Literature?"

"Math and literature, grammar."

"Interesting combination. A little unusual, I'd think."

"There's a mathematical way of learning grammar," I said. Mazy had tutored me in it.

Amos Saddlebrook's eyes widened with what I hoped was delighted surprise.

"Can I show her the house?" Karen blurted, clearly indicating she hated our topic.

"In a minute," her grandfather said sharply. "Let her finish her champagne. You know I don't like people walking about the house with drinks and food in their hands."

Karen sat back, already pouting. I was actually hoping she and I would tour the house and, while doing so, she'd say something about her early years here.

I sipped my champagne surely faster than I should.

"Having more than one interest is good. A variety will give you more opportunity in life," Amos Saddlebrook told me. "Travel, education, books, meeting new people, is something to seek. Have your sights set on anything yet?"

"No, sir," I said.

"She'll probably become a teacher," Karen offered. "She's practically one now."

"Oh? In what ways?"

"I think she means how I've helped her with her homework," I said.

Karen looked away and sipped her Coke.

"Well, you can be grateful for that, Karen," he said. "Your parents don't have to pay for a personal tutor."

She raised her eyes toward the ceiling.

"All right. You can show her the house, Karen. Leave your drinks here. Dinner will be served in ten minutes," he said. "Tommy's prepared some of your favorite dishes."

Karen popped up and looked at me. "C'mon. We don't have that much time. It's a big place to do in ten minutes," she said.

I looked at Amos Saddlebrook. His eyes were so focused on me that I was almost afraid to move. Then he gave me a slight nod, and I rose. I glanced at Daddy, who nodded slightly. He was clearly telling me this would give them the opportunity to discuss my adoption. Ava looked tense, her gaze focused on the portrait of her mother. Was there always going to be this sort of family tension? Was anyone really happy?

I followed Karen out.

"He's usually not that nice to strangers," she said when I caught up.

"I'm not a stranger. You'd think you would know that by now."

"He's never met you, so you're a stranger," she insisted. "Let's look at the ballroom first. Grandpa Amos keeps only a few chairs and tables folded up in it. When I was ten, I was permitted to attend a party he had for my mother's birthday. It was the first time I could stay for most of the party. There was a band on a small stage they put together like a puzzle."

"Puzzle?"

"You know, sliding sections. You're sure you're not from some other country?"

She led me down to the end of the hall, where we went through a double-door entrance to a large room with the same wood floor. There were two large windows at the rear draped in gold silk curtains. As she had described, there were a few chairs scattered along the side and in the far right corner a pile of folding tables. Besides its size, I saw nothing exciting about it.

"I imagine when everything is set up," I said, seeing she was expecting some sort of great reaction, "with some decorations . . ."

"You have to use your imagination a little. Balloons hanging from the ceiling, crepe paper everywhere, music piped from large speakers, and tables and tables of great food, cakes, and drinks. We had Grandpa's eightieth birthday party here. Even the governor stopped by. There were congressmen and senators, and I was permitted to bring five friends. You can imagine the competition to get the invite."

"I'm sure. Did you play in here when you were very little?" I asked. The question surprised her.

"No," she said quickly. "I was too little to be left alone. Let's go."

As we walked back to the stairs, she pointed out a more formal living room, not quite as large as the study, and then the dining room. Miss Becky and Molly were still setting up the long dark-maple wood table with the large teardrop chandelier above it. There was a mirror the length of the wall on one side.

"Grandpa's office is on the other end of the house. He has a separate entrance and parking lot for his business visitors."

I saw that the kitchen was down on the right, just across from the dining room. We just glimpsed it as we passed by, but it looked four times the size of Ava's.

"All the bedrooms are upstairs, three on each side of the stairway," Karen said. "C'mon. You can look at all that later."

I had paused to look at the art and a case that contained figurines.
"What are those?" I asked.

"Lladrós . . . from Spain or something. My grandmother collected them. My mother says they're worth a lot, but who would buy them?"

She hurried up the stairs ahead of me.

"I do remember something funny," she said when she reached the top. "This was like climbing a mountain. Grandfather still calls it 'Karen's Mountain.'"

I continued to follow her.

Everything we saw, every room, was very large, the bedrooms especially. The room she said was her mother's had what anyone would call a small living room as part of it, differentiated with a small step down. Although the vintage furniture had never been replaced since Ava left to live where they lived now, it all looked brand-new. It was obvious that the room was looked after daily. In a strange, almost eerie way, it was as if the room was being prepared for Ava to move back into any day, in fact any moment.

"What do you call this furniture?" I asked.

Karen broke into a wide smile. She knew something I did not.

"Grandpa never stops bragging about the furniture my grandmother bought and had made. This is called American Empire. My mother's canopy bed is called the Portsmouth Pineapple Bed. The posts are hand-carved. The wood is called tiger maple."

"Tiger?"

"Grandpa says they make guitars out of the same wood. You'd better tell him it's beautiful. Anything my grandmother did is beautiful or perfect."

She paused as I looked more closely at the furniture. I sensed she had something else to say, something maybe more important to me.

"My mother thinks she'll never live up to her mother in her father's eyes."

"Who said so? Did she say that?"

"I'm not really stupid, Saffron."

"I didn't say you were."

"I don't need it spelled out. I won't ever live up to my mother in her eyes, either," she said. "It's a family tradition to be inferior. What about you and your mother?"

"We were never in competition," I said. Maybe we would have been, I thought, but not like this. When a family is this arrogant, they never think anyone else could compete except other family members. In this moment, I felt sorry for Karen, even sorrier than I felt for myself.

"What about your father? Didn't he sleep in this room?"

"Sometimes. I don't remember all the details, but he was away working a lot, and then, suddenly, when I was starting school, we moved out."

"Were they married here? In the ballroom, maybe?"

"No, they eloped or something. Grandpa wasn't happy about it. My mother and him, he," she quickly corrected, "still argue about it." She paused and then whispered, "Because they didn't get married until a while after I was born."

"Oh, and then—"

We heard a bell ringing.

"Dinner," Karen said. "I'll show you the rest of the house later."

She started out. I looked again at the room in which Ava had grown up and that my father had shared periodically. You didn't have to be a brain surgeon to realize Amos Saddlebrook wasn't happy with his daughter's romance and pregnancy. It was probably very unpleasant for her being practically imprisoned here. No wonder she wanted her own home.

I could almost believe she made Daddy marry her eventually just to get out of here. Was it love or a desire to escape? How did Daddy navigate all this? How much did my mother know? It seemed to me he was boiling a pot of lies most of the time.

Maybe it was better for me not to navigate all the mystery. Where would it lead me?

I couldn't imagine more of the truth bringing happiness.

Mazy's adage resonated: *Ignorance is bliss.* Sometimes, I thought, but for now, surely here.

It wasn't possible to open a door or turn a page without my fingers trembling.

CHAPTER TWELVE

Almost as soon as I was seated at the long dining-room table, I knew that Daddy's idea to legally adopt me indeed had been discussed. I felt like some pet in an animal rescue mission. If they didn't take me, save me, I'd be forever lost. It wasn't difficult for me to have that feeling. Amos Saddlebrook was looking at me even more intently, scrutinizing everything about me. What had been his reaction to the idea? Was I auditioning for it right now? Would he start asking me more personal questions at dinner? I looked at Daddy, hoping to get some hint, but he was lost in thought again, gazing at the ceiling, maybe to avoid looking at me. Ava showed no indication one way or the other, either. She still wore that stern, businesslike expression she had the moment she confronted her father. I didn't sense any father-daughter warmth.

Miss Becky and Molly began to serve our salads, and as Karen had predicted, Amos Saddlebrook took a bottle of red wine out of the wine stand.

"I think we'll permit the girls to have a little of this," he said. "In civilized countries, young people are brought up to appreciate quality wine."

"We're not civilized in America?" Karen quipped.

He smiled. "There are pockets of it here and there."

He smiled at Daddy, who immediately smiled and nodded. He resembled a puppet. Ava remained stone-cold, with just that small dip in the sides of her mouth that told me she either was unimpressed by or disagreed with what her father had said. I noticed Amos Saddlebrook didn't even look at her to see her reaction.

"You two might as well learn the proper way to open a bottle of very good wine . . ."

I thought Karen's groan was a little too loud, but her grandfather ignored it and continued his instruction, mainly, it seemed, for me.

"Always wipe the outside lip, insert the corkscrew gently into the center, being careful not to go all the way through. Particles of cork might fall into the wine."

"And poison us?" Karen asked.

"No. Of course not. But the effect is ruined. Again, turn slowly, and steadily ease the cork from the bottle. Wipe the inside and outside of the lip once more."

"We could all go on social security by the time we get a sip," Karen said.

Her grandfather froze. I looked at Ava and suddenly saw something very new. She was actually smiling at something Karen had said. I turned to Daddy, who was looking angry. Before he could speak, Amos Saddlebrook looked at Karen sternly and said, "That's inconsiderate, Karen. Saffron's not had the experience of drinking good wine and drinking it properly."

"Yes, she has. She told me she knew how to check its color, its smell, and the taste. Right, Saffron?"

I thought I could hear thunder rolling through the great house. I glanced quickly at Daddy and at Amos Saddlebrook, but it was Ava who suddenly looked more interested.

"Why did the matter even come up for discussion?" she asked.

Karen looked suddenly terrified. Would I reveal she had snuck wine before we had left, and this after the disastrous Toby party?

"I was just telling her about some of the places my mother worked," I said. It seemed I'd be covering for my half sister my whole life. "For a while, my mother worked in a very classy restaurant and told me what she had to go through when someone ordered a very expensive bottle of wine. She had to be trained in how to open and pour it. She said it was like handling liquid gold."

"Ahh," Amos Saddlebrook said.

Ava's eyes continued to sparkle with suspicion. Daddy wore a look of relief, and Karen smiled with self-satisfaction. She had one-upped her grandfather. There was just slightly more of a crimson tint in his cheeks.

"Perhaps you can show us how it's done, then, Saffron," he said.

He nodded at Miss Becky. She took the bottle and poured the red wine into my glass, leaving enough room for what I knew was the swirling of it. *Do I do it all as perfectly as Mazy showed me or pretend to stumble in my memory? A simple thing like this could expose all our lies.*

My fingers were trembling when I grasped the glass but grew firmer when I swirled it, lifted it to look through the wine in the light, took a whiff, and tasted it.

"It needs a few moments," I said.

Amos Saddlebrook's face burst with delight and surprise. He turned to Daddy, who, for the first time, appeared as proud as any father would be. Karen looked like she was literally in pain. It was obvious she was hoping I would fall on my face.

"A few moments for what?" she asked, grimacing. "I want a sip already."

"You've seen this before, Karen," her grandfather said. "But obviously you didn't pay attention. Good red wine has to breathe, or decant, for a while. It brings out the flavor. Thank you, Saffron," he said, smiling warmly at me. "That was very nicely done."

I glanced at Ava. She stared at me, but not with the appreciation I anticipated. Instead, she was looking at me with even deeper suspicion. My heart beat faster.

"I'm amazed at the details you recall from what had to be quite a difficult life," she said.

Daddy's smile faded. Another small crisis had poked up its gleeful face. My lips trembled for a moment, and then I shrugged.

"Most of us don't realize how much we remember," I said as nonchalantly as I could. "How much sits untouched in our minds."

Ava tilted her head a bit and leaned forward. "How do you mean?"

I looked at Amos Saddlebrook. His eyes were sparkling with delight and anticipation.

I shrugged again. "Something you see triggers the image or images of things you thought you forgot or didn't realize were that impressive. Surely that's happened to you, Aunt Ava."

Amos Saddlebrook burst into a laugh. Daddy's smile radiated on his face. He looked so pleased. Ava simply nodded and sat back. No one spoke for a long moment.

"Can we start to eat already?" Karen asked.

It broke the tension. Amos Saddlebrook smiled and began. He and Daddy started to talk politics. I noticed how careful Daddy was when it came even to a slight disagreement. Ava concentrated more on chiding Karen for slumping and eating too quickly.

When our main dish of steak and a lobster tail was served, Amos Saddlebrook announced his plan to have a holiday dinner in the ballroom.

"Can I invite some friends?" Karen instantly asked. It was another opportunity to wield her power over some of her classmates.

"You can discuss that with your mother," her grandfather said. Karen groaned. "What?" he asked, catching the look in Ava's eyes. "Something I don't know about?"

"You'll probably hear about it soon," Ava said, holding her gaze on Karen. "Your granddaughter was part of a raucous party at the Tobys'. And parties are off the table for the foreseeable future."

"I thought we weren't to bring that up!" Karen cried. "Besides, Grandpa's holiday ball is not exactly another party, right, Grandpa?"

"Why don't you begin by telling me what occurred," Amos Saddlebrook said. He looked at Karen, but his eyes shifted to Ava.

"I'm being blamed for something I had no control over," Karen whined, and threw down her napkin, folded her arms petulantly across her chest, and sat back.

"We always have control of our own destiny," Ava said. "If our friends are doing something unpleasant, we step away from them."

"What if a meteor hits you in the head? You're not in control of that."

"In that case, you should have paid attention to the weather report," Ava said.

"Something untoward occurred at one of your parties, Karen?" Amos Saddlebrook asked. He looked at Daddy. "Why wasn't I told earlier? I don't like being the last one to hear about something involving my family."

"Mother didn't want to tell you!" Karen blurted, obviously hoping that would overshadow her involvement in the Toby party.

Everyone was silent for a long moment. Amos Saddlebrook dabbed his lips with his napkin and sat forward, his eyes suddenly focused solely on me.

"Were you there, too, Saffron?" he asked.

"Yes, sir," I said.

"Was it a meteor?"

"It was for me," I said.

Karen turned with daggers in her eyes.

Her grandfather nodded with a look no one could mistake for anything but admiration.

"Karen, you don't usually keep things from me."

Ava grunted like someone fighting a laugh.

He gazed at her and then back at Karen. "Well?"

I kept my eyes down and waited.

"Some boys got Margaret Toby's brother sick drunk at a party at her house."

"Sid Toby's house?"

"Yes," Ava said.

Amos looked at her, then glanced at Daddy and then at Karen. "And you? Did you get drunk, too, Karen?"

"Not really," she said. She glanced at me, and I looked away.

"I see. Well, it's good I was told tonight. I'm sure I'll hear about it at the club tomorrow. Sid Toby has a loose mouth for a bank president." He sat up. "Let's not let this ruin the dinner," he said. "We'll sort it out. Afterward, we'll have dessert in the study, where your parents have something more important to discuss with us all," he added, turning to Karen.

When she frowned, her eyebrows nearly touched.

I looked at Daddy, who gave me a small nod. The tension at the table was as thick as a fog, and suddenly, the tapping of silverware and the lifting of glasses and putting them back on the table were a discordant symphony that sounded louder than the drumbeat of my heart.

Watching everyone lost in their thoughts convinced me that the lies in this family went deeper than I had imagined. It was as if they had their own sharply penetrating roots and were moving quickly in my direction. Soon I'd be an integral part of the web of deception that held the Saddlebrooks and Daddy together. I really had so little family happiness to use as a touchstone, but I couldn't help wondering if this was true for every family, wondering if their family histories and the individual needs and ambitions of each member required as much betrayal as it did loyalty. Could I have been far better off being only with my Umbrella Lady? Should I not have longed so much to find my father and a family life? I mourned more for Mazy. In what had become her make-believe magic cottage, I was happier fantasizing. Eventually, there were no fogs at our dinners; there was only love.

Who really loved another here?

After we had all taken our seats in the study and before any dessert was served, Daddy announced his and Ava's proposal. He was looking mostly at Karen.

"Adopt?" she asked, like someone who wasn't sure of the meaning of the word.

"For all intents and purposes, her living with us all is practically the same thing," Daddy said.

"You mean her name will be Anders, too, now?" Karen asked.

The words tormented my lips, danced on my tongue. I was so close to blurting it out: *That is my name.* But I closed my eyes to shut down the urge and pressed my lips together hard.

"Aren't you pleased?" Amos Saddlebrook asked. "You'll really have a sister as well as a little brother."

I could see the turmoil in her face. Yes, having a sister sounded good, but now everything I was given and everything I wanted would be coming to me as an Anders, and although it was only through some legal document, Saddlebrook was something I could lay claim to as well as she. I could invite friends here, have parties here. In short, I was going to be too equal to her. How could she bestow anything on me and expect my worshipping gratitude?

And what about Daddy? After I was adopted, I could sit up front, and she would sit in the back. When she looked across the room at him, I could read it in her eyes. *Will he love me the way he loves her?* It was as if she was a princess who had to shift somewhat to the right to make room for another on the throne.

And yet she couldn't show any of this. Her grandfather, who I thought already saw how self-centered she could be, would condemn her. Nevertheless, she was surely thinking that he, too, could favor me more and very soon. No longer would she be showing me how to behave and with condescension granting me access to her friends, but I could very well do that to her.

Oddly, perhaps, I felt sorry for her. This total stranger had moved into her home and into her family with seeming lightning speed and had begun to take over part of her special world. Already too often, her mother was pointing to this new girl as someone to emulate. She had a new shadow cast over hers. But until this moment, she still had something much more important than anything the new girl had brought with her behavior, intelligence, and good looks. She had the Saddlebrook name, with only an infant brother to share it and all the importance it brought.

Now what?

"Is there a ceremony or something? Maybe in the ballroom?" Karen asked, still sounding a little stunned.

Amos Saddlebrook laughed and looked at Daddy. "That's my granddaughter . . . always thinking of a party," he said.

"Well, something fun should happen," Karen insisted. She sat back in a pout.

"Actually," her grandfather said, "it's not a bad idea. We should get Saffron's ideas about it, too, don't you think?"

"How can she have any ideas? She really doesn't know anyone, except one boy a little, and she went to her first party ever at the Tobys'."

"Well, that's unfortunate, apparently, isn't it?" Amos Saddlebrook said. "To base your idea of a party on that?"

"It wasn't that bad," Karen muttered.

No one spoke for a moment.

Amos Saddlebrook looked at his watch and nodded at Miss Becky. She and her assistant began to clear away the dishes.

"If it is all right with everyone, especially Saffron, I'd like to have a conversation with her in my office. There's no reason for you all to wait. I'll have Tyson bring her home."

"Why?" Ava demanded instantly. Both she and Daddy looked quite surprised.

"She's on the verge of becoming part of the Saddlebrook family. I think she should be aware of what that entails."

"And you don't think we can do that?"

"Why shouldn't she get it all firsthand?" Amos responded.

Ava turned to Daddy. "Did you know about this?"

He shrugged, lifting his arms. He looked at Amos Saddlebrook, who was fixed on him in a way more intently than I had yet seen. It was clear to me he was just about daring him to oppose.

"I see nothing wrong with your father wanting to get to know his adopted granddaughter and letting her get to know him," Daddy said.

"And all the baggage," Ava muttered. "Don't forget that."

"How come I never had a meeting like this with you, Grandpa?" Karen demanded.

"You didn't have a choice like Saffron does, Karen. You were born into it."

She looked at me. "Choice? You mean, she could choose not to be adopted?"

"We'll see," he said.

"I was supposed to show the rest of the estate to her," she whined.

"You'll be back together many, many times," he said. "Is this all right with you, Saffron?"

I looked at Daddy. For the first time since the night I had arrived and he had set eyes on me, his confidence was gone. He actually looked somewhat frightened. Should I claim to be too tired? Ava was staring at me with new curiosity. Why would I oppose it?

"I think she's still a little frightened of you, Daddy," Ava said, her eyes fixed on me as she spoke. "Maybe it's better if she gets to know you more before you have one of your famous tête-à-têtes."

"There's no fast way to get to know me, and Saffron doesn't look as frightened as you're suggesting. Saffron? We won't be that long."

"I'm not frightened," I said. "I look forward to hearing more about the Saddlebrooks."

He smiled.

"Well, are you going to talk about a party for her?" Karen asked.

"Perhaps," he said.

"I should help with the planning."

"I imagine you will," he said.

Karen settled into some satisfaction.

Amos Saddlebrook stood up. Daddy rose. Ava seemed to be glaring at me as if she suspected I might be trying to dislodge her inheritance or something.

She rose. "Let's go, Karen. I'm sure you haven't finished your homework."

Karen smiled at me to telegraph her secret about the plan she and her friends were concocting. She stood up, and we all walked out of the dining room.

"I hope you all enjoyed dinner," Amos Saddlebrook said.

"It was wonderful," Daddy said. "Our thanks to Tommy."

Amos Saddlebrook nodded. I waited to see if Ava would hug her father or even say good night. She barely managed to utter that.

"I'll have her home very soon," her father said, putting his hand on my shoulder.

"She does have school tomorrow," Ava reminded him.

Daddy looked at me, his eyes full of warnings and caution. I wished we could have had a private moment, but that was impossible.

As I stood there watching the three of them leave, I felt as if I was dangling off a cliff.

"This way, my dear," Amos Saddlebrook said, turning to the left. "I realize everything is moving very quickly for you. Let's take a half hour or so to help you catch your breath. My daughter has this intensity about everything that can sometimes overwhelm everyone involved. Patience was never a valuable asset to her and rarely is to a determined woman. Or man," he quickly added. "But measuring twice and cutting once has always worked for me."

He looked at me for my reaction. I said nothing.

"I suspect that might be true for you. You don't appear to be as hyper as Karen and other girls her age. I'm fascinated with how someone with your background developed such calm maturity."

I could think of no answer that wouldn't involve the truth. He smiled.

As we continued to walk through the hallway, he described some of the art, some statues, and the custom work in the walls and ceilings. He explained who each of the ancestors in the portraits was and paused at the one of his father and mother. He spoke softly but with great pride, pointing out who had bought what as well. Just before his office door was the portrait of him and his wife. There was also a cabinet with old papers, documents, awards. He explained some of them.

"When a family has a history like the Saddlebrooks', it's important to protect and reconfirm it. Great families build great countries," he said, smiling. He paused, thought a moment, and added, "I wouldn't consider an adopted granddaughter any less important than one born into Saddlebrook, especially one who is capable of making us prouder, but we're not exactly a club. All of our family's rules of behavior are unwritten but well understood."

He indicated the office entrance and waited. Karen wasn't exaggerating about it. It was very big, with one of the largest desks I had ever seen. As he explained, it was custom-made. I wouldn't have seen it anywhere else. The walls had stacks of books that reached the ceiling with sliding ladders, and on the left was a long conference table with at least twelve or so chairs. There was a large television set on the wall, and it had been placed so he could look at it from behind his desk. In front of the desk were two large leather chairs, and on the immediate right were a settee, a table, and two more leather chairs.

Perhaps the most stunning part of the office was its floor, a slate that appeared to have gold threads running through each panel, glittering under the light.

"Let's sit here," he said, indicating the settee. "More comfortable."

I sat, and he took one of the leather chairs. He smiled warmly.

"Don't look so nervous, my dear. With your uncle proposing such an important decision, not only for you but for the Saddlebrook family, I thought we should quickly get to know each other better. That's all this is." He leaned forward with a soft smile. "I can't depend on my daughter to do it all as well. She needs more time, age, like good wine. True for your uncle as well."

He laughed, but I was afraid to mock Ava. Nevertheless, I breathed what I hoped wasn't an obvious sigh of relief. He was calling Daddy my uncle. Perhaps, then, he really didn't know the truth.

His smile flew off his lips when he sat back. "I'm one of those cold realists about life. Lying is almost a prerequisite for being in business. But I draw the line on that with family. Families live and breathe based on their honesty with each other. I hope you feel the same."

"Yes," I said meekly. I feared what he was leading up to now.

"Good. Are you comfortable being part of this family at the moment, an Anders?"

"Yes," I said, surprised at the question.

"They're obviously comfortable with you, wanting to legally adopt you. You've already made quite the impression on my daughter and granddaughter. To be quite honest," he continued, "I had no idea that you'd be coming here to live. Your uncle and his sister did not get along?"

"No."

"Maybe that's too kind a way to put it. Did your mother talk of him much?"

"No," I said.

Under his intense and inscrutable gaze, words that enforced and compounded our great lie seemed heavier than ever on my tongue, especially after what he had just said about families. He seemed to hear me with his eyes, eyes that were reading every movement in my face. He glanced at my hands. I hadn't realized that I was squeezing my fingers into tight fists. I opened them quickly.

"She must have spoken about him enough for you to know to come here."

Ava practically had asked me the same thing.

"I knew of no other relatives, and I was afraid I'd end up with some foster family."

He nodded. Was that enough of an answer? I hoped it didn't sound memorized.

"How did you know he'd want to take you in?"

"I didn't. If he didn't, I was going to keep going."

"To where?"

"Anywhere."

I said it so firmly that he smiled.

"Should I think of that as quite courageous or quite stupid?"

I felt my face redden, the heat rushing into my eyes.

"What would a Saddlebrook have done?" I asked.

He stared a moment and then broke into a smile and a laugh.

"I do believe you're a challenge for my daughter and might be a great positive influence on Karen." He lowered his eyes. "I think we both know she needs a little positive influence from someone about her age."

I felt myself relax a little, but I could see he was still thinking very hard about me and kept myself poised for a sharper question, one that would cut cleanly through all the fiction Daddy had contrived and I was following.

"I want you to think of me as someone you can trust," he said. "I know that is not something I should expect overnight, but once you have become a part of this family, your welfare is even more important to me. Make no mistake about it. I don't want you to be blindly loyal. I want your respect. I ask only that if you do something or know something that will tarnish the Saddlebrook name, its history, and its standing in this community, you alert me to it, even before you alert your uncle and aunt, if possible. Can you promise that?"

"I think so," I said.

"For now, that will be good enough. In time, I hope we'll trust each other far more, and you will believe you know so. Exchanging truth is very important in a family."

"Maybe we can start to do that now."

"Oh?"

"I learned that my uncle did not marry Aunt Ava until some time after Karen was born, that she and Aunt Ava lived here until then. Karen doesn't talk about it much, and frankly, neither does Aunt Ava."

"Yes, that's true. I wasn't about to parade my pregnant, unmarried daughter in this community. There was talk about us behind my back, of course, but even that was subdued. Ava does have a mind of her own. She's more of a Saddlebrook than she would admit, so I put up with the temporary arrangements until . . . the right thing happened."

"What made my uncle finally do the right thing?"

He gave me that piercing look again. I didn't squirm or look away.

"I think you know. You're pretty perceptive."

"Love?" I said, shrugging.

"I suppose some of that."

"What else?"

I didn't think he would answer. I held my breath.

"Look around you," he said.

"I don't understand."

"Ambition. That's okay," he quickly followed. "I admire it, demand it of myself. I don't think of it as a fault. Just know," he said, leaning toward me, "that when you reveal it too soon, make it too clear, someone can take advantage of you. And maybe . . . make you do things that you never thought you would."

I thought I really did feel my heart shudder.

Because deep inside, where fears snuggle and wait to emerge, I could sense the most horrible one had begun to open its eyes.

He walked me to the car afterward, and just before I got in, he handed me a card.

"I want you to feel free to come to see me anytime, Saffron. This number is Tyson's, and he will have instructions to get you and bring you to me anytime you call. Okay?"

"Okay," I said, taking it.

He had such a strong, penetrating gaze, I thought. The man could get into my mind with a searchlight and find my secrets.

And he seemed to know there were many.

CHAPTER THIRTEEN

"Did he say he would make you a party in the grand ball-room?" Karen asked as soon as I entered through the front door. She practically lunged at me in the entryway. Aunt Ava had permitted her to wait up in the study, where both she and my father were watching television, both eagerly awaiting me as well.

"Before I left, he told me to start the planning for it," I said.

"Really," she said, not asked. I could see in her expression that she was both happy and a little disturbed about it. "How can you plan for it? You won't know who to invite, besides Tommy."

"Whom," I said.

"What?"

"Of course, you'll help plan, Karen. You'll make most of the decisions. What do I know about parties and people to invite?"

Aunt Ava came to the study doorway.

"Is everything all right, or did my father make you feel uncomfortable about being legally adopted?"

"It was fine. He's just very proud of his family, the history and importance in the community, and wants to be sure I will be, too."

On the ride home, I had rehearsed this answer for her, expecting the question or something similar.

"He has to be in control of everything," she muttered. "The puppet master."

"How's Garson?"

"We got him to sleep an hour or so ago. I have a doctor's appointment in the morning. He might have an infection. We'll see. All right. You two go to bed."

I just gazed in at my father, who was staring at the television set but probably not hearing or seeing anything playing. I was sure he had heard my response. I waited, but he didn't even look at me. Wasn't he worried? Didn't he want to know what Amos Saddlebrook and I had discussed, or was he simply afraid to ask anything in front of Ava and Karen?

I walked past Karen and headed for the stairway. She followed quickly.

"Well, what did he say about the party exactly? Did he say we could have live music or what? And I hope we can do the menu. My friends don't like to eat all that fancy stuff."

"He didn't get into any details like that, but I'm sure we can and will," I tossed back at her, and hurried up the stairs. She followed me to my room and stood in the doorway, watching me get undressed. I know she was trying to figure out what I was really feeling, thinking.

"Something isn't right. You're too quiet. Did he frighten you or anything?"

I paused and thought about it.

"He did, didn't he?" she said. "He's such a bully."

"He doesn't frighten you like someone full of threats. Your grand-father reeks of power. He's not someone you can lie to or deceive easily. But I'm sure you know that, too. I'm just tired, Karen. I want to go to sleep."

"Well, what did you talk about all this time? It wasn't just having a party."

"He wanted to know more about me, and he wanted me to know more about the Saddlebrook family. Just like I told your mother."

"Mother's right. He likes to be in control of our lives and always has. He puts down his rules, and we have to live by them."

I started for the bathroom. She stepped back, seeing I was so determined I could knock her over.

"I don't care about his rules. You'd just better not invite Melina Forest," she said. I kept walking. "She'll keep Tommy from paying attention to you!"

I closed the door and just stood there, waiting for my heart to slow down. I wasn't thinking at all about any party. Memories and images I had long ago tried to crush were flying back at me like sting-ing hail. The sound of the wheels of the train that brought me here was grinding away at my brain. I saw flames dancing in the kitchen. When I looked back into the smoky darkness, I screamed. I could hear it. I put my hands over my ears and pressed so hard it hurt, as if that would shut out the sound.

Karen opened the door.

"Well, I did a lot of talking waiting for you. I think they'll let us go to the party after the game," she said. "I've put a hold on everyone not doing homework in protest, even though I still have some to do. Just don't say anything that might screw it up. It could be a great party if we win the game."

She closed the door.

Parties. Party for me, party for the team, parties, parties, parties. How lucky she was, able to be so indifferent to everything else. Perhaps it wasn't until this moment that I truly realized how jealous of her I really was. It was as if I had been forced to leap over my child- hood and even now, my teenage years. Karen could be a child forever, coddled and cared for, her every whim attended to. I had calluses on my feelings that she would never see, much less experience. I knew that being a child forever really wasn't something to desire if you had self-pride and self-respect and wanted the respect of others as well. I wanted to grow up and be responsible and worthy of praise, but I never really had playtime. You need children your age to have playtime.

Daddy had forced me to replace my real difficult and painful childhood with a fictional one. To survive, I had to build my new identity out of lies, embellish the deceit any way I wanted or could imagine. How could I ever relax? This life was exhausting and full of traps. I had just lied to Karen again. I didn't trust what I had seen in Amos Saddlebrook's eyes. He did frighten me. In fact, I had been trembling all the way home and was still trembling even now. How was this going to end? I wished that it would. I wished that the bottled-up real me could breathe again.

I prepared for bed and went into my room. Clouds had shifted, and the light from a nearly full moon put a silvery glow on every- thing. After I slipped under the blanket, I lay back on my pillow with my hands behind my head and stared at the ceiling. I heard Garson's crying behind Daddy and Ava's bedroom door. I could hear Daddy's heavier footsteps as he went downstairs and, minutes later, came hurrying up. Garson's crying stopped soon afterward. The stillness seemed extra thick. I brought my hands around, closed my eyes, and turned over to sleep.

Not five minutes later, I heard the door open and, expecting it was Karen, turned over to chase her out. But it was Daddy. He closed the door softly behind him and stood in the glow of the moonlight, a silhouette, more like a shadow than a man. Maybe I was already dreaming.

"Did he upset you?" he asked in a loud whisper after taking another step toward me. "What did he ask?"

"He wanted to know about my mother and you, the long estrangement, and why I would come here. Same as Ava."

"You stuck to the story?"

"Yes, but I'm not sure what he thinks, what he believes."

"Why?"

"It's just a feeling," I said.

"It's all right," Daddy said. "You're going to be a part of this family, his family. None of it will matter anyway as far as he's concerned once you're tied to the Saddlebrook heritage."

I said nothing, but I didn't have his confidence.

He stood there.

"You were wonderful tonight. Everything is fine. Very soon," he said. I'm sure he was smiling. "Very soon, you'll be able to call me Daddy again."

He waited a moment, and then he turned and slipped out when I didn't respond.

He wouldn't have liked it, perhaps.

I might have said, *I don't know if I will.*

....

Even before we arrived at school the following day, everyone knew I was to be adopted. Karen had gone on her phone. Apparently, from the reactions I saw, she hadn't been complaining, just announcing it and, with it, the prospect of a big celebration at Saddlebrook. I knew she was using it to wield her power over her doting classmates. I hated being the cause of that, and I didn't enjoy the phony friendliness it was drawing to me, either.

"I guess I don't have to ask you how your dinner at Saddlebrook was," Tommy said when we met in the hall. Melina was with him. "Adopted. Are you happy about it?"

"Why wouldn't I be?"

"Karen will officially be your sister," he joked.

Melina told him to stop teasing. One of Karen's friends was sure to hear him.

"Sorry. You're coming to practice today, right?" he asked. "I'll take you home."

Knowing that I would be unable to attend the game made me hesitant. I didn't want to build up his expectations, but I didn't want to create any suspicions, either.

"I'll be there with Melina," I said. "We can work on some math problems while we watch."

"Once you see me out there, you won't be able to concentrate on schoolwork," he bragged with a broad smile.

"Did I forget to tell you he was narcissistic?" Melina said.

The three of us laughed. Staying close to Tommy and Melina most of the day kept me from having to put on the false face of excitement over a grand party that I couldn't help feeling celebrated so much untruth. I feared that I would look so uncomfortable that

Amos Saddlebrook would have even deeper suspicions. Lies so stretched out would surely snap.

Karen wanted me to hang with her more, especially at lunch. I was like a new jewel to wear. Whenever she had the opportunity to say it, she did. "Did you meet my new sister?"

Each time, I was tempted to say it: *I am really your sister, your blood sister, a half sister. We share the same father.*

It would be as if the ceiling was caving in, especially on her. I swallowed back the words, of course, gave my best fake smile of delight. I told her I was staying after school to watch basketball practice.

"Maybe you can tell Uncle Derick when he comes to pick us up," I said.

"I've already called him and told him you're staying to watch basketball practice and I'm going over to Adele's house with Margaret. They can help me plan the adoption party," she said, and walked away.

Right after the last class of the day, Melina and I sat in the bleachers and watched the practice. We did have our textbooks open, but she didn't push us to do anything. She saw how drawn I was to watching Tommy. I knew practically nothing about sports, any sport, but I had seen some basketball on television. While the other players seemed forced at times, struggling to press their offense and defense, Tommy floated gracefully, slicing with confidence through the air and making basket after basket as if it was as natural to him as breathing.

"He really is good, isn't he?"

"Yes," Melina said. "And although I tease him about having too big an ego, it's his self-confidence that enables him to use his skills. You have to believe in yourself more than other people believe in you."

I looked at her with more interest. She wasn't a budding beauty, by any means, but she had that same graceful self-confidence in her eyes.

"How did you get yours?"

"It just comes, I guess. I'm focused and therefore probably older than I am. There are advantages and disadvantages. Most of the girls here distrust someone so . . . responsible? It's like I'd report them for littering or something."

She peered harder at me.

"Sometimes you strike me as someone who's arrived at the same place I'm at but through much more difficult travels."

"Yes" was as much as I wanted to say. Best to turn the conversation to her, I thought. "What do you want to do? I bet you'll get into any college you want."

"I'm going into medicine," she said, as if it was a foregone conclusion. "I'm leaning toward cardiology."

"I don't doubt you'll do it."

She shrugged. "Neither do I."

We laughed. Tommy made what looked like an impossible shot and gazed up at us, at me.

"He's showing off for you," Melina said. "Coach McDermott is going to chew him out for not passing."

"Seems like I am best at getting someone else in trouble."

"Don't worry about it. He wants to get in trouble over you," she said, and we both laughed again.

"How do you do it?" I asked. "How do you not care about what they think of you?"

"Only care about what someone you respect thinks about you," she said. "Then it's easy."

"Tommy's lucky to have you as a friend," I said. "He'll miss you when he goes off to college. I bet you'll miss him, too, right?"

She shrugged again. "Everyone needs a little fantasy. He's mine," she admitted. "Don't dare tell him."

I hugged her. I didn't think anyone else in this school, including Tommy, ever had.

As soon as the coach blew his whistle to end practice, Tommy ran over to us.

"Give me a chance to shower and get dressed," he told me. "Then I'll take you both home."

"My mother's picking me up," Melina said. "We're going to do some grocery shopping."

"Oh. Fifteen minutes," he told me, and ran off.

"Are you telling the truth?" I asked Melina.

"Yes," she said. "There's something special about Tommy. He's hard to lie to," she added, rising. Of course, it had to be in my imagination, but I thought she was telling me something between the lines. She looked at our untouched text problems, shook her head, and started away.

"You're coming to my party," I shouted after her. "Don't worry about Karen."

She turned and smiled.

I sat back to wait.

When Tommy came out, he paused as if he was afraid I wouldn't be there. Then he broke into a wide smile and hurried to me.

"Well, what did you think?"

"I bet your wastebasket is ten feet from your desk at home."

He laughed and reached for my hand. I picked up my books, which he instantly piled on his own, and we started out, some of his teammates whistling and calling to him. We headed for an exit to the parking lot.

"I was thinking of applying to UCLA. Coach thinks I might get a basketball scholarship there. A scout is showing up. It's a great school, but I've also been thinking about that Southern California weather. Was it great?"

Melina's words about not lying to Tommy were still echoing.

"I don't think much about the weather," I said.

"Just took it for granted, huh?"

I was silent. *This is so wrong. Break it off before it starts,* I thought. But when I looked at him, at the joy in his face, and felt his undisguised excitement at being with me, I couldn't do it. *Lies as tools.*

"Yes, I suppose so," I said.

He laughed and nodded at his car.

After we got in and started away, he asked me about Saddlebrook.

"I was never in it. What's it like?"

"It's beautiful, lots of art and vintage furniture. I didn't see any of the grounds, really. It's more like a family museum than a home."

"Really?"

"If there is a party in the ballroom, you'll be there, and you can judge for yourself."

"You don't sound all that excited about it, the adoption, becoming a part of all this." He glanced at me. "Am I wrong?"

"Things are happening fast, maybe too fast."

"Good things, though, right?"

"Too soon to tell," I said.

It surprised him. "You came from a world in which you struggled to survive, according to all I know and heard, and you're now in the world of great privilege, where you'll have everything you want."

"'Everything' is a big word. No one has everything they want. Maybe that's good."

His eyes widened again. "I have this question that keeps floating in my mind, Saffron."

I didn't want to hear it, but I saw no way not to. "Which is?"

"Who are you?" he said.

"When I find out, I'll let you know," I said, and he laughed.

"Hey, let's do this little detour. Fifteen more minutes won't matter, will it?"

"Probably not. Where?"

"Here," he said, making a quick right down a street that eventually turned into what looked like a one-way gravel road. We turned and passed bushes and trees, and then suddenly, the lake exploded right before us. There was a clearing obviously used for cars often.

"My favorite spot on the lake," he said. "I don't suggest swimming, but we can walk down to the water."

I nodded, and we got out. He took my hand, and we crossed the rest of the clearing to a path that led to a small shoreline. The lake was glistening in the late-afternoon sun as the rays threaded through trees and then danced with glitter over the water gently lapping against the sand and rocks around us. We could hear the sound of a motorboat way off toward the other end.

"My dad's not a fisherman, but in the summer, we go water skiing. The dock's off left there. I guess it doesn't compare to the Pacific, huh?"

There is something about pure nature that causes it to tighten its grip on lies and deceit. I had no way to prove it or even to suggest it, but I thought lies were easier in the center of the city, surrounded by buildings and concrete. Signs and posters, lit and unlit, broadcast untruth all around you to sell products. There was nothing untrue in these surroundings, nothing false in the water, no whispers of lies in the breeze. Everything conspired to touch your heart and maybe your soul. If you concentrated, meditated, stopped thinking of tricky answers, ways to lie even to yourself, you would or could become a part of all this, even if only for a short while. I took a deep breath and closed my eyes. Tommy's hand held mine tightly.

"I never saw the ocean," I said.

His grip on my hand loosened. "What? How could that be? I mean . . ."

"Everything about me is complicated, Tommy. Maybe you shouldn't get yourself too involved with me."

He turned me around so we were face-to-face.

"There's nothing complicated about the way I feel about you and how fast it happened. I don't mind moving slowly, Saffron, as long as you want it. I thought you did. Have you changed your mind? Now that you're going to be part of the wealthiest family in the county, maybe one of the wealthiest in the state?"

"That doesn't have anything to do with it. As long as you don't mind the mystery."

"What could be more romantic?" he joked. Then he looked very serious and slowly brought his lips to mine. It was not only another real kiss; it was the longest kiss. I put my arms around him and my head against his chest, and we stood silently for what seemed like minutes but was probably only seconds.

"Are you all right?"

"Better get me home," I said.

He nodded, took my hand, and walked me back to the car.

Neither of us spoke until we were back on the road heading for Ava's house. Despite my father having married her and having another child with her, to me it would always be Ava's house.

"So the way this works is there is a committee in charge of organizing the party after the game. They wheel in tables of food and soft drinks with hawk-eyed teachers watching to see if anyone tries to spike any, and there is music piped in. If we lose, it will still be a celebration of our getting this far. But we won't lose."

"Did you win the first time you played against them?"

"Yes, but only by two points."

"Don't lose," I said. *Not against Hurley*, I wanted to say.

"Okay, boss."

He laughed, and we turned down the road to Ava's house.

"See you tomorrow," he said after we stopped in the driveway. "And especially at the game. Every basket I make will have your name on it."

He leaned over to give me a kiss, and then I got out and watched him back out of the driveway. Ava stepped out of the formal living room when I entered the house and started for the stairway.

"Where have you been?"

"What?"

"Simple question," she said.

"I stayed after to watch basketball practice. Karen said she had already told Uncle Derick."

"I wish someone would tell me when there are changes," she said. "Karen is staying over at Adele's tonight. That's all she told me."

"How is Garson?"

"He's on antibiotics and sleeping in the living room," she said. She started to turn back to it and stopped. "Your uncle is bringing home Chinese food. He said you told him you liked it, that you told him your mother and you had it often."

I nodded. It wasn't so hard to lie to Ava. It was harder to lie to her father.

I went upstairs.

Being with Tommy was like being able to come up for air. I tried to think of nothing else but him. How would he react when and if he knew the truth? Could he see beneath all the lies? What would he see?

I had started to change my clothes when I heard a knock on the door.

"Yes?"

Daddy opened it just enough for me to see him.

"You can't go to school tomorrow, the day of the game," he said. "Getting sick just before it will look suspicious. Start complaining about something after dinner."

"How come you're so good at this?" I asked, before he could step back and close the door.

"Good?"

"At lies as tools. Have you been doing this all your life?"

He paused.

"Ninety percent of what you hear and see out there is either half-truth, twisted truth, or an outright untruth, Saffron. Maturity means being able to handle it to your own advantage. The truth about truth is most people avoid it. In the end here, you're not harming anyone. You're making them happier," he said, and closed the door.

For a while, I simply stood there, staring at it.

"What about harming yourself, Daddy?" I whispered.

I felt like he had turned me into some creature that fed only on lies. I had nearly confessed to Tommy. Another kiss, more soft words, laughs, and promises, and the dam that held back the truth might shatter. Then what? Would Daddy have been right? Would all I'd have done be to make him unhappy and drive him off?

Act ill? I didn't think I'd have to pretend too much. When I went down to dinner, I was already feeling sick, as sick as I would have felt if I had swallowed a bubble of tar. Ava was reheating the takeout Chinese food.

"You can set the table," she told me.

I had started to do it when Daddy came rushing in, carrying Garson in his bassinet. He had a look of terrible pain and panic on his face.

"What's wrong?" Ava asked.

"He's choking a lot. At one point, I thought he turned blue."

She dropped everything and went to him.

"He feels hot," she said. "We'd better contact Dr. Ross and tell him we're going to the emergency room. You call. I'll bundle him up," she said, taking the bassinet. She looked at me. "Turn everything down. Eat what you want. Let's go, Derick!" she said sharply.

He glanced at me and hurried out of the kitchen.

Wait! I wanted to shout after them. *I'm the one who's supposed to be sick.*

I turned everything off on the stove and stood back while they got everything together and hurried out. Neither of them asked if I wanted to come along.

When the door closed and the house became empty and quiet, I realized I would never feel at home here. Judges could sign papers. Lies could be cemented. None of it could take the place of real love.

Twice I had left that behind when I boarded a train.

As I sat there, feeling dumbfounded and lost, it suddenly occurred to me that since I had been here, my father hadn't really embraced me. The facade that he had created and I followed prevented him from being "too" affectionate. A smile, a kiss, or a hug might create a suspicion.

To keep myself from thinking too much, I cleaned up the kitchen and put away the takeout food. Then I went up to my room and, for some reason I could not explain, went to my old bag and took out the coloring book. The edges of the pages were yellowed and thin.

I reached in and took out the old box of crayons, and then I went to my desk, sat, and began to color in the remaining pages. People were walking to and fro quickly. Another train was pulling into the station.

And then, out of the darkness, the Umbrella Lady was walking toward me.

CHAPTER FOURTEEN

I awoke to the sound of footsteps on the stairway and got out of bed and to the door practically in one leap. When I opened it and looked out, I saw Ava and Daddy quietly carrying Garson into their bedroom. He was apparently asleep.

"How is he?" I asked.

Ava put her finger to her lips and followed Daddy in. I stood there, waiting. Minutes passed. I thought I might just go back to bed, but finally, Ava emerged and softly closed the door behind her.

"He had epiglottitis," she said. "Lucky we brought him in."

"What is that?"

"The small lid of cartilage that covers your windpipe swells and blocks the flow of air into your lungs. It was caused by an infection.

That's why the doctor thought he needed some antibiotics. This belated teething isn't helping any. We'll watch him closely and bring him back for Dr. Ross to examine him tomorrow. His fever has begun to break, so we're feeling more confident. Did you eat?"

I shook my head. "My stomach hasn't been right since I came home."

She nodded. "You looked peaked to me."

She put her hand on my forehead.

"You don't feel like you have a fever. Better get some sleep, and maybe stay home tomorrow. If you feel better, you can help with Garson later."

"Okay," I said. She just stood there. For a moment, I thought that she was working up the courage to hug me, maybe because she needed a hug more than I did. When she didn't do it, I stepped forward and hugged her. Then I turned away quickly to avoid the surprised expression that was surely bursting out on her face and hurried to my room. A quote I had read and memorized from one of the literature books Mazy had used in my homeschooling followed me all the way into my room, like some chant. *Oh, what a tangled web we weave . . . when first we practice to deceive.*

Didn't Daddy ever read that?

I fell asleep faster than I thought I would. In fact, I overslept, but since I wasn't going to school, no one bothered to wake me. I was surprised at how bright it was when I sat up. Then I looked at the clock and quickly went to the bathroom, dressed, and peeked into Daddy and Ava's room before descending. There was no one there, so I hurried downstairs, a little worried. Had things turned badly for Garson again? Ava was in the kitchenette feeding Garson, who looked quite a bit better and more alert. I relaxed with relief.

She smiled. "His fever's gone completely."

"Oh, that's great. Where's—"

I bit down hard on my lower lip. I was literally forming the word *Daddy*.

"There was some emergency at the office," she said with a smirk. "My father is a very demanding boss, even after hearing about Garson. Your uncle will be meeting me at the doctor's office later."

"What about Karen?"

"I expect she went to school. I didn't tell her anything. She'd only use it as an excuse not to go. How are you feeling?"

What if I told the truth? I thought. What if I said I was fine? How would I get out of attending the game with Hurley? Daddy would be furious.

"Still a little woozy," I said.

"Eat something light. There's oatmeal in the pantry, or just have some toast and tea. These stomach flus are usually gone in a day or so."

"Okay," I said, and decided on the toast. She finished feeding Garson and then, after cleaning him up, told me she was going up with him to take a nap herself.

"I had trouble sleeping with one ear listening for him all night. Your uncle can pass out. I didn't trust him hearing anything."

"I'm sure you never slept," I said, and watched her go. I ate a little more than I would have with her there, and then, after cleaning up, went up to my room. Maybe a minute after I had closed the door, my cell phone sounded.

It was Tommy.

"Where are you?" he asked. "Karen doesn't know anything."

"She slept at a girlfriend's house last night. I think I have a stomach flu. It started last night," I said.

He was silent a moment.

"Do you think you'll make the game tonight?"

"I'm not sure," I said. "You won't have time for me anyway while you're out there."

"Every basket I make will still have your name on it," he said.

I could feel the tears floating in my eyes. "It better, and there better be more than ever," I said.

He laughed. "I'll call later," he promised. "Got to go. Bell's ringing."

"Okay."

"Saffron?"

"Yes?"

"I know who you are, and I like what I know," he said, and then hung up.

I held the phone against my ear, touching my cheek as well. It was as if I could hold him there, at least for another few seconds.

Then I put the phone down, picked up my literature text, and began reading the next assignment as if nothing in the world had changed.

Just before noon, Ava knocked on my door to ask how I was.

"So-so," I said. "I had a bit of the runs."

"There's some Pepto-Bismol in the cabinet above the sink in the kitchen. Try a spoonful or so. I'm taking Garson to Dr. Ross. There's soup if you want. You should keep up the liquids. If it goes on past tomorrow, we'll take you to Dr. Ross."

"Thank you."

All this time, Daddy hadn't called me. Wouldn't Ava wonder why even an uncle wouldn't be interested in how I was doing?

She started to close the door and paused.

"Your uncle called to see about Garson and asked about you," she said, as if she had heard my thoughts. "He's meeting me at the doctor."

"Okay."

I convinced myself that he was being casual about it to avoid arousing even the slightest suspicion. Daddy was so good at deception.

She left. I waited until I saw her pull out of the garage and drive off, and then I went down to get something to eat. I was actually very hungry now. I made myself a peanut butter and jelly sandwich and then hid all traces of my eating it. Tommy called during his lunch hour. I told him I was about the same and to stop worrying about me.

"Concentrate on what you have to do tonight."

"I have to see you," he said. "That's what I have to do."

"You will as soon as I feel better."

"I told Karen about you. She doesn't seem terribly concerned for a potential new sister," he said, anger coloring his voice.

"It's okay." I wanted to add that she was still a child and she was probably happy I wouldn't invade her spotlight tonight, but I said nothing more. He told me he would call me before he got ready for the game.

"Maybe you'll make a miraculous recovery," he said.

There are no miracles for liars, I wanted to tell him, but I said nothing.

A short time after, Melina called.

"That sucks. Get over it."

"Working on it."

"Good. We'll have plenty of celebrating to do. And . . . you and Tommy can celebrate privately after you're better," she said.

"Thank you, Melina. Cheer for Tommy for me."

"Yes, I will," she said. "I'll have the loudest voice."

Ava arrived before Daddy had picked up Karen at school. I heard her come in. I hurried to the stairway. She was clearly encouraged by Garson's exam.

"All the swelling has gone," she said, coming up. "How are you doing?"

"Better, but not completely."

She nodded. When she paused, I looked at Garson, who was smiling at me.

"He's already smiling at you more than he smiles at his sister."

Could Ava see it in my look? He *was* smiling at his sister. I was swallowing the truth back, which probably made me look sick.

"Go rest," she said. "I'll make you something with rice tonight."

She started for the bedroom, and after a moment, I retreated to mine. For a while, I simply lay there looking up at the ceiling. I should just go to the game, I thought, after having that miraculous recovery Tommy suggested. I should just risk it. Ava wouldn't throw me out now, even if the truth was learned because students from Hurley recognized me. She would be angry at Daddy, very angry. He could lose his job and resent me forever. Maybe we'd both have to move out. Even if we went off together, how could that end well? He'd be apart from his son, too.

I felt so trapped and so angry. I was in such a deep sulk that I didn't hear Karen and Daddy come home.

Suddenly, my door was thrown open.

"What's wrong with you?" Karen demanded. "How could you get sick today of all days?"

"I forgot to tell the stomach flu about the game."

She smirked but remained in the doorway. "Everyone was asking about you. You should have called me."

My eyes widened with surprise and outrage. It was truly as if I believed my own lies. Daddy had taught me that was the way to make them work.

"Why didn't you call *me*? I'm the one sick. And what about your brother?"

Her face softened.

"Daddy told me they were taking him to the doctor. I didn't want to hear about it. I get too frightened." She folded her arms and looked at the floor. "Mother says he's all right now." She looked up. "Daddy said he'll go with me to the game. So did Tommy call you?"

"A few times."

She nodded. From the way she was reacting now, I thought she actually felt sorry for me.

"I'll call you the moment the buzzer sounds to end the game."

"Okay. Thanks."

"I'll make sure no one moves in on you at the celebration, either," she said.

I fought back a smile. Did that include her?

"I'm changing and then going down to help with dinner. Mother said she thought it might be best for you to eat in your room. She's going to bring a special meal up to you."

"Really? I don't think I'm infectious."

"Whatever," she said. "I'll see you before Daddy and I leave for the game."

She stepped back and closed the door. Tommy called again about ten minutes later.

"How are you now?" he asked, his voice resonant with hope.

"Much better but still a little shaky," I said. "I wouldn't want something to happen and your attention be off the game."

"Yeah," he said, dripping with disappointment. "I'll call you as soon as I get into the locker room."

"Okay. Good luck."

"I met you. I already have it," he said.

I could feel the tears trickling down my cheeks after we said goodbye. I sat back against the pillows on my bed and glared at the wall, my emotions in a whirlpool. Now I really was feeling sick.

There was a light knock on the door, and then Daddy stepped in and closed it behind him.

"You're doing great," he said. "We'll get through all this. Everything's been a little more hectic with Garson and all, but I was on your case today with Amos and the judge we're using. It'll be fast, and there'll be a lot less tension for you after it's over."

"Won't I still have to stick to the fictional life you created for me?"

"Yes, but it will be lost in a fog. You'll be too busy with this life and your future. You'll have a great school life and then go to the college of your choice, no costs to worry about. Amos really likes you, too. He wants to make you a great party. Karen will be ecstatic. We've done it. Together. Let the past drift off, and think only about the future."

"Karen said you're taking her to the game."

"Yeah. And Ava's decided to call Celisse to watch Garson and come, too. She wants to keep an eagle eye on Karen at the after-party. It won't run late. Tomorrow . . . tomorrow is the start of a really new life for you, Saffron. I know it's a sacrifice for you to miss the game, but we both know it's best for now. I'll make it up to you."

He smiled. Make it up to me? The door was closed. No one would see. Why didn't he come to me to hug and kiss me? Hadn't I done everything he wanted? He was behaving as if he really believed I was sick, too, or he was terrified I would be unable to hide our real relationship. Either answer left me cold.

"Okay," I said.

As soon as he left, I closed my eyes and forced myself to vividly remember my mother. One image I could never forget was her sitting in the backyard with me and laughing at how close the hummingbirds came to her, one practically a few inches from her face, as if it thought there was nectar on her lips. There was something melodic about her laughter. It made me feel so safe in a world without tears or pain or encroaching dark shadows. Flames in a fireplace were still beautiful; candles on my birthday were still full of joy and celebration. Sometimes she sang an old song she said her mother loved. Her eyes would be so bright. I recalled the way her voice lifted with "There'll be bluebirds over the white cliffs of Dover . . ."

"Where's Dover?" I once asked her.

She laughed and said, "It's out there. You'll see."

Would I ever?

Ava brought me a bowl of rice and chicken and some tea. She was so happy about Garson that she lost any of her regal personality. She seemed warm and caring, as warm and caring as any woman who had agreed to become your mother and embrace you as a member of her family. I was speechless, really, and feeling even more terribly guilty.

"This will be good," she said. "Something substantial. Celisse is here and will help you if you need anything. She's quite capable. She's had some nursing experience in France. I wouldn't even think of leaving the two of you if I didn't believe she could handle it."

The two of you? She was including me in every way now, including me as one of her own.

I thanked her, keeping my eyes low so she couldn't see how guilty I was feeling.

"I'll be calling in regularly," she promised. "And keeping my eyes on your soon-to-be sister," she added with a stern look. "Derick and I are official chaperones. There'll be no repeat of the Toby party. I assure you."

"Okay. Thank you for dinner," I said.

She stood there a moment and then left.

I listened to all the movement in the hallway, heard Celisse's voice and Karen urging her parents to move faster. She wanted the best seat in the bleachers. No one stopped in to see me before they all left. When they did, the house became so quiet that I could hear the whistle of the wind over the roof shingles.

I rose and carried my tray out of the room and down the stairs. Celisse was sitting in the kitchenette having some tea and biscuits. Garson was asleep in the bassinet and looked very content.

"Sorry you are ill, *chéri*. Is there anything you need?"

"No, I'm fine, Celisse. I'm getting better. How's he doing?"

"He's well. A scare, I'm sure."

She had such a sweet, soft smile.

"Are you happy you came to America?" I asked, after I put my dishes and silverware in the sink.

"Ah, *oui*, but sometimes . . ."

"Sometimes?"

"I miss my *famille*. I have two older sisters, both married and both with three children. They all live in Rouen. You know it?"

"I think that was where Joan of Arc was burned at the stake."

"*Oui*," she said. "*Très bien*, but it has more to it than just that history. One day you'll go. There is much to see and learn."

"*Peut-être*," I said.

She smiled. Garson moaned, opened his eyes, and then closed them again.

"Babies are sweet," she said. "It is frightening when they get ill. So fragile. Oh. I think I have to go up and get his new teething ring. Mrs. Anders forgot to give it to me. They were in such a rush, such excitement about the school game."

"I'll get it for you. Where did she say it was?"

"On her vanity table. In a box not opened."

"Okay."

"*Merci*," she said, and I hurried up the stairs, reminding myself I was supposed to be sick. When I stepped into Ava and my father's bedroom, I paused. Ava was really in a rush to get herself together. Drawers were still open, clothes tossed on the bed. So Mrs. Perfect could be a little sloppy sometimes, I thought, and smiled.

I spotted the new teething ring box and started for it. Then I stopped and stared at what was displayed on the vanity table. She had put out some jewelry and some watches, probably deciding that these three were too elegant to wear to a basketball game. The one in the middle made my heart stop and start. Slowly, I reached for it. Just touching it sent a chill up my arm and down my spine.

It was gold, not with a round face but shaped more like a triangle. It had a tiny diamond next to each number. I turned it over. On the back was inscribed *Love, D*. I would never forget it. When Daddy first had given it to Mama, he proudly told her it was custom-made. Back then, she wore it often, practically every day. When she stopped and put it in her brown antique jewelry box, he was upset, but she had stopped wearing everything he had bought her by then.

I clearly remember hearing how our house had burned to the ground and how everything was reduced to ashes. I didn't want to hear about Mama, but I did remember Daddy deciding that combing through the rest of it was useless, and it was wiser to bulldoze away the remains and put the land up for sale.

The fire not only burned away everything we had, but it burned indelible memories into my mind. For nights and nights after, I would wake to the vision of Daddy coming into my bedroom, his arms full of my clothes to wear, his face ripped with panic. I cried for Mama, but he said he had to get me out first and fast. The flames were so big, snapping at us, as he carried me down the stairs. When we emerged from the house, I heard something crash down behind us in the house, maybe the dining-room chandelier.

People were all over the street by now. The flames were visible in the doorway. Daddy couldn't go back in. I was so dazed I thought Mama must be out, too. Where was she? I could see flames in her bedroom window. Glass exploded. I clung to Daddy, who was in his pajamas. Some neighbors were rushing over to us with blankets. The sirens were screaming all around us. Daddy had me change into the clothes he had quickly scooped up for me. Then, for a while, we both stood there watching the firemen start to battle with the blaze. I was pressed against him, softly crying, "Where's Mama?"

All of this thundered back at me. The watch seemed hot in my hand, as hot as it could have been if it had been rescued from the flames. It looked absolutely immaculate, untouched. I remembered the tiny scratch next to *Love, D.* This was the watch. For a moment, I really did feel woozy. The room seemed to spin. I put my hand on Ava's vanity table to keep my balance. The dark thoughts that blossomed in my mind didn't simply happen now. The seeds of them were always there.

I scooped up the teething ring box and walked out with it in my left hand and the watch in my right. Before I turned to Celisse at the bottom of the stairway, I closed my hand around the watch.

"*Merci*," she said, taking the box and opening it. "I'll wash it off."

I nodded, hoping she didn't see any changes in my face, and then I hurried back to the stairway. Would I cower in my room? Would I cry? Would I pack a bag and run off? When I stepped into the room, I saw the card Amos Saddlebrook had given me on the top of the dresser. I looked at it for a moment and then made up my mind. I would not cry.

I called the number.

"This is Tyson," I heard.

"This is Saffron. I need to see Mr. Saddlebrook right now."

"You're home?"

"Yes."

"I'll be there in twenty minutes," he said.

For a moment, I stood there stupidly. Then I thought, *I have to go. I have to get as far away as I can.* But first, I would see Amos Saddlebrook. I had good reason.

I changed into a pair of jeans and a warm blouse. I put on one of the pairs of running shoes Ava had bought me, and I packed my old bag with more clothes and the things I would need. I included all the money I had and then put in the watch, my mother's watch. I scooped up the jean jacket Ava had bought me. For a moment, I looked around the room. There was nothing else I wanted to take with me. I wasn't even going to take the coloring book. Instead, I left it on the bed with the old crayons.

Then I went out. I could hear Celisse in Ava and Daddy's bedroom singing some French lullaby to Garson. For a few moments, I stood there listening. As softly as I could, I descended the stairway and went to the front of the house. When the headlights of Mr. Saddlebrook's car appeared on the street, I stepped out. Tyson turned into the driveway and stopped. He got out and opened the rear door for me.

"Did you tell Mr. Saddlebrook I called you?"

"Yes," he said. "He's waiting for you."

I got in, and he closed the door, backed out of the driveway, and turned up the street. I looked back at the house. The water running in the dark pewter fountain with a sculptured little boy and girl under an umbrella glittered. It seemed like just yesterday I had first stepped up to this house, that motion detector light putting me in a spotlight. As the house drifted back, I could feel my body tying into knots of anger and sorrow.

Everything had begun with a lie, I thought. Why shouldn't it end like this?

EPILOGUE

Unlike the first time when I was brought to Saddlebrook, it seemed more like a descent through the darkness and the day, descending to a huge house that hovered over everything around it, the windows more like dozens of eyes glaring out at the world.

Tyson said nothing all the way. Maybe because of how troubled and sad I was, his tall, dark, stoic figure caused me to think of Charon in Greek mythology, the ferryman of Hades who carried souls of the dead across the rivers Styx and Acheron to the world of the dead, for that was really how I felt, so empty inside, so defeated and lost, simply numb.

He said nothing when we pulled up to the front entrance. He stepped out and opened my door. Standing so straight, expressionless, staring out at nothing, he resembled a pewter statue. It made it all seem so unreal, but I knew why I had come here and I knew what I wanted to say. Simply disappearing into the night without coming here was cowardly and in my mind gave the evil a new and stronger life. It mattered to me.

Amos Saddlebrook opened the door himself. I paused for a moment as he looked out at me, dressed just as elegantly in a gray suit with a blue tie and looking as distinguished as he had the first time.

"What's that bag you're carrying?" he asked.

"The bag I came with," I replied.

He nodded and stepped back for me to enter.

"My office," he said, gesturing toward it.

I walked ahead, entered the office, and took a seat on the settee just where I had previously sat. He took the same seat across from me as well.

"I was told you weren't feeling well," he said.

"You know that wasn't true," I replied, and then opened my bag. I reached in and took out my mother's watch and placed it on the settee and then looked firmly at him. He wasn't smiling, but there was a look of amusement in his eyes. It made me feel younger and, for a few moments, challenged my courage.

"Derick Anders is not my uncle. He is my father."

He sat back, amusement dissipating like smoke. He brought up his hands and pressed the ends of his fingers together in cathedral fashion.

"Go on," he said. "I'm sure there is more you want to tell me."

"Oh, there is more. You know that my father carried me out of a house on fire, and my real mother died in that fire. I believe you also know that I lived with my grandmother for years after, a grandmother I had never known existed. My father had never told me it was his intention to leave me on a train platform so that she would find me and take me to her home."

His face tightened, his eyes darkening.

"And I didn't know she was my grandmother for some time after I had been living with her. For years, she held out the hope that my father was coming back for me.

"But by then, my father had come here, assumed his responsibilities as Karen's father and married your daughter, Ava. I wonder if his having Garson was just another insurance policy. He used to do that, sell insurance."

"My girl," Amos Saddlebrook said, "you are quite the cynic for one so young."

"I suspect you were as well, maybe when you were even younger," I said, and he smiled.

"What makes you so certain I knew all this?"

I looked around.

"Consider who you are, what you've accomplished, what power you wield over so many in this community and the important people you know in government and in business. I doubt you'd buy a new brand of toothpaste without someone doing extensive research for you."

His smile softened. He nodded, total seriousness now capturing his face and his posture.

"Why have you come here tonight?"

"We circled this last time we spoke. You made it clear to me that my father was driven by his ambition, an ambition I am convinced you dangled in front of him so that he would marry Ava and clean up the social blemish on the Saddlebrook name."

"What if that's so?"

"You drove him to do what he did. You're just as responsible," I said.

He tilted his head a bit and widened his eyes. "For his leaving you with your grandmother?"

"No, much more."

Any friendliness or amusement was completely gone from his face.

"What more?"

I held up my mother's watch.

"I was very young but not too young to have encapsulated traumatic memories and, from time to time, be haunted by them, by the whisper in my ear, by the horror I refused to accept."

He sat forward. "Go on."

"He woke me, hysterical with fear, I thought. He had some of my clothes in his arms but said there wasn't time to put them on. There wasn't time to do anything but get me out of bed and into his arms as well. There was certainly not enough time to rouse my mother, who put herself to sleep at night. She was on some pills for her depression. I screamed for her, and he said he was coming back in to carry her out, too. He was in his pajamas. He hadn't had time to dress himself. At least, that was what I had believed."

"You no longer do?"

"No," I said. I held up the watch by the end of the band. "This is a very special watch. He had it custom-made for my mother. It has a unique shape, and on the back, he had *Love, D* engraved."

"Where did you find it?"

"On Ava's vanity table an hour or so ago."

He shrugged. "He's unoriginal. He wanted to give her the same romantic gift."

"No. If you look at the watch, you will see a small scratch by his initial. I think . . . I believe now that my mother once tried to scratch it out and only was able to do this."

He reached for the watch and studied it.

"Are you saying this is the one thing besides you that he saved?"

"He had it on him already. He was planning on giving it to Ava. His marriage was going up in flames. He'd be free to do what you wanted."

He stared at me hard. "*I* wanted?"

"This way, the way he designed it all, Ava never knew about me. I imagine he had her feeling sorry for him . . . the fire and all. He was having trouble figuring out what to do. You were dangling all this in front of him, probably increasing the pressure."

"So this is my fault?"

"That's for you to decide, but I'm thinking you'll find another conclusion."

He handed the watch back to me.

"So you intend to run away again?"

"And escape from all these lies."

"To what? Do you think you'll find a place where lies don't exist? You're using that watch like a key to open some door. Like you clearly said, you knew all this without the watch, but you kept it buried, pushed it away.

"Why did you let your father create this fictional background for you? Why did you come here in the first place?"

"To find the truth."

"A truth you already knew. I understand how painful it was for you to find that watch and let the truth free. Things like this happened to me, too, as I was growing up. Believe me. My father's picture is probably next to the word *scoundrel* in the dictionary, but I didn't go, 'Oh, woe is me. I have to pretend and accept so many terrible things.' No. I looked around and saw that there were more men like my father. Did he do good things? Yes, just like I do. I made that school happen. I've helped so many people in this community make a living, a good living, support their families and send their children to college. I make very large contributions to all sorts of causes, but I live in the business world. Lies are the currency, not dollars.

"And when or if you're caught lying, you hire lawyers who are experts in hiding it, distorting it, and basically shoving it off somewhere so you can continue. Someone's hurt, but usually they'll survive, and so many will benefit. A great many people depend on my success. And yes, your father is one of them."

He smiled again, but it was a different smile, a smug smile.

"And so are you one of them. You want to be ethically strong, morally outraged, pure, but all this time, you lied. You kept the deception going. To this day, to this moment, my daughter does not know the whole truth, and you helped make that possible."

"Aren't you angry about it? For her?"

"No. Exactly the opposite. For her, I hope the truth is never fully revealed. She's a very proud person. She won't tolerate it. Her family will suffer. Karen, who needs more tender loving care than you might imagine, will be destroyed, too. You'll leave all that behind and rush off to some fantasy world. Years from now, you'll stop and realize how much you lost, if you were only more . . ."

"Deceitful."

"Self-protective. It's very cynical, I know. If you work hard enough, you might come to a place where you'll feel more honesty. You might find someone to believe in and marry him, but you won't be able to stop being suspicious until you pause and think maybe you'll be happier if you don't know every secret, every bit of truth, if you can pretend some or weigh the wonderful things you have against being so foolishly . . ."

"Angelic?"

"Exactly, Saffron. Leave the angels their wings. You don't know for certain that what you think happened did happen. Maybe your father had that watch in a safe-deposit box. Maybe he really believed he was going back into that house, but first he wanted to save you. Maybe now that you've appeared, he really wants you to enjoy this life, to have everything you need and want, to go to a good school and then to a college you choose to become whatever you want."

"Do you believe any of that?"

"It's not important for me to believe it. It's what is at the moment. If I have any good motives, it's to protect my daughter, who thinks I don't love her. There's not enough of me in her for her to survive the truth.

"From what she's told me, what Derick's told me, I think you'll do well, and she'll be very happy to be a mother to you. As long as you're the orphan and not the true daughter," he said. "I think you can live with that."

He sat back.

"You won't survive out there, Saffron. You're too demanding. You want too much honesty. Work on it here. Look at that bag you brought. You don't want to take it with you. You want to leave it behind, way behind."

I could feel the tears on my cheeks, but I wouldn't touch them.

"How can I live with him, thinking and believing what I do?"

"You know what I would do? I'd think, how does he do it? How does he tolerate your presence? Take that from him, and turn it on him, the same self-denial. Choose your smiles, accept whatever affection you want, and punish him with your strength of acceptance. If he's guilty and he does have the conscience you wish everyone had, he'll confess someday and truly ask for your forgiveness. If it's important to you, you'll give it to him. If it's more important to hold on to the hate and rage, you'll hold on to it."

"I can't decide if you're wise or evil."

He laughed. "Maybe it's both. Stay here, live in the Saddlebrook world, and make me one of your causes. Get me to apologize for my life someday, someday soon. I'm pretty healthy, but life is finite. You'll have to work fast and hard."

I flipped away the tears and took a breath.

"Go back, Saffron. I hear you have a boyfriend who is making the school's sports history tonight. I've been following it on my mobile. He's on the way to a league scoring record. Maybe a little of that has to do with you."

I started to shake my head.

"Don't be shy when it comes to taking credit for anything good. Show them all that you're better and stronger. I assure you. In a short while, they'll all think of you as a Saddlebrook, if you're ashamed of Anders."

I swallowed hard and looked away. Who would I rather be?

"Tyson has orders to take you wherever you want, Saffron— home, to the train station, the bus station, or even the airport in Albany. Wherever you want."

He stood up. I looked at my mother's watch in my hand and then put it back in the bag and stood, too. Then he walked me to the front entrance.

"You'll be proud of what I'm about to tell you," he said, thinking hard as we stood there together. "Once, toward the end of my father's life, he asked me coldly, 'Do you want to be better than me or more successful?'"

"And?"

"I told him, 'Both.' He didn't like my answer. Your father won't like it, either, when that time comes. Sort of the gold ring out there, huh?"

"Maybe."

"Good luck to you, whatever choice you make."

He opened the door. Tyson literally leaped out of the car to open the rear door.

It felt good to see someone that dedicated to serving you. Was that terrible? Arrogant? I looked at Amos Saddlebrook. He was smiling.

I got into the car, and Tyson started away.

"Where to, miss?" he asked.

I looked back. Amos Saddlebrook was still standing in the doorway. He knew the difference a right or a left would make. Right was back home.

"Do you have an umbrella in this car?" I asked.

"Umbrella? Yes, miss. Right on the seat beside me. Always."

"Can you hand it to me?"

"Why? It's not raining, miss."

"Oh, it is, Tyson. It is."

He shrugged and reached over to grasp it and hand it to me. I just held it in my lap and sat back.

"Make a right, please, Tyson," I said.

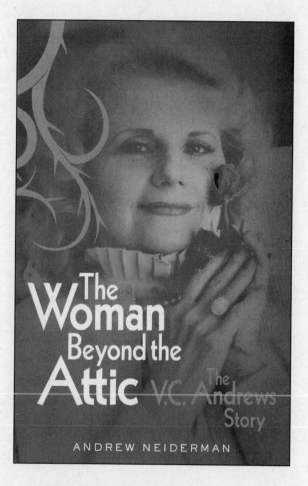

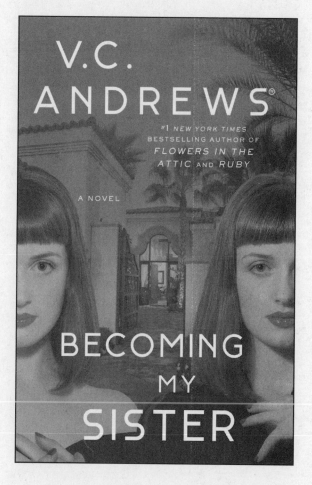